NUKES ON THE LOOSE!

There were thousands, the bombs aimed by the governments of the United States, the Soviet Union, France, China and India at one another's strategic locations and population centers.

They were all on course; and, one by one, in order of their closeness to their targets, Superman disarmed them, driven by the ringing cackle of the demon C. W. Saturn haunting his mind.

Superman threw missiles into space.

He tossed one warhead at another.

He drove the heat-seeking devices of the multiple warheads crazy with his heat vision.

He took direct hits on his chest.

He gulped down several ounces of hot plutonium.

He caught giant armloads of deadly weapons as if they were pickup sticks and threw them like darts in the direction of the sun.

And still he heard the ring of primeval laughter . . .

Also by Elliot S. Maggin

Superman: Last Son of Krypton

Published by
WARNER BOOKS

Superman: Miracle Monday

Elliot S. Maggin

WARNER BOOKS

A Warner Communications Company

Superman:
Miracle
Monday

The Journal

My typing speed is up to fifty-two words per minute. My accent, according to the ancient video-disc recordings, is virtually flawless. My grasp of Middle American slang and idioms is, like, solid man. This studio where I'm living with the fake smog out the window is a real slice, y'know?

As they used to say (everything these days is as they used to say), I'm as ready as I'll ever be. Now it's just a matter of convincing my professors. They'll come around soon enough.

Kristin Wells
1 May, 2857

Thanksgiving

The boy would be ready, Jonathan Kent decided, when he was able to feel pain.

Jonathan had already awakened his wife Martha three or four times this night with his tossing and turning, but she had not been awake enough any of those times either to stay awake or to notice why she had awakened. This time, when Jonathan screamed a shrill, horrible scream, she was awake enough.

"My land, Jonathan! What is it?"

He screamed again, catching the sound short in his throat as he woke himself up.

"Jonathan! Oh dear, please wake up, Jonathan."

He grabbed at his pillow, tensed his muscles, slowly let them go.

"Jonathan? Are you all right, Jonathan? Won't you please wake up?"

"I'm awake, I'm awake. I don't think I ever want to go to sleep again."

"What a horrid thing to say. I've never known you to have bad dreams before."

"I've never had a dream this bad before."

"Do you want to tell me about it?" She no more wanted to hear about it than she wanted to stay awake any longer, but she was ready to comfort her husband back into sleep.

"Don't even want to tell *me* about it. Go back to sleep, Martha."

"Good night, Jonathan."

"Good night, dear."

But Jonathan had to tell himself about it. It was more than a dream, of course. It was the future—the real future—and not distant at all. He repeated it in his mind over and over until he tortured himself with the experience, tortured himself into coming up with a solution.

It had begun this past afternoon, Thanksgiving Day, with the turkey. Jonathan had stopped raising livestock for slaughter a few years ago, soon after he and Martha had adopted little Clark. Martha bought this turkey from young Maynard Stone whose father, James Stone the bank president, had thought it was a better idea for his son to go into the backyard turkey-breeding business than to simply give his son an allowance. Maynard, nearly grown now, was a good boy, taking care of his father with turkey money through the banker's long illness.

Martha brought the kicking and gobbling turkey home and nine-year-old Clark helped his mother by snapping the bird's neck and plucking its feathers in the twinkling of an eye. Sarah Lang and her young daughter Lana came to the Kent farm for Thanksgiving dinner because Professor Martin Lang was off in Yucatan or the Sinai Desert or Thailand or somewhere on one of his archaeological digs. Martin called the farm at dinnertime from wherever he was to say hi and happy Thanksgiving, and Sarah told him it was the best-tasting dinner she had ever had. For all Jonathan knew it may have been. He was not enjoying himself.

All through the meal Martha went on about what a good boy Clark was and what a help he had been. Of course, she left out certain facts in her approbation. Clark had, for example, dressed and stuffed the bird in four seconds, including time out to ask Martha whether she wanted thyme in the stuffing. Also, when the bird was not done in time, Clark had finished roasting it with heat vision. And through it all, Jonathan had trouble noticing how good everything tasted because something was bothering him about the bird, about his wife, about the smiling faces of his neighbors and his compliment-collecting son.

That part of the dream was all real, from the past afternoon and evening. The rest of the dream took place in the future, but it was also real:

Sometime during the next few years a pair of bored, broke adventurers in diving suits tried to rob the Smallville branch of the Heartland Bank and Trust Company. The event in progress was broadcast over a police-band radio in Jonathan Kent's general store, the store Jonathan was planning to buy when he sold the farm later this year. Lana Lang was in the store at the time, and Jonathan covered for young Clark by asking him to go to the basement and bring up a package from storage. Clark brought back no package. Clark was Superboy, and this was the day he would tell the world he had arrived.

Clark stripped to the costume he wore under his street clothes, the costume Jonathan and Martha had made for him from the unraveled material of the blankets in which, as an infant, Clark had come to Earth. He dove through the tunnel he had built from the basement of the store to a wooded area. He found the robbers jumping into a lake from a pier outside of town. Police in their cars were unable to follow them into the water.

Superboy plopped out of the sky into the lake and spotted the pair merrily plowing through deep murk, breathing their canned air. The boy knifed through the water and gripped steely hands around a pair of aluminum air tanks. He punctured both tanks in five places. The air rushed out, and a minute later—fifty-nine seconds after police and onlookers saw the not-yet-familiar red-and-blue streak pop straight up into the sky in a spout and a swirl—people saw the corpses of the pair of drowned bank robbers surface in a dead man's float until police could fish their blue bodies from the lake.

Superboy's work was not done. Up, up and away through the sky he flew.

In a nearby national forest preserve a timber wolf was menacing a forest ranger. The ranger held an empty rifle in one hand and reached for the door of his truck with the other. The ranger had scared the wolf into growling at arm's distance while he had edged twelve feet to the truck. His fingertips reached the truck door. Then, deliberately and with no quick moves, he would position himself. In one motion he would leap into the cab and slam the door closed. The window on this side was shut, the wolf couldn't get in. He would slam on his gas pedal and leave the beast behind. He would make it now. He knew it.

11

A red-and-blue gust of wind swept down from the sky and left the animal, its jaw shattered like a dropped piece of pottery, dead on the forest floor. Superboy stopped to introduce himself and shake hands with the bewildered ranger, then soared off.

On the other side of the preserve there was a drought, the only one in the country that year. Farmers were losing their wheat crops, hundreds of thousands of acres. Superboy plowed a system of trenches and canals through the area, linking it with the Ohio and Mississippi Rivers, irrigating the countryside for all time, or until the rivers choked themselves with silt and waste, whichever came first. Fallow land would bloom again. The boy stopped to make a statement to the press.

In Minneapolis there was a little blind girl undergoing a brain operation. The tumor that had sat against her optic nerve and made her blind since the age of eight months had begun to grow, and it had to come out. The supervising neurosurgeon had delivered the child six years earlier in a stalled elevator, the only delivery he had made since he was an intern. Now he had to save her life. He was as nervous as he had ever been. It was he who had made the decision not to remove the tumor when it made the girl blind. There was about one chance in a hundred that her brain would survive this operation. The doctor guided a tiny scalpel past her optic nerve in order to separate the tumor from the bone tissue it touched, and then he remembered that this little girl whose skull lay open under his hand was someone he loved. His fingers were going to shake. He knew it. The scalpel vanished from his hand.

Suddenly, beside the neurosurgeon, there stood a handsome black-haired boy, maybe thirteen years old, dressed in a bizarre red-and-blue costume with an odd pentagonal red-and-yellow emblem on his chest. In the moment the doctor and his surgery team looked on without knowing what to do, Superboy cleanly vaporized the deadly growth and with a puff of air he cooled the space where it had been. Six days from now, for the first time since her infancy, the girl would be able to see. Superboy told the doctors and the hospital's publicity department who he was and what he had done, and he called the neurosurgeon a bumbling incompetent in front of his colleagues.

Superboy crashed through virgin forests to help build roads or dig mines. For the good of society he dropped tyrants, heinous criminals and chronic speeders into volcanoes. He was a weekend guest at the White House where he suggested that the President make him de facto Commander in Chief of all American military forces, since, according to Superboy, he would be in charge of everything soon enough anyway. The President considered the expediency of this.

Jonathan Kent knew about kryptonite. No one had yet given a name to the glowing green stone that the boy once closed up in a lead tube and buried under a corner of the Kents' old barn. No one knew it was a fragment of the exploded planet Krypton, the lost world of the boy's birth. All anyone knew was that one day, when Clark was about four or five, there was a splash of meteors in the sky over the farm. The boy decided to dart into the sky and see if he could catch one of the fiery rocks before they all fizzled into nothingness with air friction. Thirty miles over the farm the child caught hundreds of them in the little red cape of his playsuit. The biggest one was the size of a baseball. Mostly they were cosmic gravel. But as he tied the ends of his cape into a hobo knot, he felt dizzy and lost the power of flight; it was all he could do, as he fell to Earth, to catch currents of air and point himself in the direction of home. Martha heard a thud in the back of the house and found her son at the bottom of a ten-foot hole with the capeful of pebbles on top of him. She climbed into the hole, threw the cape and the meteorites away and dragged the child into the house where, almost immediately, he woke up crying.

The next morning Jonathan took the boy out to the barn, where he had laid out the rocks. Some of them looked quite remarkable: one was orange striated with blue; another was melted and bubbled with friction on one side and solid as granite on the other, as though someone had thrown a knuckleball at Earth's atmosphere; the shape of one looked to Clark like the bill of a duck.

One, the size and shape of a big marble, was undistinguished except for the fact that it glowed slightly in a dull green color. It was the radiation of that stone that made the boy fall down again in the barn.

That was years ago, and no one had talked much since then about what the stone might be. Maybe the boy had forgotten about it.

Now—Jonathan dreamed—Superboy was already being worshiped as a messiah by people who should know better. Superboy should know better. Soon he would take the power of the life and death of the planet into his hands. He was a boy—no more than a boy, with a boy's emotions, a boy's caprices, a boy's lack of restraint—with the power of the gods of fable.

The man certainly did not want to kill his son. Fathers do not kill their sons. He did not even want to punish him. He only wanted to talk to him—to make him listen, the way a boy ought to listen to his

13

father. But when Jonathan drove out to the old barn that night and took three shovelfuls of dirt out of the corner where the lead-encased meteorite was buried, the shovel hit something solid the fourth time it sliced the earth, and Jonathan shuddered.

What was he nervous about? Clark hadn't buried the meteorite that shallowly; the shovel had hit a rock, that was all. Jonathan pulled the shovel out and chopped into the ground a few inches away: it hit something hard again. Another rock, probably.

Then, what should have been a rock under the shovel pushed the blade up out of the ground, shook off some dirt, and the rock became a sooty hand at the end of a blue sleeve. The arm shoved itself out of the dirt and pushed at the shovel, throwing Jonathan to the ground. And following the arm out of the earth was the body to which it was attached—the figure of Jonathan's adopted son Clark, in his red-and-blue flying suit—the boy the world knew and feared as Superboy.

The boy glared at the man, raised the shovel over his head like a broadsword.

Jonathan screamed, "I wasn't going to—"

That was all he had a chance to say before the shovel came at Jonathan's face: he screamed, Martha shook him awake.

Jonathan was too pumped up with adrenaline to do any more sleeping that night. He knew what he had to do in the morning; then he remembered he did not have to wait until morning. Clark did not sleep more than an hour or so each night, and Jonathan suspected Clark only did that to be polite.

Jonathan groped for his glasses, draped his robe over him, shivered until he found his slippers. He padded down the hall to Clark's room and was about to knock on the door when the boy said, "Come on in, Pa."

Jonathan found the boy sitting at his desk with a plastic microscope from a Gilbert Science Set, and for an instant the man was scared again. He told himself that, at least for the moment, his experience was only a dream. "What're you up to, Clark?"

"Look in here." Clark slid the microscope along the desk toward another chair.

The boy's desk was an L-shaped affair in the corner of the room. It was a combination of an old office-style desk on the wall facing the window, and a long butcher-block platform that used to be the kitchen counter against the adjoining wall. "What am I looking at?" Jonathan asked as he peered through the lenses.

"A cross section of a grasshopper's nerve ganglia."

"Umm."

Clark thought the old man was somehow nervous. He looked into his father's eyes and saw that they were uncommonly dry. That was probably only because it was so late, Clark decided. "It's magnified forty times," Clark told his father.

"How do you know it's the . . . nerve ganglia?"

"I dissected him myself with my fingernails and my microscopic vision. Now watch."

Jonathan watched Clark as the boy held up two empty microscope slides, one next to each of his eyes, to act as reflectors. He faced the shaft of the microscope and told his father to look at the grasshopper now.

"Bigger," Jonathan said, "lots bigger. Is that the same thing I was looking at a moment ago?"

"Yeah. Watch it now."

As Jonathan looked at the insect's nerve tissue, Clark continued to stare at the microscope with some intensity, gradually bringing together the outer edges of the slides. As he did this, the object at which Jonathan was looking seemed to grow, to become more detailed. Jonathan had to cover his left eye with his hand because the right eye that was peering through the instrument began careening into the grasshopper's body like a straw into a baler. As Clark diminished the angle of his reflectors, Jonathan saw a close-up of the animal's nerve tissue that looked like a red-and-orange landscape of another world. Then closer. He saw a pair of narrow chains running parallel, and between them was a red gully made up of some sort of pulsing, viscous substance.

"See that, Pa? That's the nerve," the little boy's excited alto said. "It's a single long cell running the length of the animal's body. Now look at this."

Closer still. There was a tiny green triangular object stuck to the edge of the nerve cell. It got bigger, bigger until Jonathan realized that this was a separate complex object in itself.

"Know what that is?" Clark asked him.

"No idea. Looks alive, though."

"It is. It's a virus. It's a single molecule of ribonucleic acid feeding on the grasshopper's nerve cell wall. It doesn't know the grasshopper's dead yet. What you're looking at is magnified nearly a hundred thousand times. Pretty good, huh?"

"Not a bad trick, son." Jonathan looked up from the microscope and rubbed his eyes before he put his glasses back on. "How d'you do it?"

"With my microscopic vision. I figured out how my eyes work. I've got this weird optic nerve, see? It's got an active mode along with the passive mode everybody else's optic nerve has, which is why I can project heat and X rays with my eyes, besides just seeing through them. Anyway, all I have to do to intensify the magnification on that microscope is divert the active mode impulse of my— Are you following this, Pa?"

"Umm—barely, so far," Jonathan Kent answered the nine-year-old child. "You're likely to lose me any second, though."

"Well, anyway, it's like with these slides I'm projecting what I can see, like mirrors off the back of my eyeballs. Pretty good, huh?"

"Pretty good. Don't suppose the grasshopper appreciates it much, though."

"He didn't appreciate the virus either."

"Tell me something, Clark. Couldn't you have done about the same sort of trick with a chunk of rock or an old tree twig?"

"What do you mean?"

"I mean instead of putting a dead thing on your slide."

"Huh?" The boy crinkled his eyebrows for a moment and glanced through his foster father's eyes. "Oh, I'm sorry. I didn't know stuff like that bothered you. I just wanted to see what killed the grasshopper, is all."

"Whuzzat? You didn't kill him?"

"No. And there were grasshoppers all over the cornfield. Well, not like it was an infestation or anything, but there didn't seem to be any reason for this one to be dead. It was young, no parts missing, didn't have any digestion problems I could see. So I took it in here and found the virus. They're all up and down his nerves. He probably just twitched to death. Terrible."

"Well now, that's the best news I've heard all day."

"It is?"

"Sure enough."

"Well this virus could get into other grasshoppers. It might be all over. Could even get at other animals maybe. That's not great news."

"Son," Jonathan Kent said smiling, "when you live around farming and nature as long as I have, you learn to understand that everything lives in a balance. Grasshoppers live with corn crops, viruses live with grasshoppers, even men live with their livestock. All you've got to remember, being a thinking kind of creature, is not to tamper with the balance as much as you might be tempted to. Understand, boy?"

Clark looked through his father's eyes again. They were different from the way they were when Jonathan walked in. They were some-how more relaxed, moister in the tear ducts. "Yeah, Pa, I think I understand that."

"I was just thinking about that tonight when I woke up. Wanted to come in here and tell you."

"Right, Pa."

"Well, good night, Clark. Don't strain those active modes of yours."

"Right. G'night, Pa."

Clark wondered why his father had been so upset when he walked in, wondered why the little bit he said was so important to him. Clark tucked his questions into a pocket of his mind, confident that he would figure out their answers soon enough. For the rest of the night Jonathan Kent slept like a grizzly in January.

Graduation

The boy grew up in a universe of macrocosm and microcosm. To visit the other side of the world was, to him, what swinging on a vine across a creek was for other boys. He could see the unending dramas of underground ant colony wars and stratospheric weather front competitions as easily as he saw the mail truck barreling past the farm into town twice a day. He could alter his visual perceptions to detect waves on the entire electromagnetic spectrum, seeing alpha particles or cosmic rays as easily as he saw the visible light—but in colors that ordinary humans were incapable of imagining.

He could feel the level of the day's sunspot activity when he woke up in the morning in much the same way that those around him could tell if it was raining before they opened the shades. He could hold a conversation in one room while he listened to another one a mile away and to a radio broadcast as it flew through the air around him in microwaves.

The world was his playground and campus, superhuman senses his teachers, the anonymity of the Kent home his womb and protection.

He was alone in all this sense and knowledge, monumentally alone; but less alone, he realized, than were those other Earthmen, glued to their world and trapped inside bodies that could do no more than touch the outsides of other bodies. The boy was alone, but he was never bored.

Jonathan Kent had sold the farm for less than it was worth; bought the general store in Smallville from old Whizzer Barnes for more than it was worth; and moved into a little clapboard house he couldn't afford next door to Sarah and Martin Lang. Young Maynard Stone, the former backyard turkey entrepreneur, was now John M. K. Stone, the chief loan officer at the Smallville branch of Heartland Bank and Trust. Young Stone floated a loan to Jonathan for ten years, betting on Clark's eventual ability to pay it off. That was the way people did business in Smallville, especially with a man whose smile was as infectious as Jonathan Kent's.

Clark was thirteen when he sat on the school bus and stared through the window at the installation ceremony for a new queen bee in a hive four miles away. Lana sat next to him and talked incessantly about how incredibly old Clark Gable was starting to look and how she couldn't understand why her mother said he was such a hunk every time she saw a picture of him in a magazine and was Clark listening to her?

"Yeah, Lana. Clark Gable's a hunk. Mostly I like his name."

"Oh Clark, you're always daydreaming. I don't know why I talk to you at all."

"No, I was listening, Lana. Honest," he said, as the new queen's nuptial flight carried her above all the drones but one. Clark turned to look at the girl, taking an instant to notice her incredible red hair for the seven hundred and twelfth time, and said, "You said that he's nearly sixty and his wife at home is pregnant and he's filming a movie somewhere out of the country with Marilyn Monroe and every woman your mother's age is drooling for him all the time and you don't see how his poor wife can handle even looking at a man like that because he's so old and presumably overrated and outside the country with Marilyn Monroe and I suppose I agree completely."

Clark smiled the way his father smiled (if people knew he was adopted they had very likely forgotten by now) and Lana let out a deep breath and said, "Oh Clark," and the bus driver slammed on his brake.

They were on the Totten Pond Road, on a little hill that was the highest point for fifty miles, and the window on the right side of the bus looked out over Smallville. If Clark pointed the fingers of his right hand upward, with his thumb on the gold-leafed town hall bell tower and his ring finger at the point of the light blue steeple of the old Methodist Church, then the span of his hand held the entire town.

Clark looked up when the bus stopped short. So did Lana and the thirty-one other kids on their way to school this morning. The driver threw the handle to open the double door and hopped out. The fifteen kids on the left side of the bus gaped out their windows and said things like "Wow," and "Aww," and "Oh the poor thing," and the eighteen kids on the right side got out of their seats to see what was going on.

"This old fella look familiar to any of you kids?" the driver wanted to know. The driver was kneeling next to his left front wheel, gently stroking the fur of an ancient black Labrador retriever, dying or dead, who had just been hit by that wheel.

Clark gulped, looked at the dog thoroughly from his vantage point on the bus. The animal was not breathing, its heart had stopped; its brain was still radiating electromagnetic energy but it would not be doing that for long. It probably died of shock the moment the bus hit it. There was nothing Clark or anyone else could do for it.

"That's Tim," Pete Ross said, "the dog that lives in the chicken coop on the Johnson farm."

"Is that Tim?" somebody said.

"Aww," somebody said.

"Oh the poor thing," somebody said.

"There was so much dust on the road," the bus driver said, "that I didn't see him until I was almost on top of him. He just stood there, didn't even try to get out of the way."

"Mr. Johnson said he had arthritis," somebody said.

The driver wrapped the old dog in his coat and put him under his seat, saying that he would take the animal to the Johnson farm as soon as the students were all at the school. The rest of the ride was uncommonly quiet. Halfway through the morning, all the students who were on the bus, except for Clark, seemed to have forgotten the incident. Clark left school that day at lunchtime.

Jonathan Kent was planning on liking his new career. He was supposed to have gotten rid of the farm years ago on doctor's orders, but the advent of a son had delayed that. It's just plain common sense that a little kid can't keep a big secret in a small town, and little Clark's secret was as big as they come. Doc Hill told Jonathan then that if he kept up the hard work he wouldn't live to see another president sworn in. Well he'd lived to see two or three, he couldn't remember exactly how many it'd been. All he'd needed was a boy to share the work and to call him Pa.

Clark was older now, though, and he could keep his own secrets; and running a general store right in town just a few blocks from home was lots better for body and soul than pitching hay—as long as Martha kept the books straight. Jonathan was rearranging his display of detergent boxes from alphabetical order to size places for the second time this week when the pay phone near the door rang.

"Kent's General Store, Jonathan Kent here."

"Jonathan, is that you?"

"It was when I answered the phone. Don't see any reason it'd change now. Something wrong, Martha?"

"It's Clark."

"What about Clark?"

"He came home early from school. He's running a fever."

Jonathan was about to say something to the effect that boys get sick sometimes, but then he realized that Clark had never been sick before. "You suppose your thermometer could be wrong?" he asked his wife.

"The temperature is the least of it. He walked in red-eyed and he hasn't stopped crying since he got here. He's in his room under the covers and shivering and he won't tell me what's wrong. Jonathan, I think it could be some sort of unknown ailment we can't do anything about. That's the only sickness I can imagine him getting. I don't know whether or not to call Doc Hill."

"Lyndon? No, don't call him. I'm afraid he might still remember breaking a needle on Clark's arm when he was a baby. We'd have a devil of a time explaining if it turned out to be some space bug giving him the shakes. Just keep him warm until I get there and we'll figure out what to do."

Jonathan was a strong man, Martha knew. Underneath his glasses, his mild manners, his sheepish grin was the boy who had spirited her off in his buggy to a justice of the peace when he couldn't convince her father he could support a wife; the man who had taken a hundred twenty acres of the rockiest thicket in Kansas and twisted it into a wheatfield and a home; the husband in whose face she found love and prayer and hope when she had despaired over being unable to give birth. Middle-aged and childless, Martha Clark Kent grew to want no more from life than to grow old in the company of this unshakably good man. Then, as happened to Abraham's aged wife Sarah, the Heavens gave her a son.

Someday soon she would learn the origin of her son, the toddler she and Jonathan had found in an object she thought was a falling star one afternoon when they were on their way to look over a used tractor. She would learn of his flight from a dying planet, cast off into space by his parents. She would even learn the name of the planet— Krypton—and the names of the parents—Jor-El and Lara. But for most of the time she knew her adopted son, Martha Kent would know no more about him than that the boy had had, when she first saw him, the most angelic face she had ever seen. She wondered if all angels rode falling stars when they came to Earth.

Before Jonathan closed the gate of the picket fence, Martha had already flown out the door and into his arms with a "Jonathan! Jonathan!"

"Now what's all this about the boy being sick?" he asked as he fairly carried her back through the door.

"He won't talk to me. He may be delirious. He made his way home all right, he's just shivering and his face is so hot you could scramble an egg on his forehead. I'm scared for him, Jonathan."

"Now now, dear, he's got tougher skin than we do. Why don't you fix us a cup of tea and I'll see what the boy looks like?"

"All right." He was the kind of man—and they were scarce indeed—who quietly watched life most of the time, but when those he was watching seemed unable to handle things, he stepped in and shone with confidence.

Jonathan was in Clark's room for three or four minutes, not long enough even for the water in the kettle to think about boiling, before he came out. He wasn't smiling, but the confidence was still there.

"Growing pains, I warrant," he told her.

"Growing pains? With a fever and the shivers?"

"That's what I'd call it. Nothing a good man-to-man talk won't cure."

"Jonathan, the boy's ill. I never had growing pains like that."

"I did."

"Do tell?"

"First time I came calling on you. Was so worried I'd made a bad impression I had to stay home from school for two days."

Martha thought a moment. Then her eyes widened and she said, "Sakes alive, Jonathan. It's not little Lana. Not at their age, is it?"

"Oh no, Martha. Nothing like that. That'll come too, soon enough, but not yet. There's a lot of hurting a boy goes through if he wants to be a man. And when a boy wants to be a special kind of a man like Clark'll be—well, a lot of hurting. I left the store open and there were three robberies in town last year. You run off now and tend to that and don't worry. I'll tell you all about it later."

"Oh men!" And she left, no longer the least bit worried.

Clark was not sure whether he was awake or not, whether he was talking or not. He felt as though he was talking. He was using up the kind of energy you use up when you are talking, and he did not have a lot of that energy to spare just now. He did not feel as if he was saying anything, though. Just talking.

What was there to explain? Clark wondered. He was sick. People get sick, right? So he was sick. He did not like it, did not do it on purpose, didn't think he was going to die from it or anything. He was just sick, is all. So what was Pa talking about when he said he wanted to know what happened? He had been feeling all right. Then he was sick. After a while he would feel all right again. End of story.

Clark thought he felt as though he was going to throw up. Then he wondered what it felt like when you felt as though you were going to throw up. But Clark didn't throw up, so he must not have felt as though he was going to throw up, but it must have felt a lot like that. What did Pa want now?

Then Clark was thinking about that poor dead dog.

Living things have a kind of glow around them, like a halo. Living happy things glow in one color; living sad things glow in another color. Living intelligent things in still another color, living innocent things in yet another. There was no name for any of the hundreds of colors and shades in which living things glowed. They were not colors that could have been seen by the eyes of whoever it was that had made up the names of the colors. The boy did not feel he had to make up names for them; he had no one with whom to talk about them except himself, and he would know what he meant without the names. But dead things, especially dead things that have lately been alive, look awful. They're all gray and empty. Their glow fades slowly—as slowly as a mimosa leaf closes when it reluctantly decides that the sun is going down. Then after the glow is weak and gray for a while it disappears, leaving behind a disgusting lump that is not much besides a disorderly mess of chemicals. There is nothing else like it. No metaphor, no analogy. Just nothing, where there had been something that glowed.

Pa was sitting there, smiling sometimes, asking a question sometimes, listening all the time. Then once, just before he left, Pa put his hand on Clark's head—softly, the way Pa did things—and left it there awhile. Before Pa left the room, Clark stopped shivering.

Clark slept peacefully for another two hours, longer than he had

24

slept in one stretch since he was a baby. When he woke up, it was nearly six o'clock and his dinner was warming on the stove.

"Hello, Clark," Jonathan Kent said. "How are you feeling?"

"All right."

"Would you like your turkey soup?" Martha Kent asked, as she felt his forehead and pushed that dangling curl of hair out of his face.

"Sure, Ma."

The three ate for a few minutes before Jonathan said, "I told Ma about the talk we had this afternoon, son. Do you remember much of it?"

"Some."

Clark ate a few spoonfuls of soup and then he said, "The thing of it was, I was on the bus."

"I know."

"I was riding on the bus that k-k-k . . ."

"That's all right, Clark," Martha said, as she handed him a big dish of roast beef and string beans.

". . . that k-killed the dog."

"It's over now, it's all right."

"It's not all right! It's really not. How could it be all right? None of the other kids could've helped it, the driver couldn't've helped it, even the dog couldn't. Only I could've helped it. And I could've, too!"

"If you'd seen it coming," Jonathan said. "But you didn't."

"But I could've."

"But you didn't. We already went through this hours ago."

"We did?"

"Yes."

Clark worked on the string beans for a while. Then he put down his fork and asked to be excused. "I'd like to go for a walk somewhere."

Martha looked at Jonathan and said, "Certainly, dear. I'll keep your dinner warm if you like."

Clark walked toward the door until his father asked him to wait a moment.

"Why don't you put on that outfit we made out of your baby blankets?"

As dusk gathered that day, on the hill overlooking Smallville there was a sight no one had ever seen before. There beside the Totten Pond Road stood a black-haired boy in a costume of primary colors. A red cape billowed in the breeze at his back. Red boots, blue tights and a blue shirt stretched over powerful muscles. An irregular pentagon containing a stylized letter "S" blazed over the boy's chest and cape

A few cars slowed as he stood there, then sped past him. One man driving a buggy stopped for a second, about to call out to the boy, but went on by instead. The boy looked not at all like any of the other boys his age who lived in Smallville.

On that hill, silently and solemnly, Superboy promised himself and who or whatever else might hear his thoughts that his life would be devoted to the preservation of life; that he would use his powers whenever possible to save and improve the conditions of life and of living things everywhere; that under no circumstances would he ever be responsible for the loss of a single conscious life; that failing in any of these affirmations he would renounce his powers forever· There could be no nobler mission for a superman.

That evening Clark came home, finished his dinner and went to his room early. Jonathan and Martha sat together by the fire and read until well after midnight. At some point just before they went to bed, Jonathan looked up from his book and said, as much to his son as to his wife, "Well, Martha, looks to me as though the boy's ready "

These six hundred sixty-six pawns were acquainted with Saturn, whose exploits on Earth were legion. Although Saturn had a good many minor failures, failure never came the same way twice; and after all, he had done quite well on occasion.

Saturn got the best of a young Egyptian pharaoh, for example. He promised that if the boy destroyed all records and memory of his monotheist predecessor Ikhnaton, then the boy-king would have gold and treasure beyond his greatest dreams; and that treasure would be with him longer than that of any other pharaoh. True, the tomb of King Tutankhamen remained free of looters until the year 1911; but the boy had died at nineteen, and Saturn saw to it that the treasure remained with Tut's body, not his soul.

In 1846 Saturn was beaten by a United States senator from Massachusetts, who was actually a native of New Hampshire. Because of the senator's brilliant oratory, a jury comprised of vermin summoned from the bowels of the Netherworld was convinced to free the soul of a hapless farmer Saturn had trapped. In return, Senator Daniel Webster won freedom for all of New Hampshire until the end of time.

In 1920 Saturn won when he posed as an angel who offered eternal salvation to a young Austrian house painter in return for the Austrian's agreement to take his greater reward then and there, foregoing the remainder of his allotted years. Adolf Hitler foolishly refused, and as a result of the encounter, he was encouraged to go on to establish the Third Reich.

Saturn failed in the year 1930. A young Milano boy with no weapon or training other than his innate goodness exorcised Saturn from the body of his dying father. Because of this ordeal the boy's life was shortened, but Albino Luciani won the right, as Pope John Paul I, to a great temporal honor during the final days of his life.

A secretary-general of the United Nations resisted Saturn in 1961. Saturn undid the seat belt of the diplomat, on a mission of peace in Africa, just before the airplane in which he was riding crashed, immediately killing everyone aboard except for the secretary-general, who was thrown clear of the wreckage. Writhing with the pain of a broken back and a punctured lung in the middle of a foresaken glade, the man heard Saturn's offer of life and an end to pain if he would betray the trust of an emerging African nation. Dag Hammarskjöld died, in immeasurable pain, with a prayer and a smile on his lips.

Socrates would not fall to Saturn's temptation, but the Athenian civilization did.

Copernicus found the thin beam of truth, but Saturn easily found morally blind men to condemn him—in the name of faith.

Lincoln's strong hand and native genius led his nation from division, but Saturn managed to salvage a century of hatred and division from Lincoln's death, if not from his life.

Men marched to war and women—though they often knew better—cheered them on.

Crowds rioted.

Mobs lynched.

Demagogues roared.

Hordes swarmed.

Death, blood, destruction and mostly vengeance—it was all very impressive. C. W. Saturn found the cloud for every silver lining.

The fabric of the emptiness around Saturn dimmed a dimness that had nothing to do with light. A hundred or more meters from C. W. Saturn the space swirled and a ragged circle of ground fell in. Then a larger circle around it cracked under the surface. And more and more of the floor cracked and tumbled downward in widening, inaccurately concentric circles, until a great depression formed in the floor. It widened further, forming four corners, and its sides flattened into four triangular walls which came together in a point far below the surface of the ground. There, it ended, a wide smoldering canyon the shape of an inverted pyramid.

For a moment, there was quiet in the space that was not space. It was a moment just long enough for the crouching, slithering members of the unholy court to ache to know what it would be like to be in that ultimate of luxuries, a place where one could stand up straight. It was long enough for the residents of this place to want to go into the depression of space, to feel physically free there for an instant, suspended between the eternities of past and future; long enough to realize what sort of eternal future they would see if they yielded to the temptation; long enough to summon a wrenching combination of envy and despair from the blackest depths of their nearly inured souls, before space swirled again.

It was as though someone had sown the wind in the pyramidal depression. Sound roared. Space folded. Visions creased over one another. A pyre of yellow and blue fire rose from a point near the bottom tip and grew to the size of the hole, then bigger, until the pyre coughed flames that burned icy cold into the great crawl space, and frigid smoke blew around Saturn and the unholy company.

When the swirling stopped and the frigid flames had dissipated into the infinite cramped expanse, a new being had arrived. Sitting in the pyramidal hole was a creature that hissed hatred like brimstone through cavernous nostrils. It sat squarely on the base of the small

30

canyon, its leathery, pointed tail coiled into the sharp nadir to make itself a seat. It was large enough so that even as it sat in its slouch, its head rode higher than the ceiling above the deep throne. The craggy surface of the ceiling curved upward deferentially as the great head took the ceiling's place, returning when the head moved on. The being's skin was scaly all over, with thick black hair growing from under the scales. Its limbs wore long claws and its head was dressed in a fearsome countenance of deep-set eyes, high cheeks, long pointed ears, and horns. There were spurs on its elbows and knees, and a dark leathery skin covered its face and hands. Thick black wings grew from its back.

This was the form Saturn had designed to strike terror into the hearts of humans. It was an honor, a sign of confidence in Saturn, that the ruler chose to wear this form for this meeting. For this was Samael, the master of this place.

"C. W. Saturn," Samael said.

"I am here," was the answer.

"You have done well, successfully extending our influence and that of the physical laws of Chaos to the territory called Terra. I therefore require you to continue to the final stage of your mission: the utter moral and physical destruction of the one called Superman."

This, as Saturn had known before his return to his kingdom of origin, was what all the training and preparation had been about. Saturn would have the responsibility of ruining for all time and space the humans' greatest symbol of goodness and order. After the fall of Superman, the beachhead world of Earth would suffer the collapse of the moral sensibilities of all humans; then the very laws of physics and ultimately the continuum itself would begin to crumble. Creation would give way to Oblivion.

For this place, the place from which this intention was dispatched, was Hell, and C. W. Saturn was the agent of Hell on Earth.

Kristin Wells was intense.

She was also with it, liberated and foxy.

Outrageously foxy.

Kristin was all these things on purpose. Kristin loved disco dancing, and she ardently hoped that someday, against all odds, Sonny and Cher would get back together. She had her hair redone every month the way the model on the cover of *Cosmopolitan* had hers, and she believed that the Equal Rights Amendment should be ratified immediately. She thought worrying about electoral politics was soporific (*a drag,* she corrected herself), she was indignant over (pardon, *bummed out by*) the exploitation of women in contemporary magazines, and she was extremely concerned with *(into)* the astrological signs of everyone she knew.

The phone rang.

"Hey baby," Kristin said into the phone.

"What was the popular name of Peter Noone?" the voice asked without ceremony.

"That was Herman, y'know? From Herman's Hermits? You should get with it, baby. That was ages ago."

"Significant nonetheless."

"Really," Kristin said. "Have a nice day."

The apartment was modest but very hip. *Très chic* was what Kristin supposed she should call it. Aluminum foil lined the bedroom walls and the ceiling was papered with posters of John Travolta, Christopher Reeve and Jack Nicholson. There was a printed sign on one side of the bedroom door that said, "Save water—shower with a friend." On the side of the door, facing the combination kitchen–living room was a framed, artifically yellowed copy of *Desiderata*. The dominant feature of the living room was plants. Dozens of spider plants and wandering jews and ferns of several varieties hung from the ceiling and the tops of the window panes. Philodendra, caladia and the matured shoots of a single incredibly fecund coleus sat, in various states of care and prosperity, in pots around the room. The stove, sink and refrigerator hid out against one wall of the room behind a set of folding doors.

It was nearly eight o'clock and Kristin had to finish cutting her cuticles and glossing her fingernails before "Mork and Mindy" came on the tube. The phone rang again.

"*Ciao*, honey," she told the mouthpiece and then sang, "I'm 'enery the Eighth I am, 'enery the Eighth I am I am—"

"Pardon?" the same voice as before said.

"Never mind, cute stuff. What's cooking?"

A hesitation. Then the question: "What is a Krugerrand?"

"A Krugerrand? Is that what you asked? A Krugerrand?"

"Yes, Ms. Wells. A Krugerrand."

"Some kind of hazel nut, isn't it?"

"Afraid not."

"Oh, then it must be a South African coin containing an ounce of gold whose value rises and falls with the fluctuating price of gold. Right?"

"Correct."

She got them again. Sometimes she felt like Oedipus, she decided. Not a lot like Oedipus, she decided, only a little. She turned on the television just as Mork from Ork panicked because he mistook a candle lit in a living room for the light that warned of the coming of the interplanetary Marquis de Sade. Kristin laughed pretty much uncontrollably for the next twenty-seven minutes, through the commercials. When the show was over she looked at the clock, realized she had only half an hour to get ready for her date. As soon as she got the temperature of the water in the shower just right, the phone rang.

"Yuh?" she gurgled into the receiver.

"Identify Thurston Howell the Third."

"Suck a turnip!" and she hung up.

Pismo Grandee sat at the control console in the Field Work Training Center. To his right was his information terminal. In front of him were six monitor screens in a row, four of which he was using. Of the four students whose training exercises he was monitoring, one was in another room of the building feeding answers to oral essay questions on the Mars Colony Rebellion into his own terminal; another was practicing light-beam dancing in the style popular among adolescents in the 2130s; a third was piloting a stationary device that simulated sublight gravitation-field flying; and there was a fourth who was the program's prize student right now. Carleton Hampshire materialized on the platform behind Pismo to relieve him.

"Interesting outfit being worn by you," Pismo said.

"Very latest according to research," Carleton answered, grinning. He was wearing a loose white silk shirt with billowing sleeves, with cuffs and a collar that were simply stiffer strips of the same material. It buttoned up the front, but only as high as Carleton's solar plexus. His shoes had high heels and his slacks were tight as paint and bulged unnaturally. "We went disco," he told Pismo.

"It was mentioned when your return to the apartment was seen by me. How is her progress?"

"Excellent. I was caught in some errors of speech pattern and cultural orientation."

"Were they compensated for by you?"

"Not necessary for that to be done. Student herself compensated, deciding that since Andy Gibb was identified incorrectly by me, she was being consorted with by a wimp."

"A wimp?"

"This term was defined by her as something too low to kick and too wet to step on."

"And Andy Gibb?" Pismo fed the name into his information terminal.

An instant readout on the terminal's screen gave the dates of the singer's birth and death, the names of several of his best-known works and a brief account of his career including the phrase, ". . . younger brother of Barry, Maurice and Robin Gibb who made up a singing group called the *BeeGees*."

"Ambiguous storage of information," Carleton said, pointing to the phrase on the screen. "Unclear whether brother Andy was *BeeGees* member."

"Apparently was not. Information please: Are you equipped to sit at console with tight leggings?"

"Will inform if success is denied," Carleton said. Both men laughed at the joke. If it were nine hundred years earlier, Pismo might have asked if Carleton could sit down without splitting his pants and Carleton might have said something to the effect that Pismo would be the first to know, and they would have laughed as well.

"Good Miracle Monday," Pismo told Carleton before he teleported out.

"Good Miracle Monday," Carleton said as he worried his shape into the shape of the chair.

Carleton scanned the computer readout of the yet unfinished answer to the last question on the Mars Colony Rebellion.

He looked at a graph of the proper pattern of light-beam dancing and compared it with the student's pattern.

He noted that according to the student's readout, the third student had just landed his antigravitation device two hundred meters underground.

He punched the code for Kristin's telephone receiving device, watched the monitor as she answered it.

Before he could speak she said, "He was a shipwrecked multimillionaire in a television series called 'Gilligan's Island.' He was played by an actor named Jim Backus."

"Excuse?" Carleton was confused. It was Pismo who had asked her the question.

"Thurston Howell the Third. The question I hung up on when I was in the shower."

"One moment."

As Carleton punched the name Thurston Howell the Third into his terminal Kristin said, "You been asleep, baby? I shoulda been. I went out to a disco with this real turkey. I shouldn'ta bothered to take that shower. The guy had this open shirt and no chest hair. Really

34

tacky. Guys with no chest hair should never wear open shirts. It's just my opinion, know what I'm saying? He looked like the Pillsbury doughboy. Really, y'know?"

Carleton saw that the information on the readout mirrored Kristin's answer to Pismo's question of several hours ago. Carleton was not offended, even though he was the "real turkey." No Earthman in the twenty-ninth century grew chest hair. It was the only measurable natural evolutionary change in nine hundred years.

Carleton asked his question. "Who was Secretary of State in 1970?"

"Politics. What a royal drag," Kristin whined, playing her role. "Lessee. 1970? Nixon was President, that means the Secretary of State was Henry Kissinger, right?"

William Rogers was Secretary of State in 1970. It was Kristin's first incorrect answer in nearly two weeks.

In Kristin's apartment, and on the screen through which an instructor of the Field Work Training Center monitored her, it was a bright spring day in the city of Metropolis, sometime around the year 1980. Everywhere else—in the ancient city of Metropolis that lay outside Kristin's walls; in the Confederation of Nations of which Metropolis was effectively the capital; in the Martian Principalities, the Venusian Protectorate, the Jovian and Saturnian Satellite City-States; in the Union of Outer Darkness comprising the far-scattered civilization of Uranus, Neptune, Pluto and the artificial comets; on barren bases and mining colonies throughout the Arm of the Milky Way wherever Earth humans had extended their consciousness—in all these places it was a day in the year 2857. More importantly, for Earth humans everywhere it was a special day, the third Monday of the month: Miracle Monday.

On Miracle Monday the spirit of humanity soared free. This Miracle Monday, like the first Miracle Monday, came in the spring in Metropolis, and for the occasion spring weather was arranged wherever the dominion of humanity extended. On Uranus's satellites where the natives held an annual fog-gliding rally through the planetary rings, private contributions even made it possible to position orbiting fields of gravitation for spectators in free space. On Titan, oxygen bubbles were loosed in complicated patterns to burst into flame with the methane atmosphere and make fireworks that were visible as far as the surface of Saturn. At Nix Olympica, the eight-kilometer-high Martian volcano, underground pressures that the Olympica Resort Corporation had artificially accumulated during the preceding year were unleashed in a spectacular display of molten fury for tourists who walked around the erupting crater wearing pressurized energy shields. At Armstrong City in the Moon's Sea of Tranquility there was a holographic reenactment of the founding of the city in the year 2019, when on the fiftieth anniversary of his giant leap for mankind the first man on the Moon returned, aged and venerable, to what was then called Tranquility Base Protectorate, carrying a state charter signed by the President of the United States. The prices of ski lift tickets on Neptune inflated for the holiday. Teleport routes to beaches and mountains on Earth crowded up unbelievably. Interplanetary wilderness preserves became nearly as crowded with people as Earth cities. Aboard the slow-moving orbital ships that carried ores and fossil materials in slowly decaying loops toward the sun from the asteroids, teamsters partied until they couldn't see. On worlds without names scattered throughout this corner of the Galaxy, where Earth's missionaries, pioneers and speculators carried their own particular quests, it was a day for friends, family, recreation and—if it brought happiness—reflection.

Pismo reflected for a moment on the envy he felt for Kristin Wells, who would, before the next Miracle Monday come to the Metropolis of the twenty-ninth century, live through the first Miracle Monday, walk these streets as they were in the age of the great barbarian builders and explorers. Kristin Wells would meet the legendary Superman. Her mission, like those of the scores of others who managed to convince someone to finance a trip to the deep past, would probably find nothing new for the historic records, but it would be worth the trip. Meanwhile, Kristin Wells trained for a stay in the past and, in her spare time, watched Superman by timescan.

Pismo had found a point in time and space, some months before the events of Miracle Monday, in which Superman was stopping a tidal wave from engulfing downtown Metropolis. There was no record of natural tidal waves in this area in recorded history, but Pismo, Carleton and Kristin reconstructed the probable causes of the phenomenon.

"Fascinating," Pismo said.

"Remarkable," Carleton said.

"In-freaking-credible," Kristin said and smiled.

The Wave

Always there have been the heroes.

Achilles single-handedly drove the army of Troy back behind their walls under a sun that was carried across the sky in Apollo's chariot.

Young David killed the giant Goliath with the spin of a smooth rock in a land where walls fell at the sound of trumpets and the Creator of Heaven and Earth spoke through the mouths of men in rags whose eyes burned with the lights of Eternity.

John Henry laid hundreds of miles of railroad tracks over trails blazed by Davy Crockett, who could wring the tail off a comet by smiling at it.

John Kennedy, with intellect and force of will, averted the annihilation of a civilization whose athletes could run a mile in less than four minutes, whose pilots could orbit the planet in less than an hour and a half and whose humblest born could grow up to be president.

And Superman . . .

Real or imagined, the heroes lived; they lived in the world not as it was, but as it should have been. Real or imagined, the heroes lived under the responsibility that came with the good wishes of those who aspired to what they stood for; lived in a realm decorated with fancies not available to mortal men and women; lived with conceptions of reality more idealistic than those that were practical for their contemporaries; lived by values far beyond the reach of those who walked with feet and lines of sight against the ground.

It was in a Universe where there was a right and a wrong and where that distinction was not very difficult to make that Superman calmed a tidal wave before it washed fury over the city of Metropolis.

It was a frigid day toward the beginning of February. About a week ago there was a minor earthquake off the western coast of Greenland. No one was hurt. In fact, no one particularly noticed it other than a few seismologists who reported the event to whoever it is to whom seismologists report such things. This information found its way from whoever it is to the news media whose job it was to decide what was important for the world to know about.

Clark Kent, the anchorman and associate producer of the WGBS Six O'clock Evening News, reported the quake to his assigned portion of the world in seventeen words during the seventh and next-to-last segment of his daily report. The *Daily Planet* told its share of the world about it in thirty lines on the left-hand column of page sixty-four. The bulk of the world—those who did not watch Clark Kent or read the *Daily Planet*—found out about the quake similarly from various sources, and the world promptly forgot it. It seemed a very forgettable occurrence, although indirectly it nearly destroyed Metropolis.

Most of Greenland, including the portion mildly shaken by the earthquake, was covered by a glacier several kilometers thick. The major effect of the earthquake was to prompt a fairly insignificant mass of the western edge of this glacier to shatter into hundreds of pieces, many of which were about the size of a sperm whale. The whale-sized chunks of ice bobbed in the water a bit, then they floated out to sea.

A hundred or so kilometers east of northern New England there was a nuclear power plant. The plant contained a fission reactor which supplied power to most of Maine, New Hampshire and Vermont. The plant was originally built because of a political compromise. For several years a group of concerned but politically naive people who called themselves the Oysterbed Alliance—taking their name from the town of Oysterbed, Maine, where their organization was born—demonstrated against the proposed building of the reactor in a certain

38

coastal city. If not for the intransigence of the governor, the plant would certainly have been moved to another site when surveyors discovered that the proposed town was directly over a minor geological fault. Instead, this basically swinish governor chose to take an unshakable stand against the Oysterbed Alliance, making them a scapegoat for all the ills of the state in his reelection campaign. New Englanders tend to be uncommonly astute in detecting swinishness among their political leaders. He was defeated for reelection by a man who, as it turned out, did not want the reactor in his state at all. Neither did the governors of the other two states whose power companies would benefit by it. As a result, the plant was built on a massive platform, floating on tremendous pontoons over the virgin sea.

Six months after the pontoon reactor began its operations, there was a tremor in the town that had been its originally planned site. Authorities called the tremor an *icequake* because it was caused not by the fault in the ground, they said, but by a sudden thaw that followed eighteen consecutive days of weather in which the temperature did not rise above seven degrees Fahrenheit. On the nineteenth day, the ground shook suddenly and violently free of the ice.

The marine equivalent of an icequake happened when the icebergs that were loosened by the Greenland quake floated a few kilometers south. A reactor of this sort, it seems, wastes more heat than it directs into electrical power. Hence, this reactor spread more energy across its immediate area of no-longer-virginal ocean than it generated to provide power for the three northern New England states. So when a few score icebergs, lately dismembered from the glacier, floated from the frigid waters that dominated the North Atlantic, into the vicinity of the white-hot breeder reactor and the nearly boiling seawater that cooled it, the bergs hissed into water and steam within minutes.

Because of this the sea suffered a trauma, a physical concussion. The sudden clash of radically differing temperatures in a fairly large area caused the ocean to leap like a cat off a hot iron.

The ocean, as much as air, rivers and mountain ranges, has currents and textures. One such current, part of the backwash of the Gulf Stream, flows southwest from the vicinity of Greenland to the area of Metropolis. Generally this current is rather insignificant and had been unnoticed by oceanographers and other people whose job it was to notice such things, much as Plains, Georgia, was generally unnoticed by mapmakers until 1976 or thereabouts. The advent of the nuclear reactor in the path of this current, in fact, generally had the effect of raising Metropolis's temperature by a degree or two. This day, however, the frigid sea grew and hissed with an unnatural terror.

The water off the coast of New England was expelling its shock southward through the current.

With no precedent and less apparent reason, a wall of water two hundred meters high and twice as deep, rode the ocean surface to the edge of Metropolis harbor.

Water of that mass and at that height would hit the ground and buildings with the force of a monstrous sledgehammer wielded by an arm as big as the city itself. Dockworkers, tourists, businessmen and women crouching under biting wind on their ways back to work after a late lunch looked up into the sky.

From the east came a looming elemental monster, a wave times a thousand.

From the west, over the city, streaked a familiar red-and-blue figure, grim, determined, dwarfed by the adversary that threatened to deal the city a crushing blow.

They had no hope of survival, these people within sight of the great wave, no hope other than this man who flew. Some of them saw the tiny figure accelerate in the direction of the wave, heard the whistle of his flight under the thunder of the oncoming juggernaut. They saw him, if they saw him, for only a moment, because by the time he reached the harbor he was flying faster than any mortal eye could follow, into the cresting mountain of sea.

As Superman crossed the sound barrier, he lifted his eyes and mind from the city he was determined to save, and he focused all his considerable being on the sea-spawned monster before him. At a velocity of three to four hundred meters per second he would reach the wave within three quarters of a second; during this time he would be able to shoot thirty or so blasts of heat vision at the wave's front, steaming out holes half a meter in diameter and several meters deep.

By the time he reached the wave Superman was flying chest-first, his body spread-eagled. The water's downward motion in order to fill the holes burned out of the body of the wave had subtly slowed its progress. Superman crashed his bulk through the face of the wave at a speed of Mach one and, for an instant that was longer than the instant it took for him to fly from shore to wave, there was a Superman-shaped hole from the front through to the back of the wave. A fraction of a second later the sonic boom from Superman's flight hit the wave in the face.

The body of the wave was rippled with shock. It could not support its own mass for the distance to the shore. It was less than three seconds since people in the crowd near the piers had spotted Superman streaking toward the harbor. They were still looking up at the point in the sky where Superman flew by three seconds ago, and the hero's job had just begun.

Instead of a mountain of water swatting down the financial district, there would be a huge slab of water clapping down on the outer harbor, sending hundreds of smaller angry chunks of water to slice apart the coast.

Superman was underwater looking up. He saw the wave moving nowhere, standing for an instant before it yielded to gravity, like a mortally wounded dinosaur who did not yet realize that its next move was to fall down.

Now Superman had to begin to move really quickly.

He circled underwater counterclockwise because if he went clockwise he would very likely have created a waterspout. He circled slowly for the first few milliseconds, nearly as slowly as sound travels. Then, once he established his own internal rhythm, he went faster. Then faster. And faster.

In a circle whose diameter was that of the dying wave he spun faster.

Upward he moved in a corkscrew through the water. Faster.

As he cracked the surface, the harbor swelled around him. Faster.

The wave above, looking for a place to fall, swept itself up into his rhythm. Faster.

The mountain of water flattened and spread into the shape of a dish. Faster.

Its edges rose with his motion like clay spinning against the hands of a potter. Faster, faster, faster.

By the time the faces of souls lately doomed to drown turned from the fading form of their hero above to the looming force of doom from the east, there was a giant swirling cylinder of water heading into the sky over the harbor. And the sea was as crisp and calm as the sea could properly be on a frigid February afternoon.

Up, up and away the last son of Krypton corkscrewed above the tallest buildings, above the sparsest clouds, over the realms of the strongest birds.

Then, suddenly, like a ski racer missing a gate, he spun out into the open sky. He whirled his body back to face the dispersing mass of seawater in the lower stratosphere, focused his narrowest line of sight on the lowest part of the mass, and a pair of optic nerves like none described in any medical text on Earth kicked into operation to reflect intense heat off the front of Superman's lenses, searing straight through his indestructible corneas and out his eyes.

At the speed of light, twin beams of infrared radiation—pure

41

heat energy—bored out of the man's eyes at the falling mass that, less than a minute ago, was a tidal wave born of glacial earthquake and nuclear excess. In the time it took for the water to drop through the radiant beams of heat vision, a great cloud of steam swelled through the stratosphere above the city of Metropolis.

Sometime during the coming eighteen hours, that great steam cloud would freeze and crystallize in the February air. Countless tiny six-sided crystals of former tidal wave would ride air and gravity to the ground, and Metropolis would wake up the next morning swathed in a blanket of snow sixteen inches thick.

Like matter and energy, forces of nature cannot be created or destroyed, only transformed and diverted. A blizzard, the Man of Steel had reasoned as he spun his circles, was something with which the city was equipped to deal. A killer wave was not.

The streets were paved with slush. The bus he had to drive this morning was twelve years old if it was a day. The guy getting on was smiling and saying good morning as though he were someone running for office; instantly the driver disliked him. Most people in this town actually liked this man with the silly grin and the inoffensive good looks who broadcast the news over WGBS every evening. As Clark Kent gained his footing on the slippery floor of the crowded bus the driver lurched the vehicle, hoping to trip up and embarrass the reporter whose face unnerved him the way a peaceful afternoon bothers the leader of a marching band. Instead of tripping Kent, the driver found that his bus was stuck.

Clark folded himself over a seat and waited patiently for the bus driver to conclude that he had another reason to be angry today. There was another bus, of course, plowing through the snow a few blocks behind. Nobody on this bus would mind transferring to that one and the city looked rather attractive in white anyway.

Clark Kent would be a few minutes late for work today, but he didn't think he'd mind that either.

The Announcement

Basically, the idea was to escape from the Galaxy Building and get well on the way out of town before the associate producer arrived and told everyone to do something else. The escape was Jimmy Olsen's idea, and Ev and Jerry didn't much care whether it worked or not. They played along because the alternative to following Olsen upstate was probably to sit on the Fifty-ninth Street Tramway and shoot film of cars sliding into one another's fenders on the bridge below. Going along with Olsen would, at worst, make for an interesting day and, at best, it would give Ev and Jerry a story to tell their grandchildren someday.

Reporters, secretaries, technicians, staffers of one sort or another were beginning to blow out of the snow into the WGBS-TV newsroom adjoining Studio B. When Jimmy had arrived at work—as was his custom, snow or no snow—fifteen minutes early at eight forty-five, he turned on the United and Associated Press tickers in time to get a list of the major anticipated stories of the day. Clark Kent, the associate producer, was responsible for assigning reporters to their stories. The moment Jimmy saw the name Lex Luthor type itself out on the rolling yellow paper, he started wanting Clark to arrive at work late.

Years ago James Bartholomew Olsen Senior had told Jimmy that once a man knew what he wanted, he was halfway to having it. By that reckoning, Jimmy reasoned, Clark ought to be late for work half the times Jimmy wanted him to be late for work. Whenever a story about Luthor tapped itself out over the wire, Clark invariably assigned it to himself. Clark was almost never late. Jimmy looked out at the snow and figured that he had a lot of potent wanting saved up.

Because of the snow, Jimmy thought it was fair to wait for Clark for an extra fifteen minutes. When Clark was still somewhere out there at ten past nine he decided that no one would haggle over five minutes. He signed out the four-wheel drive newsvan and hustled Ev and Jerry into the freight elevator.

"Excuse me, sir," the freight elevator operator said, "but you ain't carrying any freight."

"Pardon?" Jimmy said as he pressed the button for the basement and blocked the elevator operator from keeping the door open.

"Freight. You've got to carry freight. Packages or heavy equipment or something."

"Oh that's all right. See my press pass?" Jimmy smiled as he pulled out a laminated card from inside his ski jacket. He wore the pass on a rawhide shoelace around his neck. "I'm with WGBS News, you see, and Ev and Jerry here are my cameraman and sound technician. They carry heavy equipment all the time."

"But they ain't carrying it now. This is the freight elevator."

"Right. Yes. You're new here, aren't you?"

"I've been working here for twelve years."

"Right. Well, you must've seen a lot of strange things. A lot of strange things happen here, you know."

"Not on the freight elevator."

"Not until today, huh?"

"Eh?"

"Well, thanks for the ride," Jimmy said as he pulled Ev and Jerry by the elbows off the elevator into the basement garage. "Hope your next twelve years are just as interesting."

They couldn't take the regular passenger elevator down, Jimmy said, because they might run into Clark coming up. They couldn't leave through the lobby because that was the way Clark came in. They couldn't drive toward the East Side although that would have been the best route out of town because they might see Clark plodding through the snow, having missed his bus and unable to hail a cab, and the crew in the newsvan would have to offer him a ride and explain where they were going. Unfortunately, when Jerry, at the wheel of the oversized minibus, turned left onto Fifty-second Street, Clark Kent stepped off a bus that happened to be driven by a very patient and pleasant member of the overworked Transit Workers' Union.

"Uh-oh," Jimmy said and slouched in his seat.

"Jimmy?" Clark asked himself and then waved and yelled, "Jimmy! Where are you going?"

"Gotta watch Luthor escape. See you later," Jimmy yelled back and told Jerry to throw on the four-wheel drive and get out of there fast and to hell with the snow. Before Clark Kent had slogged across the street, through the lobby, up the elevator, and into the newsroom, Jimmy and the newsvan were on the Westway heading upstate.

Jimmy turned on the car radio and slid up and down the tuner until he found a weather report. Evidently it was snowing nowhere except in the immediate vicinity of the city. It was bitterly cold for hundreds of miles around, but outside Metropolis the air was crisp and clear. Maybe Superman really had caused this storm. Jimmy would have to remember to thank him for seeing to it that Clark was late the day Luthor showed up on the morning newswire.

The rolling yellow sheet from the Associated Press had said, simply, that Lex Luthor would hold a press conference at the criminal's residence, which happened to be on the grounds of the Pocantico Correctional Facility sixty miles north of Metropolis. Luthor's conference would be at two in the afternoon, and Warden Haskell would meet with the press an hour earlier. It would be at least noon before the newsvan broke free of the blizzard. The sound man drove and the cameraman navigated through the slow line of traffic filing up the Westway as Jimmy slouched among the equipment in the back of the van and wrote the story that had not yet happened:

Last year, the criminal scientist Lex Luthor escaped from Pocantico Prison eight times. The year before last he broke out eleven times, and one of those times he broke back in and then out again to retrieve something he had left behind. He has broken out only once so far this year, but it's only the beginning of February. He has broached walls, dug underground, flown overhead, set up disasters or mirages of disasters, and slipped away in the confusion. He has simply vanished, leaving no explanation for his disappearance. Today,

45

however, he did something he hasn't done before. He called a press conference to announce plans for his next prison break.

Jimmy assumed that was the most likely reason Luthor might want to meet with reporters. It was not that the criminal had ever wanted to talk with a reporter before about that or anything else. It was not that Jimmy had any special information other than what he had learned from the AP report. It was not even that Jimmy had flashes of extrasensory perception. It was simply that, having been around news and newspeople constantly since the age of sixteen, by the time Jimmy was in his mid-twenties he was as aware of the patterns and probabilities of important events as he was acquainted with the phases of the moon or the floor plan of his apartment. Very little took him by surprise. His effusive and volatile personality was largely an unconscious attempt to provide himself with some internal excitement, since he was effectively jaded as far as the external world was concerned.

By the time Jimmy looked up from his scribblings, Jerry was wheeling the newsvan on a snowless highway through Scarsdale and it was half past noon and a forty-five-minute drive to Pocantico without traffic. Jimmy suggested that Jerry drive faster. Ev strongly suggested that the trio be prepared to split the cost of any speeding tickets because Clark was a stickler for obeying the law and the station would not cover it. They would be late for the warden's show, but they would catch the main event.

In a cubicle on the third level of the four-tiered maximum security cell block at Pocantico sat a man who possessed probably the greatest intellect of any Earthman of his day. Luthor was talking to himself.

"Ladies and gentlemen," he said. "No, gentlemen . . . no, esteemed members of the press—the mass media? Umm."

Luthor got up from his cot, paced back and forth over the length of the cell, stared up at the gray back wall of the cell as if it had a window in it. "Simple," he told himself. "Direct, concise, simple. You're not running for office."

He sat on the cot again, sat back against the wall and picked up his yellow legal pad and his pen. "Three main points," he mumbled, and he listed them:

1. Have discovered new energy source which can be developed and made practical immediately—

46

2. Have petitioned Justice Department for permission to work on development either in or out of prison & have submitted funding proposals to 20 major industrial corporations in return for 49% share of new process—all rejected—

3. Submitted proposals out of courtesy and in all good faith—not surprised by rejection—therefore will demonstrate process by using it to escape sometime during next 7 days—

Luthor looked over his note pad and his three points, paced up and down the cell some more, waved a hand as he mumbled approximately what he had to say that afternoon, and looked up through the bars at the other inhabitants of Cell Block Ten. All the men in sight were quietly watching him, wearing various expressions of hero-worship and awe on their faces. Luthor smiled, tossed the pad on his cot and said in a clear, loud voice, "Any questions, class?"

Somebody hollered, "All right!" and two hundred or more men within earshot whooped and applauded for the greatest criminal of all time.

A kilometer away and thirty meters underground, Warden Haskell, the man who ran this prison complex when Luthor was away, was briefing the press.

"As you can see," Haskell said, "these walls are sixteen inches thick and this door weighs seven hundred pounds and takes three men to open it even when it is unlocked. We were very careful, by the way, in choosing the titanium alloy this is made of to see that there was no lead mixed in the material. Hence Superman will be able to monitor the prisoner if he so chooses. The lock, part of which you can see in the doorjamb here, consists of eight bolts which have to be opened both here at the midpoint of the door, and in my office by a special electronic control for which only the Attorney-General and I know the combination. Any claims the prisoner makes to the effect that he is being held incommunicado will be unfounded, as you can see from this press conference as well as the fact that we will provide him with—"

The reporters, fifteen men including four television technicians, were standing in the large super-security prison cell listening to the warden when they heard a crash out in the hallway. Then a man yelled "Stop!" and there was another crash and the warden walked out to see what was happening. There he found three strangers standing with their legs spread and hands on the wall while one of Haskell's prison

47

guards held a gun and another one frisked them. Haskell wondered what was the matter until he recognized one of the three strangers.

"Curtis," he said to the guard with the gun, "what's the problem here?"

"Unauthorized personnel, sir."

"Unauthorized hell," Jimmy Olsen said as he pressed his hands against the wall. "Didn't anybody ever read the First Amendment to you guys?"

"This individual showed me a false press pass," the guard said, "and upon detection he became indignant and tried to force his way in."

"When're you guys gonna learn to talk English?" Jimmy wanted to know.

"Mind your manners, punk, or I'll break your face," the guard told him.

"That's enough, Curtis. You too, Murphy," the warden said. "Back to your posts. I'm sorry about this incident, Mr. Olsen. I'm Warden Edmund Haskell. I don't think we've met before."

"I was planning on being pleased to meet you, Warden." Jimmy extended a hand.

"The men are on edge today because of the heavy security around moving Luthor. I hope you understand. What's this problem about a press pass?"

"I don't know." Jimmy pulled his card out from under his shirt as the guards trudged off and Ev and Jerry went to check their two cases of camera equipment that had been thrown against a wall. "Here's my pass if you want to see it. It got me past three checkpoints just fine until I got down here to the dungeon."

"I see," Haskell snorted as he read the information that hung around Jimmy's neck.

"You see what?"

"I'll have to have a few security drills, Mr. Olsen. This card shouldn't have gotten you *this* far. It's your season pass to the indoor courts at the Metropolis Racquet Club."

"How do you like that?" Jimmy looked at it. "I wonder if my socks match."

Jimmy, Ev and Jerry followed the warden into the dungeonlike room and the other reporters tapped their feet, looked at their watches and gave each other impatient looks as Jimmy's crew set up their sound film equipment. Nobody said a word of complaint, though, as the warden waited for Jimmy Olsen before continuing his remarks. It was great to be a star.

The room was ostensibly built for occasional high security cases. The federal grant said that some examples of the room's uses would be for suspected assassins, spies during wartime, an emergency bomb shelter, terrorists whose friends were likely to try to break them out of jail, that sort of thing. It would not do, Constitutionally, to build a special facility for a single prisoner, since that would constitute cruel and unusual punishment. During the construction of the facility, no one besides reporters mentioned the fact that the super-security cell was being built in the prison where Lex Luthor had spent slightly more than half his time since he became too old for the East Kansas Juvenile Reformatory. But sure enough, the very day Luthor decided to call a press conference—something most convicted felons do not often do—Warden Haskell decided to announce that the new facility was complete and ready for its first occupant: Lex Luthor.

"As I was saying earlier," the warden went on, "any claim that the prisoner might make to the effect that he is being held out of touch with his attorney, his friends, his colleagues in either criminal or legitimate pursuits—anyone at all—will not be borne out. As you can see, there is a functioning private telephone on the wall between the television and the camera through which the prisoner is monitored, although numbers of all outgoing and incoming calls will be recorded automatically, and you will notice that there is a switch under the camera with which the prisoner can turn off our audio monitor for up to fifteen minutes of any twenty-four-hour period. Thus, the room simultaneously provides redundant security and maintains a convict's legal rights to limited privacy."

Luthor had been bragging during these past days that he would escape this week. The man was not generally given to boasts of either the hollow or the dense variety. Haskell was the ninth warden at this prison in eight years. Four had been fired; two had had nervous breakdowns; one had had a heart seizure after seven months here, following a history of anemia; and one had actually turned out to be one of Luthor's many fictional alter egos. This last case was such an embarrassment that the governor lost his own job over it. Haskell had entered public service twenty-nine years earlier in order to have job security. He was eight months from retirement and he did not intend to screw up as had his predecessors. No one would blame Haskell if Luthor escaped from him every once in a while. The man had not stayed in jail long enough to go to trial more than once since he was a teenager. But if Luthor managed to get out after announcing his plans to the press, Haskell would have the same job security as the forgotten pitcher who was dumb enough not to walk Babe Ruth after the hitter pointed out the place in the bleachers where the next pitched ball ultimately landed.

"Well, I wouldn't dream of taking any time away from our star inmate," Haskell concluded. "I wouldn't want to be accused of emotional brutality." No one laughed but Haskell. "There will not be any time for questions, gentlemen."

"Wonder why," the reporter from Newark said, loud enough for Jimmy to hear him.

Almost immediately, there was a shuffling and the muffled sound of men's voices from the hall. Before anyone could get out of the room, three prison guards, each with a .38 calibre pistol in one hand and a set of complicated work orders on a clipboard in the other, rushed in and ordered everyone into the hallway. The warden went with them to stand on one side of the door as a horde of prison guards—none of them was shorter than six-feet three—burst through the translucent, wire-reinforced glass door at the far end of the hall. Ev and Jerry recorded the scene for Galaxy News. As far as any eye or any camera could detect, no one was saying a word, but as the swarm oozed into the narrow space, reporters could gradually make out the sound of a man's mouth moving faster than any biologically sound mouth ought to be able to move.

"Hey cauliflower-head," were the first words that the reporters were able to distinguish from the clapping of cleated boots, "don't you ever have trouble getting fitted for earwax? . . .

"Watch those size fourteen hooves of yours, Elmer. I don't want instant fallen arches. Look, when you get a new pair of shoes can I have those? I need a spare rudder for my yacht. . . .

"Will you look at old granite-face here, about to crack his first smile since kindergarten? Last time he did that they had to call in an orthodontic stone mason and a cement truck to repair him. . . ."

It was unmistakably the voice and attitude of Lex Luthor, dwarfed and invisible among shoulder-to-shoulder prison guards. The lump of guards passed, knee-to-knee, holster-to-clipboard, through the hallway toward the reporters and the warden, then turned right into the super-security cell like water over a dam. The only way to determine where among the swarm Luthor walked was to try to figure out at what point the stream of invective sounded the loudest before it faded into the reinforced room.

"That was my groin you hit, ape-arms. Wanna find that clipboard in your spleen some morning? . . ."

Luthor could say anything he chose to the guards. Once, when Luthor was working a rock pile, a rookie guard shoved him onto a heap of stones that cut his face. Luthor never said a word to anyone else about the guard or the incident. All he did was suggest to the young man that he apologize. Luthor told the guard that he did not even have to act as though he was sorry, only that he should say the words. When the guard declined the suggestion, Luthor simply heaved a sad breath, wiped a grimy hand over his face and went back to work. One morning not long afterward, while accidentally dozing for a moment during the night shift, the young guard woke up with the initials *LL* carved in his forehead. Luthor was accounted for during the time it happened. He certainly would have arranged for an alibi had he done it himself, but he had nothing to do with it. It was simply the work of one of the inmates, angry over his hero's indignity, serving notice on the prison administration—as the inmates did in one manner or another from time to time—that Lex Luthor was not to be touched.

"Hey, where's the innkeeper? Where's former Warden Half-skull? You out there, Warden, scraping the governor's shoe polish off your tongue again? Hey, I don't like to kiss and tell, but I think one of your hired thugs just tickled me."

Eventually the entire company of prison guards flowed into the super-security cell and the wind began to die down for a few moments. Seven guards came back out of the room and solemnly assembled in the corridor—one on either side of the cell door facing three who lined up opposite them looking into the open room, and two at the translucent wired-glass door at the end of the hallway.

"All right, gentlemen," Haskell said to the company of reporters who were amazed by the security precautions, "I think we're ready."

The newsmen, with their note pads, flash cameras and video equipment, all filed into the room. Spiffily uniformed men, pistols and clipboards in hands, lined all four walls, and in the far left corner, dressed in fatigues and a cherubic grin, stood Lex Luthor, lighting a pipeful of tobacco.

"I do wish you'd thought to put some ashtrays in here, Half-skull." Luthor dropped his match which fell straight for half the distance to the floor and then spiraled the remainder of the way from the height of Luthor's knees. Imprisoned, handcuffed, dressed in dull gray, surrounded by eighteen men, all of whom were appreciably more massive than he, the bald, stocky man looked for all the world as though he were in charge.

Luthor greeted the reporters, taking care to pay special attention ("Your acne clear up yet, puss-face?") to Jimmy Olsen. He made his three-point statement, embellishing it suitably; Haskell once again assured the reporters that the room was quite escape-proof; during the drive back to Metropolis Jimmy began writing the story of Luthor's escape, which would certainly come in handy sometime during the coming week.

In two weeks Warden Haskell would be transferred to the East Kansas Juvenile Reformatory where his salary, and consequently his retirement pension, would be reduced by about 20 percent.

Demons

Nearly everyone had a personal demon. Few people called them demons, but that was what they were.

Perry White, the editor of the *Daily Planet,* and Franklin Roosevelt, the thirty-second President of the United States, collected stamps.

Lex Luthor had a younger sister named Lena who was a toddler when Lex left home and who did not know she was related to the infamous criminal, but whose life and career Luthor followed.

Sherlock Holmes played the violin, as did Albert Einstein, who realized during his final years that he was in danger of dying before he formulated his Unified Field Theory and so banished his demon, in order to spend all his intellect chasing the tail of time and space.

Lois Lane wrote poetry and hid the pages in a corrugated cardboard file box whose inside she once lined with lead foiling.

Jimmy Olsen, unknown to any of his friends other than Clark Kent, took the name Marshall McShane to host a Sunday afternoon country music show on a college radio station called "Music You Can't Hear on the Radio."

Morgan Edge, the president of the Galaxy Communications, ran six miles a day.

Kristin Wells, Lois Lane's two-day-a-week girl Friday, had a passion for expensive discos and for obscure volumes on recent history.

Steve Lombard, the former quarterback and current WGBS sports reporter, spent weekend afternoons, when millions of American men are watching football games, eating popcorn in front of old movies on television.

Jimmy Carter taught Sunday School.

Martha Kent collected antique bottles.

Lord Greystoke learned languages, human and otherwise.

Edward R. Murrow smoked cigarettes.

Superman had Clark Kent.

In fact, Superman loved Clark Kent as much as he loved anyone or anything else. He loved his alter ego as he loved the memory of the two good people who had taken him as their son; as he loved this adopted world that had accepted him as its hero; as he loved Lois Lane. Clark Kent was a person as real and individual as any man ever created by the mind of man. Superman even gave Clark a demon: Clark videotaped television commercials that particularly amused him, and showed them to friends who were polite enough to sit through them. Superman spent appreciably more time creating the reality of Clark Kent than he spent doing anything else. Clark Kent spent more time walking the Earth than Superman spent flying above it. Superman valued his creation as he valued a human life.

Right now, something was bothering Clark Kent and had been bothering him since he first saw Jimmy's film of Luthor's announcement, but Clark could not for all his reason figure out what it was. He sat in his tiny office running the film through an editing machine for the seventy-third time. He would have run it faster if not for the fact that the film would have melted with friction. It was nearly five fifty-eight in the evening, two minutes before air time. He would have to memorize the entire film this time through, frame by frame, if he was going to allow himself the customary ninety seconds to type and edit the anchor script for his hour-long news show. He would spend most of those ninety seconds, of course, walking down the hall, at the speed of a normal, slightly clumsy Earth human, from his office to the news anchor desk in Studio B.

"Good evening, this is Clark Kent with the Six O'Clock WGBS Evening News," were the next words he said, and slightly more than a million people heard him say that.

As it happened, slightly fewer than a million people saw the film of Luthor dropping the match that first fell and then spiraled to the ground. More than a hundred thousand of Clark's viewers, at that point in the show, were sniffing through the refrigerator, thumbing through the newspapers, sorting through the mail or whatever. Almost everyone whose television was turned on, however, heard Luthor declare his intention to escape. A few clucked their disapproval A few wondered if Luthor had, as he claimed, discovered some new miraculous source of energy. Most of them dismissed the claim, not realizing that Luthor was not a dishonest public servant but rather, an honest criminal. Clark suffered no such oversight.

Here were some of the other stories Clark mentioned on the news tonight:

Eleven hours after the snow had stopped falling, much of the city continued to be winter-bound.

The price of gold hit its first new high of the year this afternoon, and the price of imported oil did the same thing for the third time in the past six months.

The head of state of Laos charged that the Prime Minister of Thailand was responsible for an outbreak in Laos of cholera, and the Laotian intended to put the Prime Minister on trial in absentia.

There was a plague of locusts in the sky over Brussels, Belgium.

And so forth.

Through these and all the other stories, Clark spoke his lines dutifully and professionally, as he watched a mental picture, frame by frame, of Luthor announcing his intention to escape. Clark had no illusion that Luthor might have slipped a clue as to his specific methods in the words he chose. The criminal was quite a bit cleverer than that. No, it was something else.

The show was supposed to end with a mildly amusing film narrated by Lloyd Kramer, which showed cars on the bridge below the Fifty-ninth Street Tramway sliding on the sleet and ice, bending up each other's fenders and breaking lights fore and aft. It was a fine report, actually, narrated in a flip, irreverent style. It had been a good story, in fact, during every major snowstorm of the past three years. Three years ago was the first time Clark had assigned the story, and by now it was getting dog-eared. Clark did his job with consistent efficiency and a startling lack of imagination.

Here is where Superman makes a mistake:

It is not a big mistake by the standard of the mistakes Superman is in a position to make. It is indeed a mistake, however—not an intentional cover for the purposes of reinforcing his Clark Kent disguise, and because of who made it, this mistake becomes just a touch horrifying.

The show was supposed to end with Lloyd Kramer's amusing version of Clark Kent's standard soporific snow assignment. It didn't. During the final segment of the "Evening News," anchorman and associate producer Clark Kent momentarily takes over the function of the director, Josh Coyle, who spends the two or three minutes of the final segment feverishly editing together videotaped scenes from the day's newsfilm to show with the credits at the conclusion of the program. The reason Coyle has to do this during the final segment is that only at this point does Coyle know exactly how many seconds he can allot for the credits. Coyle began putting together the closing videotape as soon as he cued the final commercial which preceded the last segment of the show. Consequently, Clark Kent's sole function during the two or three minutes that he is effectively the director is to cue the final tag film. That is, it is Clark's job simply to tell the technician in the booth with Coyle which film to slip into a little slot, and precisely when to do it.

What Clark Kent was supposed to tell the technician, as the final commercial ended and Josh Coyle played with his tapes, was, "Cue the tramway film for seventeen seconds." This meant that the final segment would consist of Clark talking for seventeen seconds, followed by Lloyd Kramer's film.

What Clark Kent actually said was, "Cue the Luthor film for seventeen seconds." Then, as the technician sitting next to the preoccupied Josh Coyle slipped the wrong tape into the videotape player and the live image of Kent at his anchor desk in Studio B returned to a million people's television screens in the Metropolitan area, Kent read from his prepared text: "A few hardy and perhaps a few foolhardy souls did, for reasons known only to them, venture among the elements today. Our man Lloyd Kramer watched some of them this afternoon on the Outerborough Bridge from his vantage point on the Fifty-Ninth Street Tramway. This is what he saw."

Clark Kent, running through his mind the same scene that was now reenacting itself on a million television screens, and Josh Coyle, splicing and cross-editing videotaped scenes only hours old with the skill of a ping-pong champion, noticed the error simultaneously, less than a minute before the end of the show, when Coyle's job was complete. Angry with the technician whose fault he thought the error was, Coyle flipped a switch on the director's override console and pointed at Kent from his booth, signaling that the anchorman was now back on the air. Before the director turned to vent his anger on the young technician, Clark apologized on the air.

"We usually call these things technical difficulties," Clark told his audience. "That's simply an easy way of saying, 'Sorry, my mistake.' I gave our technician the wrong cue, and he rolled the wrong film. We'll get Lloyd and the snow, I trust, on the eleven o'clock report."

"See?" the technician in the booth told Coyle. "See? He did say 'the Luthor film.' See?"

"For all of us here at WGBS News, this is Clark Kent wishing you a good evening," and Josh Coyle's videotape collage of the day's newsfilm rolled underneath the credits to signal the end of the program.

As it turned out, this particular mistake was not a bad thing for Superman. It helped, to some extent, to reinforce the reality of Clark Kent as a fallible human being. But the fact remained that it was Superman, not Clark Kent, who made the error.

C. W. Saturn occasionally lost a battle, but he did not make mistakes.

Fifty miles to the north, at his home in the village of Tarrytown, Warden Haskell of the Pocantico Correctional Facility had been late in turning on the WGBS Six O'Clock Evening News. The story in which he was interested, Jimmy Olsen's account of Luthor's transfer from Cell Block Ten to the new super-security cell, was the lead story that night and Haskell had missed it.

Mrs. Haskell was a newspaper reader rather than a television watcher. She came into the living room with the morning's *Daily Planet*, the afternoon *Post* and the message that dinner would soon be ready. During the remainder of Clark Kent's broadcast, Mrs. Haskell sat on the couch next to her husband reading stories about her husband's day, about Lex Luthor's past career, and about the locusts that swarmed over the streets of Brussels. Mr. Haskell did the crossword puzzle until he was stumped by 24-across, which was a thirteen-letter word meaning "deliberately, for dolphins." That was when Haskell looked up at the screen and was alarmed to see the mistakenly rebroadcast film of Luthor lighting his pipe.

Haskell bolted from the couch and his wife asked, "What's wrong, Eddie?"

Without answering her he grabbed the kitchen telephone to call the prison's director of maintenance. The man was not at home, and none of the custodians on duty that night was near a phone at the prison. Haskell would try the maintenance director's number every half hour that night until someone answered. Despite his errors in judgment and his doomed retirement pension, Edmund Haskell was a very bright man. He knew what was wrong with the film.

Coyle always had trouble criticizing Clark Kent. The newsman was so self-effacing, so willing to acquiesce to a put-down, that Clark was still only about midway through an elaborate apology when the frustrated director threw his hands into the air and walked off. Clark appeared to be talking to himself, with Coyle's back toward him, when Lois Lane walked into the studio.

"Come on, Clark," the woman said. "You wouldn't want to stand in the way of young love, would you?"

"What?" Clark was riffling through the pages of the script for the news show whose ending he had just botched. He looked up and said, "Oh. Lois."

"Busy for dinner?"

"Me? Busy?" Clark was genuinely surprised. "You're asking me out to dinner?"

"Gloria Steinem and Helen Gurley Brown both said it's all right. I figured I'd better do it."

"Of course I'm not busy."

"Terrific, Clark. I'm trying to get Jimmy to meet Kristin, that new girl who's typing the final copy of my book. You just make believe you're my date, all right?"

"I'll try to put on a good act."

Lois Lane was Clark's idea of a remarkable woman. She was almost anyone's idea of a remarkable woman. Not yet through her twenties, she was successful in her field, famous, envied, intelligent, and one suspected that if she was not wealthy, it was only because she did not care to be. She was regularly named to the annual list of the year's "Ten Worst-Dressed Women," a promotional device used by a California dress salesman who sought notoriety by picking fights with people whose names were more famous than his. Last year a writer for *People* magazine placed her on a list—along with names as diverse as Jacqueline Onassis, Kate Jackson and Lillian Hellman—of the "World's Ten Most Eligible Women." She asked Clark to spend time with her, she supposed, because he was safe.

"Hey, Clarkie, cutting out so soon?" The voice from behind was that of Steve Lombard, the sportscaster. "Whatcha up to, Lois-babes?"

"No good, Grizzly. Come on, Clark, I don't want to miss Jimmy." Actually, the rush was over the fact that Lois wanted to miss Lombard.

"Hey, stick around for the free feed. I'll buy ya a margarita, Lois." Lombard had hooked Clark and Lois by their elbows and Clark noticed that the former quarterback was maneuvering them toward the swinging door to the hallway.

"See that elbow, big stuff?" Lois asked as Lombard glanced out the window of the door, deftly positioning the pair in front of it.

"Yeah."

"It's as close as you're going to get."

And then Benny Boghosian, as was his custom, wheeled his snack cart unceremoniously from the hallway through the door, which hit Clark, who softly and carefully defied gravity to lift himself slightly off the ground and into the left side of Lois where Lombard had aimed him. Lois fell smoothly into the arms of the former quarterback.

Of course, there was nothing else Clark could have done about Steve's prank, nothing else he could do about the scores of similar pranks pulled in front of women on whom Steve was determined to make some sort of an impression. But Clark could never get even overtly. Steve was as much a tool of Superman's constant fashioning of the fictional Clark Kent persona as Clark was a function, very often, of Steve's apish nonsense. That was what was so infuriating about Steve.

There was a bloody mary for the sportscaster on Benny Boghosian's lunch cart, compliments of Galaxy Communications's president, Morgan Edge. Clark noticed it with his heat vision. It would be unbearably bitter this afternoon. Clark apologized to Benny and to Lois, who took his hand as they left. She took Clark's hand to make it clear to Steve that she was not impressed with him. She held Clark's hand once in a while, for one reason or another, and she often had to tell herself not to notice whatever it was that she felt in her hand when she did. She had no conscious idea what it was she felt, but she resolved not to think about it for fear that she might decide she liked it.

"Maybe it's his money or something," the sportscaster said, downing the drink in one swig, " 'cause it sure ain't the way he dresses." Then he noticed his throat.

"You know who Kristin is," Lois said to Clark in the hallway. "I told you about her. She's the one typing up my book on that bank robbery down in the Village. The one where the kid saw the Al Pacino movie and went out and held ten people hostage for eight hours and got talked out of it by the disc jockey on WNEW."

"Right. Are you done with that already?"

"Except for the final proofreading. I'm not much on style, Clark, but any editor can be sure that Perry White taught me to make my deadlines. Anyway, Kris is a really nice girl. A little spacey, maybe, but she's pretty new in town and she's been hanging around those awful singles' bars and I promised to treat her to dinner today. Then it occurred to me that she and Jimmy would be perfect, so I told her that you and I had a date tonight and that I'd forgotten about it, but she could certainly come along, and wouldn't it be nice if we got another man to make it a foursome. Pretty clever, huh?''

"Clever as a fox, Lois.''

"I found her through one of those temporary office help agencies, but I only need her two days a week and they almost never call her, so I told her about Lena. You remember my friend Lena Thorul, don't you, Clark?''

"That's not the one with mental telepathy, is it?''

"Telepathy. Not mental telepathy. Mental telepathy is redundant. Yeah, that's the one. Lena's writing a book, too, on psychic phenomena, and she can't type at all. So that fills in another two days a week for Kris. She's even covering her rent! Now you're briefed on her.''

"Why do I want to be briefed on her? Now I won't have anything to talk about.''

"You never have anything to talk about anyway, and it has to look to Jimmy as though you and Kris are old friends, so it won't look as though we're setting them up.''

"Aren't we setting them up?''

"Of course we're setting them up.''

"So why can't we tell them?''

"It's like a bear in the woods. Don't you know anything, Clark?''

"A bear in the woods . . .''

By now they had walked down the hall to the elevator, taken it down from the twentieth floor where the WGBS News offices were, to the sixth floor which contained the editorial department of the *Daily Planet* where Lois worked. Halfway down the hall, between the elevator and the cubbyhole that was Lois's office, she stopped, made Clark stand still, and faced him.

"When you run into a hungry bear in the woods,'' she explained, "you have to lie down and play dead. That way the bear doesn't know what's been at you and he'll leave you alone. If you run away the bear's likely to kill you.'' She walked on.

"Oh.''

"Right! Well, it's the same with Kristin and Jimmy. If we lay them out like dead meat neither of them will be interested.''

"I see.'' The fact that he didn't see at all pleased him immensely. Generally, his curse was to understand too much.

Kristin Wells turned out to be what Jimmy Olsen would probably call a knockout. Jimmy was not in Lois's office, though. Kristin was there alone, doing the crossword puzzle in the morning edition of the *Daily Planet.*

"Porpoisefully," Clark said as he walked in behind Kristin and she jumped.

"Oh. What did you say?"

"Twenty-four across, the one you're having trouble with. It's *porpoisefully*. Like dolphins. Thirteen letters."

"Hey man, you're right. Outrageous."

"Kris Wells,"—Lois was formal in a very breezy manner—"this is Clark Kent."

"Sure, Clark. I watch you on the news every day."

"We're old friends," Clark told his new friend solemnly.

"I bet Jimmy's upstairs getting free food. I'll run up and get him. You two become older friends. I'll be right back."

Clark sat down on the windowsill and awkwardly clapped his hands once. Kristin watched him, watching herself being careful not to let on how thrilled she was at meeting Superman.

"So," he said and paused. "You like doing crossword puzzles, do you?"

"We were having a perfectly good time," Lois was telling the phone two days later, "and then he got sick to his stomach over the lobsters and left."

"Just like that?"

"Just like that."

"No 'excuse me' or anything?"

"Oh, lots of 'excuse mes'. Lots of 'pardons' and 'terribly sorrys' and all that stuff. Clark's got all the manners his milkmaid mother ever taught him and then some. Just no stomach."

"Well, I don't know, Lois," Lena Thorul said from the other end of the line. "The thought of picking out your dinner from a tubful of crawling things never much appealed to me."

"You're one thing. Clark Kent is— Do you have any idea how tall he is?"

"Tall?"

"At least six-two."

"Really? He never looked that tall to me."

"That's not taking the slouch into account. I saw him next to Steve Lombard—y'know, Grizzly the football player? Oh, that's another thing. Remind me to tell you about him before I forget."

"Grizzly the football player. Got it."

"Right. Where was I?"

"Six-foot two."

"Right. At least six-two, maybe more. I'll admit everybody

61

looks tall to me, but he's taller than Steve. Really. Do you believe a big strong guy like that whom everyone in town watches on the news every day and trusts to tell them stuff they don't know—this guy never even knew that they throw live lobsters into boiling water?''

"Come on. Are you sure this is recently?"

"Really. It was two days ago. Yeah, the night Luthor escaped."

"Ohh—"

"Oh, I'm sorry, Lena. I forgot about that." Lois had momentarily lost the fact that Lena was what she called an empath. Lena had emotions that were psychically heightened, and one of the things she became unaccountably emotional about was Lex Luthor. Lois knew why this was, although Lena did not. Lois apologized: "I just remember headlines the way other people remember days of the week. I didn't mean to mention that."

"It's gone. Forget it. What about Clark?"

"Clark? He's impossible. He can't be for real."

"I told you when I met him, Lois," Lena Thorul, recovered, dropping to her most conspiratorial tone, "and I'll say it again now. Clark Kent's got a lot more going for him than he lets on. I can tell these things. You could do worse."

"I bet I can do better."

"Be careful about that. You've been believing what you read about yourself in *People* magazine. How's it going with the test pilot anyway?"

"Superman?"

"Who else?"

"The same." Lois paused, wondering if Lena could read her mind across the city or through the telephone line. "I don't want to talk about him. I'd rather talk about Kris. She should be there any minute. Listen, would you try to talk some sense into her?"

"I've been trying to do that with you. Why would it work any better on her?"

"You're younger than me and you're older than her."

"This from someone who makes a living with words."

"Grammar is the editor's job. Listen, Lena, she hangs out at discos."

"So?"

"So? Have you ever been to one of those places?"

"As a matter of fact I have. My husband took me to Regine's once and the music actually cleared my head. There aren't a lot of

62

things that do that. Some nineteen-year-old guy tried to pick me up, though, and we haven't been back. What's wrong with Kristin?"

"She's a smart girl. She types as well as anyone I know—certainly better than I do—and if you ever get into a discussion of American history with her you'll be amazed at the things she knows. She can tell you more about the Second World War than my father, and he was a colonel. But she's a total air-head about men. She does this space cadet routine."

"How do you mean?"

"Well, Steve Lombard came into the restaurant by himself as soon as Clark left. He must have heard me tell Jimmy where we were going, because the last time Steve went anywhere alone I fell off my moa."

"Your mower?"

"Moa. It's an extinct bird. Jimmy actually seemed to like Kris—and you know how Jimmy feels about my introducing him to someone. Ever since my little sister packed him in, he's acted like I was his mother anytime I wanted him to meet anyone I thought he'd like. There was this woman pediatrician I knew once who—"

"Kristin. You were talking about Kristin."

"Right. Steve came in and acted like it was a surprise we were there. I think he saw Clark leave, although he said he didn't. He sat down next to me and all of a sudden Kris was mesmerized."

"Was he wearing an open shirt?"

"An open shirt. Yeah, he was. Why do you ask?"

"Just something that popped into my head."

"Yeah, and he was doing his usual come-on number with me, and Kris said out of nowhere, she says, 'I don't believe how much hair you've got on your chest.' "

"Really? She said that? In front of Jimmy?"

"Well, she and Grizzly went off to someplace on First Avenue and Jimmy and I passed on it. I think he was really hurt."

"I would think so."

"And Steve Lombard? That lumbering, swaggering—"

"Hold it, Lois. That's the doorbell."

Lena Thorul was one of those rare people to whom the psychic gift was precisely that—a gift. It was something she did not cultivate, fake or particularly want. Lena was writing, on Lois's suggestion, an anonymous autobiography she would call *A Burden of Prophecy*. Two days after Clark Kent left Lois Lane, Jimmy Olsen and Kristin Wells sitting in a restaurant, this perfectly rational young woman who happened to be highly psychic left Lois waiting on the telephone and walked across her living room to answer the doorbell. On the other side of the door she found something unholy, an apparition whose form she could not bear to see. She wailed and fell to the rug.

Kristin was as startled as Lena. She bent over Lena for a moment to see that the woman had fainted. She wrung her hands in her confusion, then noticed the telephone out of its cradle.

Kristin picked up the receiver. "Hello?"

"Lena? I heard a scream."

"It's not Lena. Is that Lois? This is Kris."

"What happened?"

"I don't know. Is Lena the tall blond lady?"

"Yeah. What happened?"

"She fainted. She opened the door and I said hi and didn't even get as far as telling her who I was and she was felled in a faint."

"Was felled in a faint?"

"I mean she fainted. The chick fainted, man. Checked out on the rug. What's her scam?"

"I don't know. She's a psychic and sometimes funny things come over her."

"Oh, she's an empath. You told me. I know what to do about that. I'll take care of it," Kristin said and hung up.

Kristin rifled the food stores of the apartment for any source of vitamin C, which Lena needed, Kristin knew, in great quantity. The girl opened several small cans of frozen fruit juice concentrate and forced the contents in spoonfuls down Lena's throat. In a few minutes the older woman was back to normal.

Across town, Lois Lane wondered how Kristin or anyone else for that matter could know what to do for an empath who had suddenly fainted.

Lois was incorrect about one thing for certain in her conversation with Lena. Steve Lombard had not seen Clark Kent leaving the restaurant two days ago. It was Clark who had run, with one hand on his stomach and another on his mouth, into the vestibule between the restaurant and the sidewalk, but when the sidewalk door opened it looked as though it was pushed by only a stiff wind.

Up, up into the darkness gathering over Metropolis soared Superman.

The Discovery of Magic

To a stranger, every highly developed technology must look like arcane ritual. The impression on the first extraterrestrial who studied an operation of brain surgery, for example, must have been reminiscent of the impression physicians had when they began to note the herbal therapy practiced by Ozark healers, or the reaction of anthropologists to social customs of the natives of Samoa. What is an alien to think of a rite carried out in a sterile room by veiled men and women wearing nova-white robes, a ritual that involves the removal and subsequent resecuring of a hairless human's scalp with bizarre specialized tools?

Such arcane rituals accompanied every new discovery that civilization added to its repertoire. The discovery of tools was accompanied by the rituals of woodcraft and stone masonry. The bronze age brought the smelting of ores. The locomotive was accompanied by coal-tending and first-class compartments. The telephone evolved with dial tones, busy signals, conference calls, and adolescence. Internal combustion brought drive-ins, traffic jams and the Organization of Petroleum Exporting Countries. Now Luthor brought to civilization's environs a new discovery, and the collection of rituals he formulated to go with it showed signs of being no less distinctive than any that went with previous discoveries.

Luthor called his discovery *gas-wave physics*, and until he saw the coverage of his press conference on the Six O'Clock WGBS Evening News, he had planned to put off his ritual for a few days. What Luthor saw on the television screen alarmed him. He would certainly have been more alarmed if he had noticed the three guards and one electrician who came to the super-security cell on the warden's orders that night at two o'clock to check the heating system. Luthor was doing something like meditating at the time as part of his ritual. Of course the three guards and the electrician thought he was asleep. The guards were glad to avoid the customary verbal abuse, although the electrician, who did not know any better, would have liked to meet Luthor. As a matter of fact, the electrician was very careful not to find the air current that the warden insisted was in the room, so that the workman would have an excuse to come back tomorrow and see what Luthor was really like. Tomorrow, of course, Luthor would no longer be there.

All sorts of conflicting emotions flew around in Luthor's formidable brain when he watched Clark Kent on the evening news. Kent was the good boy that Lex Luthor never was, the conventionally successful and respected man that Luthor never grew up to become. These days, on the few occasions Luthor had to talk to the newsman, Kent called him Mr. Luthor and acted as though they had never met other than in connection with Kent's job and Luthor's infamy. Luthor supposed he acted the same way toward Kent, except for that one time he had idly threatened Kent's life, the time Kent nearly had him convinced to change his ways. But years ago they were both in Smallville, and in Smallville things were different.

At the age of twelve no one but a potential saint is flawless, and in America saints don't generally live past the age of nine. That was what Jules and Arlene Luthor had in mind when they brought a child into the world—a saint. When their nine-year-old son Lex clearly showed himself to be something other than that, they decided to have another child and move to the heartland where their son, for what he was worth, and their infant daughter could have a proper upbringing.

In the city, Lex learned how to pick locks, slash tires and extort classmates' lunch money in return for "protection." In the country he learned how to steal fresh watermelons, break into ice cream parlors for midnight snacks, and from Clark Kent he learned how to scare cows into losing their milk.

Lex had always showed signs of alarming honesty. If he neglected, for some reason, to tell a new acquaintance not to trust him, then Lex could certainly be trusted. He was careful, upon meeting each of his eighth grade teachers, to smile and say, "Don't trust me," before he said hello. Although Brooklyn's public school curriculum was woefully behind that of Smallville at the time—and has been ever since—Lex immediately led all his classes academically. And once he convinced each teacher that he was smarter than anyone else in the class, he proceeded to convince each teacher that the teacher had no business presuming to teach him anything about anything other than humility.

When Lex interrupted Donna Hughes, his mathematics teacher, while she was in the process of showing the class how to derive the formula to solve quadratic equations, Mrs. Hughes slyly invited Lex to finish the derivation. He did, faster than she could follow, and he did an encore to that performance by deriving a formula that generates prime numbers. Mrs. Hughes, along with nearly every other mathematical scholar since the time of Euclid, was under the impression that there was no formula in existence which consistently generated prime numbers. Lex erased his formula before the teacher closed her mouth and could summon the presence of mind to copy it down.

When Robert Knodt, the science teacher, got it into his head to convince his students that chemistry was relevant to their everyday lives, Luthor managed to dull the teacher's point. Mr. Knodt set up a simple experiment which he had designed to measure, during a period of a few days, the relative efficiencies of different kitchen-food wrappings at keeping out moisture. These commercial food wrappings ranged from ordinary wax paper to the rolled plastic wraps that were just then beginning to come on the market. Lex volunteered to bring in one of his mother's wax paper bags, whose inside he first coated with a nonporous, nearly undetectable clear plaste that Lex made from one of Arlene Luthor's fiberglass kitchen curtains. Mr. Knodt was at a loss to explain how the wax paper turned out to be more resistant to moisture than any of the supposedly nonporous wrappings. The wax paper, in fact, seemed to be 100 percent resistant. Lex told Mr. Knodt and the class what he had done, but when the science teacher asked Lex if he was interested in patenting his new substance, Lex claimed to have forgotten how he had made it.

And when Carol Roberts, the social studies teacher, suggested that Rutherford B. Hayes did not actually win the presidential election of 1876, but that his party had bought southern electoral votes in an illegal political bargain, Lex disagreed. The boy launched into an involved polemic on constitutional law to prove that although there was a political deal, it was actually perfectly legal. The irrefutable logic of his tirade reached above the heads of the class not long before it also eluded Miss Roberts.

Except that on these occasions, and on several others, Lex noticed the faintest hint of a grin on Clark Kent's face. Clark knew something he was not letting on, and Lex decided for some reason that he liked Clark. For a while Clark seemed to be the boy's only friend.

Lex liked Clark less and respected him more when Clark took the blame for the silly prank Lex pulled one night at the Herman farm, but Lex finally told Clark not to trust him after that. Clark had not trusted him since.

No time to think about that now, Luthor decided as he sat watching the Six O'Clock WGBS Evening News in the Pocantico Correctional Facility's super-security cell. He had contrived to be transferred to this dungeon for a reason, and now that he was here there was work to do.

Since the last full moon, when he did not eat for three days, Luthor had been on a completely organic diet. This was one of his new rituals. It was not particularly healthy for him, Luthor knew, but it was no less healthy than his normal diet of hormone-infested meat and canned food-coloring and preservatives flavored with traces of vegetation. A diet of whole grains and fruit juices was necessary for what he had to do. In order to deal with the forces he had to harness for his escape, Luthor had to cleanse his body as much as possible of all traces of inorganic matter. That was the key.

It was no more difficult, in prison, to get organic food than it was to get illegal drugs. The price was higher there than it was outside, that was all, and that was no problem for Luthor. It would have been difficult to get any such substances into the super-security cell, but Luthor had not eaten anything since that afternoon, and he had been planning to fast for a few days just to be sure his body was cleared of inorganic chemicals before the escape. The plan was different now. He had to get out before someone—before Superman—noticed his little indiscretion on film.

Luthor could no more bring inorganic matter among the nether regions through which he had to go in order to escape, than he could kill a rock. Luthor had teleported before, even to get out of prison. There were lots of ways to do it; all of them except this one was prohibitively expensive. Most of the methods Luthor knew for the transfer of matter through space, by other than three-dimensional means, were only theoretical. All but one of the proved methods involved equipment which was not produced on Earth, equipment that could only be manufactured in the total vacuum and zero gravitation of outer space. Luthor had never found it feasible to set up a major manufacturing operation in space. The enterprise would certainly give a massive boost to the American economy, but that was of little concern to him, and there were easier ways to break prison.

Luthor considered teleportation to be basically a waste of time and energy until he made his new discovery. Before this, he had generally regarded people who studied or promoted the various mystic arts—from meditation to astrology to demonology to whatever—to be charlatans, fools or madmen. He still believed this. The more he thought and studied and read, however, the more his mind summoned up an old image. It was an allegory in which a swarm of scientists, social theorists and scholars in their academic robes and laboratory coats carried heavy backpacks full of slide rules, significant survey samples and advanced degrees up the sheer face of a hostile mountain. Some fell off. When the survivors among the company of hard-nosed realists reached the summit, they were amazed to find a collection of mystics, sorcerers and wild-eyed prophets already there, engaged in pleasant conversation and the consumption of the contents of a community hookah. The mystics had no idea where they were or how they had gotten there. They knew only that this was their destination and that one day sometime ago a giant hand had plucked them out of the darkness and gently deposited them on the mountaintop. The scientists and other realists, though, had the satisfaction of having climbed the mountain.

What Luthor had recently discovered, what was essentially going to make it possible for him to walk through a wall and emerge a free man, was the nature of the human soul. Lex Luthor, climbing the sheer face of a hostile mountain, had found positive evidence of the existence of the souls of every living thing.

He even knew what souls were made of. He called the material *gas-waves*—the state of Creation that lay between matter and energy. The three conventional states of matter, as far as anyone knew, were solid, liquid and gas. There was also plasma. No one was quite sure where plasma fit in. The other thing that the stuff that made up Creation could be, as far as anyone knew, was energy. Energy and matter, broken down to their innermost parts, were made of the same stuff. The energy state of all matter was inherent in the matter, and the matter that energy could become was a part of the energy. Everybody knew that, even Robert Knodt. Matter could turn into energy—as it did in the process of nuclear reaction—and energy could turn into matter—as it did when a star collapsed into a black hole—but as far as anyone knew, matter and energy could not be created or destroyed.

As far as anyone but Luthor knew, there was nothing for the stuff of Creation to be besides matter and energy. Souls were certainly examples of the stuff of Creation, but the stuff of souls was neither matter nor energy. Souls were made of gas-waves. The mystics and crackpots whom Luther envisioned sitting serenely at the top of the mountain when he and the intellectuals got there had another name for gas-waves. They called them *ectoplasm*.

The crackpots, in their benign ignorance, had a name for just about everything Luthor had discovered or could postulate in connection with gas-wave physics. His ancillary discoveries and postulates were indeed so numerous that the possibilities were staggering. There was the possibility of other dimensions existing on different vibratory planes of gas-waves, in the same space as our own perceptible Universe. It was possible that the alteration of an individual's gas-wave pattern was the key to traveling backward and forward in time. It was now possible to manufacture antimatter. There might also exist, moving among the countless universes of Creation, angels, devils, demonic possession, miracles, leprechauns, warlocks, and other worlds seen in dreams. There certainly was, at the very least, a new universe to perceive, and Luthor knew the same kind of excitement that the man who had first tamed fire knew.

Luthor had told no one of his discovery. That was his way. Who was there to tell? It did not matter anyway, he knew now, if he did not transmit the knowledge to another mind before he endangered his life. He had realized, as a result of his discovery of gas-waves, that he would never die. There was a God.

This was news to him.

The discovery had started simply and innocuously, as such discoveries often begin, with a question in Luthor's mind. It was this: Where do thoughts go once they've been thought?

It was the sort of question a child would ask. It was the question of a neophyte, of a stoned junkie, of a moron, or of a genius. I mean it, he insisted to himself as he lay at four in the morning on his cot on the third level of Cell Block Ten. Where do thoughts go when you're done with them? Do they fly off into the ozone somewhere like a light beam or a radio wave? Do they drop toward the pull of gravity? What is a thought? Is it energy or matter? A tiny physical change occurs in the brain whenever it digests a new bit of information. Does that mean thoughts are organic? Is a concept a physical entity?

Luthor had gotten up from his cot in Cell Block Ten—slowly,

carefully, so as not to joggle the ectoplasmic thought that had ridden the edge of sleep to his mind—and reached for his note pad.

What is energy? he had asked himself. He went through a list of prerequisites a thing had to have in order to be energy. There were a few calculations, a few inconclusive proofs, and Luthor learned that thoughts could not be energy. Then he tried matter. This was more difficult and it took ten pages of tight calculations, but Luthor was able to prove that a thought was not a material object. Nor was it an immaterial construct of space and time. It was a thing, and it was a function of the brain, which, as far as anyone knew, was made of matter and energy. So a thought was made of something that matter and energy could produce or become, but something that was never before conceived of by the mind of a rational man.

Does any of this make sense? he asked himself.

Yes, it does, he answered. All of it.

Luthor spent the remainder of the time he was in prison this time around figuring out that (a) thoughts were made of gas-waves; (b) so were souls, emotions and certain intangible needs; (c) all space and time that was not occupied by matter or by quanta of energy was occupied by some form of gas-wave; and (d) if Luthor made public or tried to publish any of his findings, they had no more chance of being accepted by the worldwide scientific community than a woman discoverer of a cure for cancer had of winning the Nobel Prize after she had posed for the centerfold of *Playboy*.

The soul—the gas-wave nature, the ectoplasm, whatever one felt like calling it—of every entity of organic matter was as much a part of that entity as the energy that drove Luthor's digestive system was a part of his body. Furthermore, any entity with a consciousness was capable; if it knew how to steer that consciousness, of temporarily transforming its matter and energy into pure gas-waves and transporting it through a prearranged route to rematerialize as matter and energy at the conscious entity's destination—through any physical barrier. Walls, fire, nuclear radiation, Superman, any power of this world could no more stop the motion of a gas-wave entity than a hand could swat starlight out of the sky.

So now Luthor was prone on the cot in his super-security cell underneath Pocantico, oblivious to the guards and the electrician checking the heating system, although he was quite conscious. What he was doing was what the crackpots at the summit of his allegorical mountain might call "meditating," or "finding his center." What Luthor would say he was doing was exercising his consciousness in such a

71

way as to transform the energy and matter of his being into gas-waves, so that he could walk through a hole in space at the end of the room where the workman was checking the heat, and emerge whole and healthy somewhere far away from the Pocantico Correctional Facility.

Less than an hour after the workman and the three guards, thinking Luthor was asleep, left the room and wove their way through the checkpoints between the underground super-security cell and the outside world, Luthor got up from his cot. Walking with tiny steps, almost floating, Luthor made his way to the point in space where, that afternoon, he had stood and declaimed at the representatives of the press who had come to hear what he had to say.

Then he walked through the wall.

Liquefied Natural Gas

It may have been that Superman was an alarmist by nature, but this sort of thing infuriated him. He seemed forever to be slugging it out with the forces of Chaos. For example, the evening before Luthor's escape—the evening Clark Kent complained of an upset stomach over the plight of lobsters being boiled alive, and Warden Haskell seriously began to fear for his job—Superman made his way through the sky over Metropolis. There was a nutshell-sized explosion, a pop of gas caused by a cigarette tossed off by a merchant marine on a tanker, the Monrovia II, holding a cargo of liquefied natural gas in Metropolis Harbor.

Things like liquefied natural gas amazed Superman. LNG, as it was commonly called, was one of the most volatile substances known to humanity. If it leaked out of a tanker, which, Superman had to admit, it had never done anywhere until today, its fumes could spread through the air for miles and any minuscule spark—a match, a skidding rim against a worn brake lining, the flint of an empty pocket lighter—would ignite the very air into a hellish conflagration. What would follow would be, without doubt, a holocaust whose like has gone unseen since the leveling of Nagasaki. Yet this substance was shipped by the truckload and the tankerful to the harbors and through the streets of the densest population centers of the country.

Superman avoided making value judgments on any issue short of blatant criminality or imminent disaster. He had never endorsed a candidate for public office, though there had been those he would have liked to repudiate. He had never taken an active hand in any war, though he had saved lives about to be taken up in war, and he did not think he would stand for the use of nuclear weapons. When the Metropolis Convention Center was built with faulty roofing materials he simply let it be done; later, he caught the chunks of roof when they came down under the weight of the first blizzard of the center's first winter, and delivered a chunk of the roof along with its forged stress analysis report to the district attorney. He did everything he could in order to avoid interfering in natural social and scientific mistakes of humanity, the mistakes by which the race learned. But in a case like this he did not know whether it was good or bad to rein in his better judgment.

Superman was convinced beyond all reasonable doubt that if he, Superman, were not around to bail people out of spectacular disasters, then industrialists and shippers would not take the air-headed chance of transporting LNG through the places where children played. They would not fly jumbo jets that had cracks in the engine mounts. They would not build skyscrapers in earthquake zones. They would not operate nuclear power plants without sufficient technological information. They would not put whales, snail darters and blue-green algae in danger of extinction. He was sure that his presence on Earth was the reason they took those gambles, and that was why he was infuriated.

At dusk a skeleton crew of nine men mopped and sniffed and hung around and envied those who had shore leave from the tanker Monrovia II. As the big ship bobbed in Metropolis harbor, a gathering whistle dropped from the sky. Crewmen on the deck jumped and spun around and fell on their stomachs when the bright human figure careened through the starboard hull and shattered a steel plate sixteen inches thick as he flew through it.

Superman flew into the hold as though its walls were onionskin, and out behind him belched a pillar of flame, curling like cables of muscle into the sky. The petrochemical atmosphere in the hold was catching fire and there was a man inside. Superman had to risk letting the burning gas into the atmosphere in order to get the man out.

The young ensign was lying facedown on the catwalk grid in

front of the leaking cargo compartment. For the moment, he was lucky. The liquid in the hold was gradually steaming into its gaseous state and seeping out a pinhole in the compartment wall. Falling down under his first burning breath of LNG fumes, the man had scraped his belt buckle against the guardrail of the catwalk. Superman, with his special visual perceptions, could see waves of the escaping gas rolling over the man's back and catching fire from the spark of the belt on the railing.

Superman knifed through the spreading spit of flames, simultaneously examining the pinhole. To a degree that would be imperceptible to any instruments on Earth less sensitive than electron microscopes, the hole in the steel alloy wall was pulsing. Pressure was building on it from inside, and the container was about to burst into snips of metal.

Facedown, at the level of the hole, the ensign's nostrils were just out of the stream of the rising gases, but his body would not be spared from either the spreading vaporous flame or the shrapnel of the shattering container. The fire and the explosion raced each other for the ensign's mortality, and Superman joined the race.

Superman's sense of smell, always attuned to the entry of a molecule of LNG fumes when such a tanker was in town, had led him to this hold at the instant Hell was about to shake free here. Superman had a thousandth of a second lead on Hell, and by all the stars of Creation that was not nearly enough time.

The bits of thought, the electronic impulses racing back, forth and elsewhere through Superman's brain at the speed of light, lost all concern for anything else and measured time in microseconds.

He knew the man was going to be hurt. It was Superman's unwanted responsibility to decide how hurt.

As the Kryptonian plunged fists-first at the man on the catwalk, the fire was at his heels, moving toward the man like a spark along a fuse.

With a burst of speed through the air Superman reached the catwalk before the fire did, spreading his cape with both arms above his head as an awning against the licks of flame that were now crowding the hold.

Flame was below now as well. The only place in the hold sheltered from the fire was in the shadow of the spread cape.

During the few millionths of a second between the time Superman let go of the cape to let it snap back into shape and the time he snatched up the fallen ensign, Superman studied the habits of the flames and gases immediately around him. There would be a tube of

75

air six meters long and roughly the diameter of a man forming for an instant or two directly below the catwalk.

Superman held the man by his shoulders, stomped on the catwalk and, as the grid of aluminum clattered toward the bottom of the hold, he shot the man feet first through the cylindrical pocket of air.

The ensign flew at the intensifying wall of fire that raked upward between himself and the outer hull wall.

The hero launched himself, swirling his arms like a rotor, in front of the unconscious man, beating a path for him through the inferno.

What Superman would do next was to crash through the hull and ease the pressure inside enough to put off the coming explosion by about a quarter of a second. During that quarter second the man would fly out behind him and land in the water. As the officer hit the water with third-degree burns on his body and second-degree burns on his lungs, he would go into shock, but not as badly as he ordinarily might, since his body was already massively assaulted. The hero would shoot upward toward the main deck and drill his body through the hull for its entire perimeter immediately below the deck and crash through walls and supports to the main support beam under the deck.

On the main deck, seven of the eight remaining crew aboard the Monrovia II were jolted by the force of Superman's crash into the hold. At that instant an automatic alert sounded, and the crewmen knew nothing except that they ought to head for air and grab something bolted down. When a few on board saw Superman's exit moments later, they thought that he was the source of the huge explosion that followed on his heels. Actually, the explosion was the first of the LNG tanks going up like a Fourth-of-July ash can. The last member of the crew made it to open air just in time to see the horizon begin to drop.

The top half of the shattered hulk that used to be the Monrovia II was serenely rising into the air and those not holding on to something were thrown onto the deck. The air rattled with more explosions from below and the men prone on the deck of the Monrovia II, who now realized roughly what was going on, were afraid to breathe that air. High over Metropolis harbor the surface of the former Monrovia II seemed to hover for a moment. Then it began to fall.

Underneath the dismembered deck, Superman had let go and bolted downward, plucking the unconscious ensign from the water and, in the same motion, darting back upward like a falcon toward the deck that was beginning to pick up speed in the direction of gravity.

On his way back to the sky Superman puffed and inhaled into

and out of the ensign's injured lungs. He cleaned the lungs of fumes and cooled them down before he looped over the port side of the falling deck and gently deposited his charge. The lungs would work by themselves until the man could be brought to a respirator.

A quick calculation of the speed with which the deck was alredy falling and the distance to the surface of the river below told Superman that he had just enough time to call to a terrified crewman who lay on his stomach nearby, "This man has lung injuries. Get him medical attention as soon as possible."

Then Superman was gone again, below the falling deck and grabbing the main support beam. The descent of the deck slowed.

Superman set the jagged bottom of this slab of metal and masts on a pair of adjacent empty parking lots on Eleventh Avenue. He would repair the damage to the hurricane fence separating the lots later.

At dawn, when Superman would finally get around to removing the broken chunk of ship and replacing the fence, the owner of one of the parking lots would already be there, livid over the mess. When Superman managed to leave the lot spotless and ready for the day's business, the lot owner would stalk off to the police department to demand that Superman be forced to pay for parking a tanker in his lot overnight. The parking lot owner would be the high point of the duty sergeant's day.

Now, Superman left the crew to their own devices on the remainder of the ship. There was a shipload of deadly liquefied natural gas unwinding from its shattered tanks into the city.

Superman swept along the waterfront, snatching up three policemen, nine would-be muggers and four prospective mugging victims from the vicinity of the pier where the bottom half of the Monrovia II had exploded.

Two at a time, by the waist, the legs, or the shirt collars, depending on the degree of legitimacy of the reasons each had for being on the waterfront, Superman carried these sixteen people three blocks away and plopped them, disoriented, onto the sidewalk. If that was not far enough away, Superman knew, then no one else in the city would be safe either.

Again, soaring back toward the pier, Superman grabbed up a corner of his red cape in each hand, and as he reached the spreading cloud of LNG fumes, he picked up speed and altitude, catching the wind in cups of his cape and pulling up a wake of deadly fumes behind him.

Upward he raced into the air, his cape spread in his arms, then plummeting down again like a missile, to rise again with the cape spread and a load of poison gas following him. He cleared the air until, after thirty trips to the stratosphere and back, the air over Metropolis harbor was cleaner than it had been an hour earlier.

Superman had saved the city.

Clark Kent had blown his dinner date.

He watched the invisible fumes swirl upward from the stratosphere, already free of the planet's gravity. Then he took off into the direction of the night.

During the time he was saving the crew of the tanker his mind was occupied with only that. Now, as he moved eastward over the Atlantic he began to clear his head again with the joy of flight and power. He swooped low over the nuclear power plant floating off the coast of New England. He checked the level of radiation escaping from its cooling system. As night dropped over Newfoundland he picked a foundering fishing boat out of rough seas and deposited the boat, the fisherman aboard and his two sons, back in port six miles away.

In Reykjavik he averted a barroom brawl. In Scotland he lifted a swimmer out of Loch Ness because the swimmer had not seen the loch's most famous inhabitant until the monster paddled by underneath. In Munich he delivered the local police a company of six would-be bank robbers whom he had found in a tunnel under a vault. In Belgrade, unseen as far as he knew, he caught a chunk of an ancient and obsolete communications satellite most of which had disintegrated on its way to Earth. The surviving chunk would otherwise have hit an oil refinery and caused an awful mess.

That night, Superman was seen or heard, or his presence was otherwise felt, in seven countries of Europe, twelve of Africa and eight of the Middle East. It was morning in India when he swept out of the sky to snatch two children at play out of the path of a madly careening bull who would have trampled the children outside the main marketplace in New Delhi. Then it hit him.

As he held the two muddy children, the tape of Jimmy's Luthor film ran through his mind again, and in his mind's eye he saw the match that lit Luthor's pipe drop and spiral gently to the ground. And he saw the tower of liquefied natural gas fumes spiraling similarly upward toward the roof of the Earth's atmosphere.

Superman indecorously plopped the two disoriented children on the roof of an awning that shielded a merchant's delicate art prints from the Indian sun, and he swept off through the sky, taking the New Delhi marketplace's wind with him. Madly, angrily, he stroked over half the world, backward through the morning into the dying night to the west. It was not yet four in the morning at the Pocantico Correctional Facility sixty miles north of Metropolis. From a world away Superman flew there, realizing that there was an air current in Luthor's super-security cell where none should be. Underground, against a wall, a match that fell from a man's hand had been caught in a spiral of air either entering or leaving the room where there should have been no opening. Why hadn't he seen it earlier?

Somewhere hundreds of miles from the super-security cell under-neath the Pocantico Correctional facility Lex Luthor, whole and healthy, lay gathering his strength. He had known he would have to do this, but he had not realized how achy his muscles and joints would be.

He had escaped. He had walked through his "demonpass," his pathway through the Netherworld, and emerged here where he could easily stow away on a transport back to the city. Luthor had indeed been on a strict diet to make his body completely organic, since only organic substances could pass through this process. He could do nothing, however, about the mineral deposits that collect in the joints and muscles of the human body. These deposits, mostly infinitesimal bits of aluminum from cookware that gets into food, are permanent fixtures in the body unless drastic measures are taken to remove them. Luthor had just taken such a drastic measure.

Luthor, in throwing his body through a hole in space that would accept only organic matter, had ripped this residual inorganic matter out of his body and left it behind. He felt as though he had pulled every muscle in his body in all directions at once. He had.

For a moment after he collapsed, Luthor thought he felt a chilling breeze blow past his body. He was too busy with his pain. He ignored it.

The human was clever indeed, but absurdly foolhardy to pass this way, thought the demon.

Certainly the mortal who entered and moved a short distance through Hell's borderland had protected himself, with copious meditation, from possession; but he was still a fool. Any corporeal being who comes here creates a path for the denizens of this place to enter the human's own world. Maybe there were still humans who did not know that. More likely, the avarice endemic to the race moved them to do, for personal profit, things that were immeasurably dangerous to the survival of the race as a whole.

The demon thought to possess the body of the one who had led it here, but this strangely hairless mortal, even in his pain, continued to protect himself. The demon saw that although he was somewhat twisted and bent, this Luthor possessed remarkable moral strength.

No matter. If this Luthor had not led the demon here, then some other fool who thought himself a sorcerer would have done it soon enough. And if Luthor would not allow himself to be the vehicle of the demon's triumph, then there would be another more vulnerable.

The demon rode a cold wind to the center of life's energy in the world. C. W. Saturn, the bringer of Chaos, had returned to Earth.

Superman arrived too late. There was no use alerting the prison authorities either to his presence or to Luthor's escape. That bad news would travel quickly enough.

Superman looked over the super-security room into which he had slipped, unknown to the army of guards around it. He knelt down beside the wall where Luthor had stood and dropped his match this past afternoon. There was no trace of an air current left. There seemed to be no trace of Luthor left, other than the prison fatigues lying crumpled on the floor. Clearly, Luthor had used some form of teleportation to get out of here.

Hello, Superman thought. What was this? On the floor where the match had fallen, on the immaculately sterile floor of the new super-security cell, there were minute traces of some mineral. Aluminum, Superman saw by the molecular structure. He poked a finger at a few microscopic flakes of the metal and could feel that they were warm, but cooling off toward room temperature. They could have been as warm as body heat only a few minutes ago.

Curious, Superman thought. These would be difficult circumstances out of which to drag some sense. Superman would figure it all out, though. He had to figure it out, and he always did what he had to do.

From the Journal of
Kristin Wells

For the first time in the seven months I have
been here, I feel as though I am accomplishing
something. I can tell because I have not particularly
felt like sleeping for the past two days. I have
simply had no desire to sleep when I can read or
work instead. It is quite pleasant, actually. My
typing speed is nearly ninety words per minute
now, and this acquired ability has both brought
me into Superman's circle of friends, and provided
me with an income on which I am able to
support myself.

There are a number of things to note for
this journal, concerning events which have
occurred since my last entry several weeks ago.
These include, firstly, my acquaintance with a very
interesting woman named Lena Thorul;

secondly, certain events which have happened of late that correspond with historical occurrences leading up to the events of Miracle Monday; and thirdly, a general feeling of belonging and well-being that I have felt for the past three days since I spent a social evening with Superman, in his secret identity, and a number of his friends.

Lena Thorul is a schoolteacher of Lois Lane's acquaintance who has taken a sabbatical from her job and is spending the year in Metropolis writing a book about her experiences as a psychic. Her abilities in this area, I noted upon meeting her, are quite real, although she has made no conscious effort to develop and refine them. Ms. Thorul made a few serious errors in her evaluation of my own current frame of mind. She said, for example, that there were two strong opposing forces battling for control of my psyche at the moment, and that this inner conflict is causing confusion and emotional imbalance. This is sheer nonsense, of course. I was chosen for this assignment, in part, because of uncommon emotional stability, and as any fool can see, I feel quite directed and fulfilled at the moment.

I am more interested in Ms. Thorul, however, because of the sense I had upon meeting her that she was somehow familiar. I thought at first that she might be a sightseer or another historian from my own time, here to look in on the upcoming historic events, and I looked up her name in a book I was able to bring with me from the twenty-ninth century. Of course, it is a terrible security risk to place any artifact of the future in a previous time period, but I received special permission to bring one that I have since found invaluable: Michael Fleischer's twenty-first-century work, *The Encyclopedia of Supermanic Biography*, which contains a brief alphabetical reference to every person and event, and an outline of the major writings, that concern Superman, as far as scholars were able to determine during the century following his arrival on Earth. My copy is the abridged one-volume edition, but it does have a reference to the name *Thorul*, to wit:

> Anagram of the word *Luthor*, adopted as the legal surname of Jules and Arlene Luthor, parents of Lex Luthor [Cf. *Luthor, Lex* and other refs. as noted] during the final twelve years of their lives, following the first incarceration of their fourteen-year-old son at the East Kansas Juvenile Reformatory. Jules and Arlene Thorul were killed in an automobile accident in Midvale, Vermont, and were survived by their estranged son and a seventeen-year-old daughter.

There is no mention in my edition of the daughter's name, but Lena Thorul is approximately the correct age.

If Ms. Thorul, an empathetic psychic, is in fact the younger sister of Lex Luthor but does not know it, then it is reasonable to assume that she is likely to be high-strung during a period immediately following a mysterious prison escape by her unknown brother. Such an escape occurred three nights ago, and last night, when I met Ms. Thorul, her immediate reaction to me was extraordinary. She swooned and fainted. When she revived she said that she had mistaken me for something else, and could not remember what. Ordinarily, such a greeting from a psychic might be some cause for alarm, but in this particular case it was, of course, an extension of her unseen anxiety over Luthor. I will be working for Ms. Thorul two days a week.

My second area of concern is corroboration of events recorded in my own historical training with those that are actually happening around me.

Excuse me, I was daydreaming for a moment. Actually I have a list of events somewhere. Plagues, natural disasters, milk shortages, that sort of thing. We all learned about them in history classes ever since the age of five. Or six or something.

I did say excuse me, didn't I? That's silly, of course, since there's no one to say excuse me to. Or is that, "to whom to say excuse me"? I seem to be forgetting basic twentieth-century grammar. Eighteenth to twenty-first century American social history is my field of expertise, you know.

"You know?" Am I actually talking to the sheet of paper I'm writing on? That's silly too. Hold it.

There. I am better now. I was talking about—that is, writing about—historical corroboration. I have been keeping a record of news events which seem insignificant to the media, but certainly are not. As I was saying—writing!—I have been keeping a list but I can't seem to find it at the moment. I do remember a tidal wave that Superman turned into a snowstorm over Metropolis, and the first eruption of a volcano in southern Mexico in several centuries. I can't seem to remember the name of the volcano, but it's very famous. No sign yet of the worldwide eczema outbreak. I do wish I could find that list. It's here someplace. I'm generally very organized about these things. It's having to live in this tiny studio apartment in the middle of this noisy city. I can't find anything in this mess. How could these people live this way? Well, I'll find the list sometime.

The third thing is how comfortable I've been feeling here for the last three or so days. Except that I haven't been able to get much sleep. There was a tidal wave detected several days ago heading toward Metropolis harbor, but Superman somehow caused a snowstorm which stopped it. There must be some way he discovered of stopping the tides with snow.

My third point had to do with how comfortable I've been feeling for the last two days or three. Except I don't have any space, you know? If I only had more space I'd be in solid, except that I'm worried about why Lena Thorul fainted when she met me. She's psychic, I may or may not have mentioned, and she may have seen something about me that I don't know yet, like I'm getting sick from lack of sleep.

The third thing was that I'm starting to feel like I like it here because I'm making friends and feel like I fit in but actually don't. I want a cup of coffee. I met a young reporter named Jimmy Olsen who I think was a friend of Superman's in the twentieth century. He had red hair and freckles and no hair on his chest. I read that somewhere. No, maybe that was Andrew Jackson. I always get those two mixed up.

I just went to boil some water for instant coffee and I found a hot mug of it on the counter next to the stove. I must've made it myself without even thinking. I couldn't have made it myself, because I'd at least remember hearing the kettle whistling. I must've just made it because it's really hot. And it's black with no sugar, the way I've been drinking it the past three or two days. Good. It tastes bitter. Maybe I'm being watched.

James Bartholomew Olsen Junior was a Super-manic Era journalist who won the Pulitzer Prize four times between 1980 and 2014, when he was killed on Mars. He was filming an exclusive interview with Prince Anand Patwardhan of the Confederacy of Martian Principalities in Sagantown, then the Martian capital, when the city was destroyed by the com-bined forces of the North Atlantic Treaty Organiza-tion and the Warsaw Pact. His daughter, Noel N. Olsen, was the eleventh secretary-general of the United Nations; his older son, James Bartholomew Olsen the Third, was chairman of the board of Galaxy Communications and later director of the United States Information Agency; and his younger son, Clark Perry Olsen, was the archaeologist who found conclusive evidence of Superman's secret identity.

That seemed to type itself on the paper. That last paragraph. Maybe my typing is getting better

than I realized. All I did was write that stuff. I
didn't remember it all until I read it there. But that
can't be true, since I typed it myself. I must have.
I saw my hands moving. I need some sleep, but I
can't. Actually I looked away from the typewriter
for a moment, although my hands must have stayed
on the keys, because I felt the keys, I think, under
my fingertips and when I looked back I saw that
paragraph about Jimmy Olsen's career. I must
have typed it. I wonder where that cup of coffee came
from. I'm scared.

The third thing I wanted to mention was how
comfortable and stable I'm feeling for the first
time since I got here seven years ago. Months. Seven
months ago. Actually, what I'm really worried
about is that somebody might see my Superman
encyclopedia even though it's not going to be compiled
for another seventy years. Or somebody might see
this journal I'm keeping and figure out that I don't
belong here. Or I might go out to the movies or
to that Don Williams concert with Jimmy Olsen like
he wants me to do and I might mistakenly tell
him not to go to Mars. Or I'm worried that Lena
Thorul sensed something horrible about me. Or
that I can't get any space with all these people
around me all the time. Or that I don't belong here.
Or that I'll be too scared to go to sleep for the rest
of my life until I die. Or that I'll die.

I was feeling perfectly fine when I started
typing this, and I still feel fine. No I don't. I didn't
feel fine then either. I haven't felt fine since I
went out to dinner three days ago. Or is it a week and
three days ago? Haven't I been typing this thing
for at least a week? I feel like something inside me
is trying to tear me apart. Like there are two
forces fighting over my head. Me and something else.
I don't know what.

I need some space, man. I'm burning out.

The Warning

Again the phone rang. "Lois?"

"Yes, speaking," she said as she went on trying to type a story in her cramped office.

"This is Lena."

"Lena? You sound funny. Is something wrong?"

"No, not as far as I know. Tell me something."

"Almost anything if I can do it fast."

"How do I get to Superman?"

"If I find out I'm sure as hell not going to tell you. What else do you want to know?"

"Seriously, Lois."

"Seriously? I thought you said nothing was wrong. Oh, hi Clark. Sorry, Lena, Clark just walked in."

"I just wanted to show you this, Lois." Clark held out his copy of the morning *Times*.

"What did you want Superman for, Lena?"

"I got something in the mail. A letter to him addressed care of me."

"It's Russell Baker's column," Clark said. "I thought you'd like it."

"I'll read it," Lois said, "if you'll be a dear and just leave it there on the desk. No, not you, Lena. I'm sorry, Clark. I mean I'm sorry, Lena. I'm sorry, Clark."

"I'm sorry, Lois," Clark said. "I'll see you later."

"It's really very strange," Lena said.

"Strangest thing I've heard all day," Lois said. "Not you, Clark I'll see you later."

"All right, Lois," Lena said, and hung up.

"No, I didn't mean you, Lena," Lois said to the dead phone.

Lois sat with the phone in one hand, Clark's *Times* in the other and a look of clinical fascination on her face as she looked at Clark in the doorway.

"Sorry, Lois," Clark said and turned to go.

"Clark?" She decided to ask him.

"I'm sorry, Lois."

"Do you know how to find Superman?"

"Sometimes," he said.

"Sometimes. Yeah, me too."

"I heard he had dinner with Perry and his wife last night."

"Really? Maybe she's a better cook than I am."

"No, I don't think so," Clark volunteered. "Perry just wanted him to give his youngest son a pep talk. You know, Arnold, the one who always seems to be flunking out of college?"

"That's nice. I knew there had to be some sort of mission involved. Did it work?"

"I don't know. He just started at Stony Brook in January."

"Maybe if I adopted somebody really pitiful. Somebody with mange or rickets or something."

"Excuse me?"

"Never mind, Clark."

Clark left, hoping no one would ask him why he was grinning. Kristin Wells, walking the other way down the hall to Lois's office, smiled back at him, although Clark noticed that she had a slight tic above her left eye. He also noticed the freckle on the tip of her nose which seemed to be slowly driving Jimmy Olsen crazy. Poor Jimmy.

Lena Thorul was on the phone again with Lois, who had called Lena back to apologize for being so scattered when Lena had called earlier. Lois had no idea where to find Superman.

"The way he does things," Lois said, "is he sort of finds you. I hear Orson Welles is like that, but I don't suppose it's quite the same thing."

"Well, that's all right," Lena said. "I just had this feeling that I'd be able to find him if I called you."

"I'll let him know if I see him."

"Oh, thanks, Lois. It was just a feeling. Listen, now I've got to get off. There's someone at the door. I'll talk to you soon. Say hi to Kris."

Lena answered the door.

"I hear I've got some mail," Superman said.

"Oh," she said. "I don't suppose I should be surprised. You do this sort of thing all the time, don't you?"

"I'm afraid I do." He came in and closed the door.

"Well, here it is, then. Your letter."

It was a business-sized envelope whose return address said that it was from a person named Max Maven of Los Angeles. The name was vaguely familiar.

"I met him when I was a little girl," Lena said. "when we lived in New England. He's a mentalist. You must have heard of him."

"Yes, actually, I have. He does a very good act, according to most reviewers."

"Well, he was very strange. One day I ran into him at the candy store in town and he said that someday I would be his messenger."

"His messenger?"

"I don't usually look into people's minds unless there's a good reason. I respect people's privacy. But I tried to figure out what he meant by reading his mind, and it was completely shielded from me. No one's ever been able to do that before or since. I don't even remember saying anything to him. He just looked at me as though he knew me and said our paths would cross again. Does that make any sense to you, Superman?"

"I can't say it does," Superman answered, holding the letter at arm's distance and reading it through the envelope, "but that is probably not a relevant question in a lot of situations."

"I recognized him as the boy I met that day when I saw him on a talk show. He had lost some hair and wore all black and did all sorts of remarkable things. Told people their birthdays, quoted what people were writing on a pad out of his sight as they were writing it—that sort of thing. He looked a lot different, but I recognized him anyway. Oh dear, I hope I'm not bothering you with something trivial, Superman."

"No, no, not at all. Thank you very much."

"I just thought you had a kind of faraway look when I was talking."

"Did I? Just a premonition, I suppose. You know about those, don't you? I'll have to be leaving, Miss Thorul. Thanks for finally delivering your message."

"You're welcome," she started to say, but by the time she reached the second word of the phrase he was gone.

Superman streaked across the bending sky over America, wondering what he would find in California. The letter, which Superman had taken with him and was now allowing to burn to a cinder as he held it, catching the friction of Superman's flight, was brief enough:

Superman—
    Meet me at my home sometime during the day you receive this letter, or I will send Lena Thorul a photostat of her birth certificate.

Max Maven had signed it and followed that with his Los Angeles address. Superman did not enjoy being coerced.

Although she did not know it, Lena Thorul had been acquainted with Superman for quite some time. She lived in Smallville when she took her first steps and left town shortly after she spoke her first sentence.

Superboy, one day, had foolishly given her older brother a strange glowing yellow sphere which Superboy had found in a big cavern under the woods near town. Lena's brother intended to see what it was, but Lena got to it first. She happened to touch the sphere and the plate over an electric socket at the same time and the sphere melted to sludge. Lena's brother, Lex, saw the thing melt, and saw the baby's hair stand on end for an instant. She did not seem to be nearly as distressed over the incident as Lex was. He could not decide whether to be angrier at himself for leaving the thing lying around, or at Superboy for not realizing he had picked up an artifact of an ancient exploration party from the nation of Atlantis.

Lena learned to talk quickly—too quickly—after the day her hair stood on end. She also showed immediate signs of second sight. She always knew where to find her toys, as well as her brother's and father's lost tools. She also knew, for a while, that Lex was still alive when her mother had told her that he had died in a mountain climbing accident, but she was discouraged from asking about him. In the

90

course of the more than twenty years since the incident of the melted globe, Lena's extraordinary mind had been asked to repress a lot. Lena was fairly successful at keeping that mind out of other people's affairs and out of her own past.

If Superman were to make a list of the ten things he would least want to happen, having Lena Thorul see that the name on her birth certificate was *Lena Luthor* would certainly be on the list.

In Los Angeles there was another letter, a longer one this time which showed at least some regard for etiquette. It was taped to the performer's apartment door:

S.M.—
 I trust you chose to enter through the door. Unfortunately I am not here at the moment, but you will probably be able to find me at the Magic Castle.

Mystically yours,
Max

This is not a likable man, Superman decided.

The Magic Castle was a private club in Hollywood and one had to be a member or a member's guest to get in. Max Maven had neglected to consider the possibility that the doorman would refuse to allow Superman entry and that, once refused, Superman would not consider entering by force. The doorman was not unaccustomed to people in capes and odd costumes and simply did not believe the man was who he claimed to be. For a moment Superman considered telling the man the contents of his wallet, but he saw a friend inside who turned out to be a member of the club.

"Ray!" Superman called. "Ray, do you care to rescue this gentleman from an unforgivable invasion of his privacy?"

Years ago, when he was fifteen years old, Clark Kent had read *The Martian Chronicles.* Clark was so impressed that Superboy flew off that afternoon to meet Ray Bradbury, the man who had written the book. What Superboy found was a man who had never flown in an airplane, who wrote stories about rocket ships, a Californian who did not know how to drive a car, a man relatively unconcerned with politics who was, at least that day, obsessed with the idea of convincing Walt Disney to run for mayor of Los Angeles. Bradbury had a lifetime pass to Disneyland, which was where he and Superboy spent the rest of the day. Superboy had never been there before, and no one there believed he was really Superboy anyway. Children were more interested in getting the autograph of Mickey Mouse, and adults were confused by his presence since they thought that only Walt Disney characters paraded through these streets in costume.

Bradbury's wife drove them to the amusement park in Anaheim. Bradbury utterly refused to allow the boy to fly him there, and neither of them had a driver's license. Walt Disney, whom Superboy and Ray Bradbury found in his secret apartment overlooking the main entrance to Disneyland, again refused to run for mayor, but had his chauffeur drive the novelist home. Superboy flew back to the Smallville Public Library and read everything that Bradbury had ever had published.

"Hey Supes," Bradbury called from the vestibule of the Magic Castle, "is that the real you? What do Walt Disney and John C. Fremont have in common?"

"Neither of them ever ran for mayor of Los Angeles," Superman responded.

"It *is* you," and Bradbury told the gatekeeper to let the costumed man in as his guest. "It's not really him," the storyteller whispered to the doorman, "but you know how these method actors are." He pointed to his head and turned back to the hero. "We're late, Supes. There's this great mentalist act going on in the main hall. Ever hear of a guy named Max Maven?"

The room where members of the elite of America's stage magicians sat at small tables with their various guests eating brunch was not even dimmed. Max Maven brought his own atmosphere with him. He was not particularly tall, but his presence was not to be ignored. His black hair swept back into the shape of a pronounced widow's peak, and he wore a black Vandyke, a black dinner jacket and a single earring. Max was doing card tricks, so nobody much noticed when a big man in a Superman costume walked in and took a seat at Ray Bradbury's table.

"Your card, sir," Max said as he held up the deck in one hand and the jack of spades slowly wriggled its way up from the middle of the pile.

"Umm, Max," the gray-headed illusionist at the table whispered to the younger magician whose show this was. "Hold up, Max."

"Speak right up, Harry," Max said in his clear stage voice.

"I wish I could tell you it was my card," the old magician said, "but it's just not."

"What do you mean it's not?"

"I mean my card wasn't the jack of spades."

"The hell it wasn't." The performer was losing his cool. "What're you trying to pull?"

"Hey calm down, Max. You wouldn't want me to say it was when it wasn't."

"You trying to embarrass me in front of my peers, Harry? That's it, isn't it? You're jealous, right?"

"Look, Max, this happens to everybody Better here than on television, right?"

"Better never. Listen, I don't need you, Harry "

"Max."

"I don't need some old has-been fixing my tricks, understand me, Harry?"

"Max, everyone in the room knows my card wasn't the jack of spades. The only one who doesn't know is you, it seems It was the—"

"I don't want to know, dammit!"

"Max, I'm surprised at—"

"I don't need you, or this lousy club, or any of you for that matter. Listen, I went to a good college. I was going to be a doctor. I don't even need these cruddy cards to make a living, and you all know it."

With that, Max Maven tossed the entire deck into the air and, as the cards flew randomly around the room, he stormed out in a rage. In an uncommon breach of the rules of chance, fifty-one of the cards landed facedown on the floor of the room. Only one card landed face-up, and it landed on Harry's table. Max was gone by the time the gray-haired illusionist broke the silence of the room with the whispered phrase, "Oh, that son of a dog!"

The card on his table, the only card that had landed face-up, was the four of clubs, his card. Max had put one over on the experts.

Superman found Max in another room, a library furnished with wide plush chairs and paintings of great magicians of the past. A huge oil painting by J. C. Leyendecker of Harry Houdini hung over one fireplace facing the opposite fireplace and an equally large Walt Simonson acrylic of Merlyn. Between Houdini and Merlyn, between Leyendecker and Simonson, between hearths, sitting on the red carpet with his back against an unoccupied easy chair and reading a book by Carlos Castaneda at which he was laughing out loud, was Max Maven.

"You put on a pretty good show," Superman said.

"Shh," Max said. "I've got to finish this paragraph. This is funnier than Nixon's autobiography."

Superman turned to go but Max looked up.

"Good of you to come," Max said.

"Finish your paragraph?" Superman turned back.

"Yeah. I read pretty fast for an Earth human. Can we go into another room and talk?"

The pair found the exercise room on the top floor of the building. The room was padded on walls and floor and adjoined a shower and sauna which no one was using. No one was using any of the gleaming, expensive-looking equipment. Harry Houdini had been a physical fitness buff. A number of contemporary magicians were as well, but none seemed to be today. Max sat down on an exercise bicycle and began to pedal slowly, his arms and torso rising up and down as he spoke, and Superman stood with his hands clenched at his waist.

"Is the name 'C. W. Saturn' in any way familiar to you, Superman?" Max asked him.

"Yes, I believe I have heard of that name."

"Where, pray tell?"

"Mythology. It is one of the recurring names of the agent of evil also known sometimes as the devil, Satan, Lucifer, Mephistopheles, Old Scratch, the Adversary, He Whose Name Cannot Be Spoken, the serpent, or simply the Evil One, as well as several other names in every known language and culture on Earth."

"You're forgetting Pandora, or don't you believe in equal treatment of the sexes? Are you sure you are justified in labeling it mythology, Superman? Can you truly believe that in all your travels, all your exploits, you have never run across any real, solid, unimpeachable evidence of evil in the world? Not a single event of certifiable, card-carrying injustice that you can't explain away as a social problem or a result of somebody's misdirected good intentions? Don't you think there is a source of pain as surely as there is a Creator?"

"Mister— What am I supposed to call you?"

"Max will be fine. Or Your Excellency if you prefer."

"Max, my interest in the reason you blackmailed me into coming here is diminishing dramatically. How did you find out about Lena Thorul anyway?"

'How did I find out what?'

Superman paused a moment and watched the magician's smile as it grew wider. "You don't know about her at all, do you?"

"Actually, I don't know much, although I suppose I could find out if I tried. I do know that she's psychic, and that she clearly has something from her past that her mind and several of her friends are keeping her from finding out. I took a shot in the dark and guessed that it would turn up on her birth certificate. Clever, no?''

"Yes, Max Maven, no one can deny you are a very clever fellow. Thank you for a very entertaining magic show,'' Superman said, and he was no longer in the room.

Max kept pedaling and said to the air, "It has to do with Lex Luthor if I'm not mistaken.''

Max knew Superman was gone, but he also knew that the sound waves of his voice would catch up with the hero's super-hearing before Superman got very far.

"On the night Lex Luthor broke out of jail, C. W. Saturn found a conduit of entry to Earth,'' Max continued. "I assume that his method of escape somehow allowed the arch-demon's entry. Saturn, or any denizen of what we call the Netherworld, can only gain entry here through the foolish use by an inhabitant of our plane of the forces of magic. Need I repeat any of that to you, my good man?''

Max turned back to the door of the room to find it open, with Superman standing in the opening and looking into Max Maven's face.

"Who are you,'' Superman asked him, "and how do you claim to have this information?''

"Want to see something?''

Max dismounted from his exerciser and rummaged through a rubbish container for a newspaper, which he found.

"Doubtless you've seen this before,'' Max told Superman as he rolled one section of the newspaper into a cone and filled several paper cups with water from a cooler. "Usually it's done with milk, for some reason. Please bear with me. I am a showman, you will agree.''

Superman watched impatiently as Max chattered through the charade of pouring the water, paper cup by paper cup, into the cone, making believe he was holding steady a cone full of liquid, and suddenly whipping the empty paper through the air and crumpling it, the water apparently having vanished into thin air.

"Can you tell me how I did that?'' Max asked him.

"Of course.''

"Please indulge me.''

"There is a small plastic balloon of the long narrow variety in the sleeve of the arm with which you held the cone. A plastic funnel around which you held the cone caught the water and fed it into the balloon, where it is now, chilling your wrist under that shirt. Now will you answer my question about what you know and how you know it?''

"Oh, haven't I told you that? I've got second sight. Mine is probably as strong as Lena Thorul's, although that is only because I have spent years developing it. I had a dream, you see. Now watch this.''

Max pulled the water-filled balloon from his sleeve and dropped it into the rubbish. Then he began to roll the remaining newspaper into another cone as Superman rolled his eyes up to the ceiling and began to tap one foot on the floor.

"No no, Superman, I would like you to watch this time even more closely. Watch the level of my pulse and heartbeat too, and whatever else you can keep track of as I do this. Sunspot activity. Gamma rays in the air. My Krilian aura. Whatever.''

Superman watched. Max Maven took a paper cup from the water cooler's dispenser and with one hand he filled it repeatedly with water and emptied it into the cone. He did this six times before his forehead broke out into a sweat, eight times before his pulse rate reached one hundred twenty, ten times before the walls of his aorta were strained to a dangerous pressure, a dozen times before the glow of Max Maven's Krilian aura made Superman squint.

"Enough. That's enough," Superman said. "I'm impressed. The water isn't going anywhere as far as I can see. How do you do the trick?''

"Magic," Max Maven said.

"Excuse me?''

"Actually, I was hoping you could tell me where the water went. I suppose it must go somewhere." Max leaned against a wall and breathed heavily as he spoke, willing his heart to slow down.

"Sir, will you—''

"Excellency," Max said, "not sir. Max or Your Excellency. I thought we'd agreed.''

"Would you please get to your point?''

"I've already made my point.''

"Which was what? It may have gotten lost in the confusion.''

"C. W. Saturn," Max Maven said, "has entered the plane of Earth to do some bad stuff. I don't know what, but I learned in a dream that it involves you. I believe that Luthor managed to devise some method to rip a hole between our world and Saturn's. The hole must be found and plugged up, destroyed, whatever. Meanwhile, Saturn is here, getting ready to give you the fight of your life. He'll probably destroy you, and the rule of order with you. I just thought you might like to know that.''

''How do you know that?''

''The same way I know my shoes are tied when they don't fall off my feet. The same way you knew enough to tell me to stop willing the water from the cooler to disappear before I had a heart attack. I just know, that's all I can tell you. I also know that you wear glasses a good deal of the time, although I haven't the faintest idea why. I suppose a lot of people in the world know about Saturn coming around, although none of the others believe their own senses or have the presence of mind or the social consciousness to let you know. Or maybe it doesn't matter whether you know or not. I did want to meet you, after all. I thought you might have some good stories to tell. Do you?''

Superman thought a moment, then said, ''This power you have. This thing you call magic. Is that what you do in your act? Is that why you're such a successful performing magician?''

''Hell, no!'' Max was indignant. ''I'm not a magician onstage. I make miracles. I want to prove to the world that I'm the greatest mentalist in the world. If those guys out there found out I've really got the power, I'd have to do demonstrations for crackpot parapsychology studies at some backwater college. You tell anyone and make me a lab specimen, and I really will find out what the secret is about Lena Thorul.''

Superman stared at Max and shook his head in amazement. ''Then why did you show me that trick? What was that all about?''

''It's my job to perform miracles. Art for art's sake. It's your job to save the world. You have your own purposes for your art. If I hadn't done the trick, you wouldn't have believed me, would you?''

''Max, you are the most confounding creature I have met in quite a long time.''

Max smiled a wide smile that would look quite alarming walking toward an unarmed person from a dark alley. ''Obviously,'' he said, ''you have not yet encountered C. W. Saturn.''

Hot Springs

"Busy?" the voice on the telephone wanted to know.

"You mean now?" Lois answered with another question.

"Well, thirty or thirty-five seconds from now, actually."

"Umm, no," she said, scooping up the loose scraps of paper she had scattered on the bed, "of course not."

"Feel like a picnic for dinner?"

"Sure. Do you want me to bring wine or an ant colony or something?"

"No ants. I promise."

"No ants? What kind of picnic is that?"

"You'll see. I'll be there in two seconds."

Two seconds? He meant it when he said two seconds. She grabbed the papers that held the first scratchings of a silly, sappy little poem about the man on the phone, threw them into her cardboard file drawer, and went to open the living room window.

What a remarkable city this was, he decided as he threw himself upward from the window of the apartment at 344 Clinton Street.

He knew it was remarkable. He had seen a lot of cities. Metropolis, he knew, threw off a brighter glow than any other gathering of life he had seen anywhere in the Universe. He was glad he lived here. This world was teeming with life and this city, whether the world knew it or not, for all its concrete and radiating heat and clogging of air and waterways, was the focal point of life on planet Earth.

In no other place that he knew of, had any form of life gathered such an orgy of creativity in so small a space. There were nearly eight million humans here at any given time, and sometimes there were as many as fourteen million of them here at once, along with countless octillions of pets, microorganisms and entities of super-consciousness that came with them. The humans worked and grinded, conceived and grunted, through a period of eight hours or more every day; then they unwound the excess creative force from their beings at the dinner tables, taverns, churches, and meeting halls in and around the city. They spewed the unused energy of their day out over the town and into the collective consciousness of the planet even as a skyscraper throws the heat it cannot hold out its edges and its asphalt roof to ride the stratosphere and ward off the imminent ice age.

If Metropolis were to die tomorrow, if the bodies of its myriad souls dropped in their places and its structures were lost into inertness, going the way of some latter-day Pompeii, then the undirected life energy that the city left behind could drive whatever was left on Earth for millenia through the shock, until the force itself could create a new Metropolis. This city was the closest thing in the Universe to a perpetual motion machine.

Between 344 Clinton Street on the Upper East Side and Lois Lane's apartment in Chelsea were the unusually crowded hotel district, Central Preserve, the strip of Sixth Avenue that held the corporate seats of every major energy, recording and film distributor, and every broadcasting network in the country, Governor's Plaza, the theater district, Foundation Center, three major colleges and twelve minor ones, the garment district, midtown, and the homes of thousands of all conditions of people.

He swam through it all, drinking the power into his own, osmosing the energy through his cells, looking, touching, listening. He loved the stink of this town. Even this man relaxed sometimes, as he would do tonight, but the organism that was this city never let up. He did not have any idea how long he would live, and he had little idea of why he was here. He might live forever, since he saw no evidence that a man like he was would ever die. Or he might, like Achilles, die tonight after a short but glorious life. There was indeed glory in the legend he lived, but that glory was only for others to perceive. His own glory, here and now, in this city that was his home and captor, was the joy of being who he was.

He was Superman.

Precisely two seconds after he hung up the telephone in Clark Kent's apartment, not a microsecond more or less, Superman rapped on Lois Lane's living room window just as she was about to open it.

"You're half a second early," she said.

He knew he wasn't, but he apologized anyway.

He told her to grab a swimsuit and then he scooped her up and whisked her into the night. He flew slowly through the clear winter sky over the city, letting Lois watch the world spin below them. Soon they lost the lights of the city into the east and flew over the clouds as the waxing moon made streaks of color dance through the mist of Metropolis.

"Wrap up now," he said and unsnapped the red cape from under his shirt. "I'll let you know when we catch the sun on the horizon."

"Where're we going, Hawaii?"

"Not that far," he said as he enclosed her loosely in the indestructible cloth, "too many ants." Gently he accelerated as the G-force wrapped her close to him and the deadly air friction washed over the cape like soapsuds.

When the sun poked over the western sky, they were flying over Missouri. Superman dipped through thin clouds, turning so that he was flying feetfirst, and slowed down as gently as he had accelerated.

"You awake in there, Lois?"

"Mmm, yes."

"Want to see where I grew up?"

She peeked from under the flap of cape on her head, but she had to let her eyes readjust before she saw the familiar checkerboard of the Great Plains covered in white. Rushing at the pair from the western horizon was a little town dominated by a pale blue church steeple to the right and a gold-domed village hall on the left. As they got closer Lois saw the famous water tower with the sign that said:

Welcome to Smallville
Home of SUPERBOY

"There's where Lana Lang lived, and next door was Clark Kent. Look—old Chief Parker walking his dog. There's the movie theater, the only one for miles. It's got three screens now. The bank that was robbed the day I went public. The statue of me as a boy in the square

101

over there obstructs the view of that nice old gazebo. Somewhere out there, where the Stone Poultry Farm stretches for miles now, is where my cradle from Krypton crashed."

"You never told anybody exactly where that happened, did you?"

"Never did."

"A secret?"

"No, not really. I guess I didn't want them to make it into some half-baked shrine."

"What've you got against hero worship, hero?"

"Oh, people shouldn't pick living people for their heroes. Somebody who's dead can't disappoint you anymore."

"What's that?"

It was a long narrow slab of concrete in the snow with some charred planks and slats around it, the ruins of a small building.

"Oh, that. A workshop I once built for a friend. Burned down. I don't know why the town doesn't use that lot for a park or something."

He didn't want to talk about it, so he arced down from the sky toward a group of four young boys snowshoeing through the woods and called out, "Jonny! Jonathan Ross!"

The blond boy who knew him was the only one of the four who could gather the spit to say, "Superman!"

"You fellows are pretty far from home and it'll be dark in less than half an hour. You'd best start heading in."

"Okay, Superman," and they all waved at the man and woman soaring back up toward the clouds.

"You say hi to your dad for me, now."

They were gone into the sky again, Lois sheltered in red and pressed against his shoulders by the speed. When Lois Lane next saw daylight, the Rocky Mountains, swathed in an eight-foot base of snow, flowed majestically beneath them. Lois thought Superman had changed his mind about where they were going.

"Aha," she said. "The bathing suit was just a clever ploy. You were planning on forcing yourself mercilessly upon me in the wilderness all along, you cad you."

"It is a wilderness, my dear Miss Lane," he said, "but I am capable of getting quite a lot more merciless than this."

"Can't tell by me," she said, shedding the cape when they landed on a rock outcropping near a bubbling spring. "What is this place?"

A narrow stream of water flowed from a crack between two rocks on the mountainside into a mostly frozen river that was no more than six or eight long strides across. Where the stream hit the river, there was a constant hiss of steam. Around the intersection of the two flows of water were a few square meters of snowless scrub grass, with a heated pool half the width of the otherwise frozen river on one side, and on the other side unearthly configurations of ice that were made directly from steam. It was a valley boxed in on all sides by six peaks, a misty oasis in this crisp frigid desert.

"Welcome to my newest discovery." Superman bowed at the waist, his cape draped over one arm. "Our own private hot spring."

"It's stunning. Where are we?"

"Near the northeast corner of Utah. I think this place is really undiscovered. It would be pretty tricky to get even a helicopter through the air currents into this valley. May I dust off your seat?" He grinned as he clapped the cape over a flat rock and then reached into the pocket in the cape's lining for Lois's studiedly scanty swimsuit.

"What else've you got in there?"

"A handful of marbles, a rabbit's foot, two frogs and a road map to Metropolis."

While she changed into the swimsuit he turned his back, ostensibly in order to dig in the nearby snow for a small floating table and the picnic dinner that he had buried there a few hours earlier. The snow melted at the touch of hands that were still warm from friction. Dinner was his own concoction, made out of mushrooms, walnuts and fresh vegetables, with a mixture of fruit juices that Martha Kent had once taught him how to make. He defrosted and cooked the platter with the wink of an eye. He sat down in the steam-heated pool, surrounded by winter, with a tableful of picnic goodies floating on little pontoons in front of him. She sat in the warm water opposite him and rinsed off her hands in the pool.

"So, Miss Lane."

"Yes, Mr. Clean?"

"Do you come here often?"

They ate dinner, talked for a while, imagined animal shapes in the mountains through the steam, swam, sat in the natural sauna, and when night fell, they cooled off by rolling around together in the snow. When she wrapped herself again in the red cape he accelerated even more gently than he had before, until somewhere over eastern Colorado they reached the velocity he wanted. He rose higher in the sky and began to weave back and forth as he flew, delicately rocking her to sleep, helped by the thinness of the air. She would have been a touch disappointed to know that he kissed her lightly on the forehead when he left her in her bed and soared off to save worlds until morning.

Lois Lane woke up before dawn, dry and warm, still in her swimsuit and under her blankets. For now, she thought, this was enough for her. She turned over and fell back to sleep.

The Auction

The arrival of the dignitaries at the Grangerford-Shepherdson Galleries that afternoon in early March was the most impressive show that that end of Seventy-second Street had seen all day. Seventy-second Street was accustomed to good shows.

That morning at a little past three, a turbaned Iraqi diplomat attached to the consulate on Third Avenue ran out of a hotel on the corner of Seventy-second and Fifth, ordered a cab to a halt and demanded to be taken to his consulate. He threw a hundred-dollar bill at the cabbie and told him not to stop for anything. The diplomat railed in two languages and four dialects about a female agent of the Pakistani government who had lured him into the hotel and planned to extort secret information from him. He sputtered this way for no more than half a minute before the cab screamed into a stationary oil truck and was totaled like a fallen angel food cake. The Iraqi leaped out without a thought for the driver, who was thrown clear and, except for his dignity, was uninjured. The diplomat scurried around the wreckage and ordered the driver of the oil truck to finish the trip to the consulate.

105

The truck driver would have done it, since the diplomat had stuffed several fifty-dollar bills into his fist, if a pair of policemen had not gotten there first. Both doubled over with laughter at the scene.

Later, during the morning rush hour, a well-known actress led a procession of people clustered around a horse-drawn wagon from the park to a brownstone on Seventy-Second Street where the president of a large seafood distribution company lived. The wagon carried a plain wooden coffin. When the group reached the businessman's house, the actress proclaimed a boycott of canned tuna in order to protest the slaughter of dolphins caught by fishermen employed by the company. Then the group of people cheered and turned over the coffin, which cracked open against the steps leading to the executive's door, spilling hundreds of cans of tuna into the middle of the morning rush. The seafood mogul was, at that moment, sunning himself on a beach in Florida.

Around lunchtime a well-dressed man with an attaché case walked toward the corner of Seventy-second and Lexington where another well-dressed man with a zip-up leather folder was waiting for him. As the one man exchanged his attaché case for the other man's leather folder, a freakish bolt of wind somehow threw both containers open. Out of the leather folder flew thirty loose sheets of photocopied diagrams and records, and out of the attaché case flew three hundred wrinkly, laundered twenty-dollar bills. Both well-dressed men panicked and tried to fly after all three hundred thirty slips of paper, but they slipped on the ice at the curb. Before either of them hit the ground, Superman swooped out of the sky, caught all the money and records, as well as the two men. He whisked the whole bundle off to the police station at Seventy-Second Street and First Avenue—enough evidence to send more than a dozen oil company officials into a court battle which would, at the very least, deplete two corporations' budgets for legal affairs.

The best show on Seventy-second Street that day, though, was put on by Wainwright McAfee, the eminent artist's agent and art collector, and Lucius D. Tommytown, the eccentric billionaire. The Grangerford-Shepherdson Galleries had scheduled, for two o'clock that afternoon, an auction of some of the sculptures done by the late Jeremy McAfee. Wainwright McAfee, Jeremy's younger brother, claimed that he wanted his brother's art pieces for their sentimental value. According to one report, Tommytown had remarked that McAfee was as sentimental as any brother could be whose brother's effects were likely to appreciate to the value of a king's ransom. Tommytown also said, according to this report, that he wanted them more than McAfee did, and that he would prove it. On the day of the auction McAfee arrived first.

At half past one, a pair of small trucks, each carrying a huge spotlight, crawled down Seventy-Second Street and parked in front of the venerable gallery. A man dressed in a black dinner jacket and ruffles hopped out of one truck with a cordless microphone. He had on white vampire makeup and prominent canine teeth. His hair was perfect. A policeman, one of those who had been on duty when the actress unloaded her tuna cans down the block, asked the vampire for a parade permit. The vampire produced one; it was perfectly in order.

Men from the trucks set up loudspeakers, and the spotlights sat on either side of the gallery building, blocking off half a lane of traffic on their side of the street. The spotlights flashed clear blue beams into the overcast afternoon and the vampire began to speak into his microphone in the middle of a sentence as though he had been doing it all day:

"And the excitement here is mounting as the great event draws closer. The crowd waits with bated breath to see which celebrity of the art world will appear next, to bid for the works of the late great Jeremy McAfee here at the Grangerford-Shepherdson auction. It's a giant of a— Excuse me? Is it? Yes, ladies and gentlemen, I've just received word that the next arrival will be Wainwright McAfee himself, the brother and sole heir of the renowned artist. I think we can already hear him coming down the street."

Predictably, from down the block toward the park came the insistent whirring of a pair of sirens. Twin Harley-Davidsons carrying the two meanest-looking hell drivers Seventy-Second Street had seen for some time blared out a path for twenty-six feet of heaven-white Fleetwood limousine. Clapping with the wind over the giant car's hood were a pair of flags, one American and one Irish. The car ground to a halt in front of the gallery and between the searchlight trucks as the choppers reared up on hind wheels and roared off toward the river.

A long narrow chauffeur with ebony skin and shiny black boots, a black coat and black turtleneck, strode around to the passenger side and opened the backseat door. Wainwright McAfee, a great white buffalo of a man, got out in full ivory glitter, swept back a collection of hair that might last have been used by Arthur Fiedler, and offered a hand to the lady he escorted. Her skin and flowing gown were as black as the chauffeur.

The pair acknowledged the cheering crowd that had gathered around the lights and loudspeakers, nodded to the vampire, and waltzed

107

into the gallery building. Then the vampire, the chauffeur, the limousine, the loudspeakers and searchlights, and the crew who came with them, all packed up and rode off as though they had never been there.

Among the crowd were thirteen heavily bearded men wearing the dark hats and coats over fringed shawls of the Hasidic Jewish community. These were retiring, taciturn men, a mystery and often apparently invisible to most of the denizens of this city. The men stopped their walking and astute murmurings when they came to the crowd watching the vampire announce the arrival of Wainwright McAfee. They stood there for the entire display, the thirteen of them, through the vampire's verbosity, through the spectacular arrival of the art collector, through the packing up and leaving. Nearly the entire crowd, who now blocked most of Seventy-Second Street, stayed for a minute or two after McAfee disappeared and the company who had heralded him dispersed. They were perhaps wondering if some more sense could be made of the event before they had it explained to them on the society page of the next morning's newspapers.

As the throng showed signs of leaving, however, the witnesses to this street madness were further confused. The thirteen Hasids strode, shoulders hunched and heads down, into a line in front of the gallery. Simultaneously, they threw off their coats, hats, pants, shawls and false beards, and there in the March chill, arm in bare arm, stood a leggy row of twelve chorus girls in feathers and net stockings, and one disco-suited barker who held up the lapels of one of the discarded coats on whose lining was embroidered the words: THE TOMMYTOWN FOLLIES. The barker, tall, thin and bald with just a thick pair of muttonchop sideburns to decorate his face, looked to be Lucius D. Tommytown himself, his renowned basso booming over the din of the city.

"Gather 'round, folks, don't be shy. It's the Tommytown Follies here for your entertainment pleasure. No contributions please. Girls, how about a number?"

In approximate unison, all twelve chorusers sang the tune of "Let Me Entertain You," and the crowd piled in on three sides of them. Among the crowd were six process servers who had been tipped off to the fact that the elusive billionaire would make an appearance at this auction. The six fought and elbowed through the mob, showed identification to police who were keeping the street in a state of stable chaos, and the six descended almost at once on the big-voiced barker who clapped and sang along.

As the process servers stuffed their subpoenas into the disco king's hands, pockets and coat, one of the chorusers, a tall, husky, long-haired lady with hair over most of her face, grabbed up one of the discarded coats and bolted up the steps to the gallery entrance

"He's not Tommytown," the choruser yelled in a decidedly masculine voice. Tommytown pulled off the long wig to reveal a monstrous pair of muttonchop sideburns framing a fleshy pate as he wrapped himself in the coat. "It's me! It's me! You missed me!" he howled and disappeared behind the gallery door.

To get into the auction, one had to identify oneself as something other than a process server. The spurious Tommytown tore off the fake sideburns and politely handed each of the six subpoenas back to its respective server. Then, the remaining dancing girls and the hairless master of ceremonies shook hands through the crowd and made their way across the street to four waiting cars. Inside the gallery, by the time a valet greeted Lucius D. Tommytown with a dignified Artis-A suit and helped him into it, the auction was ready to begin.

The room where the auction took place looked more like a church sanctuary than an auction hall. Potential bidders sat in pews before a platform which was decorated with McAfee sculptures of all shapes and sizes. There was a lectern on the platform where the auctioneer stood, and a table at stage center where the auctioneer's aides would bring the items that were not too large to be lifted. The only thing that detracted from the churchlike quality of the room was the nature of the sculpture itself.

Jeremy McAfee was one of those contemporary artists whose classification art scholars and critics left to a later, more ambitious generation. Fitting him into a pigeonhole was too much work. For Dali and Picasso they had found words. For Calder they had gone so far as to make up new words that seemed suitable. For McAfee they were at a loss. Some thought McAfee was a charlatan, tossing together disparate shapes and colors for no reason other than to make a buck and confound art critics. Others insisted that he was a genius, beyond classification, whose creativity and innovation knew no bounds. Both points of view, astonishingly enough, were correct. Jeremy McAfee, lately killed off in a helicopter accident while he was allegedly dangling from a rope ladder making a sketch of the sunrise over Castile, actually never existed.

Neither, of course, did the artist's brother Wainwright McAfee exist, nor, as it happened, did the spectacularly wealthy Lucius D Tommytown. All three were rather brilliant constructs out of the mind of a man who stood behind the back row of the hall as the auction began; a man who, under his Pinkerton rent-a-cop uniform, mustache and graying blond toupee, was Lex Luthor. These people, along with a score of other owned-and-operated people in a number of different lines of business, were part of a great clandestine holding company that had evolved, over the years, from Luthor's far-flung illegal and semilegal enterprises.

Luthor started out as a tinkerer when he was still a young boy. He could easily have landed a job—if he had not gone off to reform school before he was old enough to get working papers—as an inventor with any major industrial firm, commissioned to spend all the money he needed to research any area of study that struck his fancy and produce whatever wondrous gadgets he wanted. He tinkered and invented anyway, even in stir, because his mind would not sit still. When he started putting together bigger gadgets—some of which were illegal, some of which there would have been laws against if lawmakers could have foreseen them, and some of which district attorneys wanted for evidence against him—Luthor had to find some way of stashing these objects where nobody could locate them.

The solution was to put them on display in museums as sculpture. Luthor invented Jeremy McAfee to pose as the artist who created the criminal's more outlandish constructions. So McAfee's "Collage of Flight," a large plastic and aluminum triangular kite with a propeller at each corner of the triangle, was actually a particularly efficient copter-glider device for one or two riders, sitting now in the courtyard garden of the Museum of Modern Art. The Whitney housed a corkscrew-nosed missile which could actually hold as many as six passengers while it tunneled twelve miles underground. Decorating the marble steps in front of the Bronfield Distilleries building out on Fifth Avenue for passersby to admire, was a ten-meter-tall, nuclear-powered, fire-belching, mechanical dragon that Luthor was saving for a special occasion. Luthor had dreams of building a harmless-looking obelisk at the site of McAfee's home near Gibraltar in Spain, an obelisk which would actually be a geological-activation station that was capable of sending an impulse through the ground under the strait to a similar site on land Luthor also owned in northern Morocco. This impulse would cause the western Mediterranean to pulse and roil until it constructed a levee of earth and rock across the Gates of Hercules, damming the sea from its principal tributary, the Atlantic Ocean, and making Luthor the proprietor of a hydroelectric plant that could provide more power than the world would need for a thousand years. He would do it, too, if those guys in the Persian Gulf got any more uppity.

Luthor did not yet have any particular purpose for this trip outside the world of the Pocantico Correctional Facility other than to see to the liquidation of the assets of Jeremy McAfee. He decided, while standing at the rear of the auction hall, that the guys in the Persian Gulf were already uppity as hell, and that maybe it was time he actually did dam up the Straits of Gibraltar and take the world off the oil standard. When he left here he would find a phone booth, dial a secret number and tell B. J. Tolley, his chief of operations, that she should set the Gibraltar Plan into operation.

The auction was beginning. The first item up for bid was something by someone other than McAfee. Luthor let it go by. The second was a McAfee sculpture called "Crystal Cave," a conical mound of glass and granite prisms about a foot high on their stand, that took two orderlies to carry it to the altar at center stage. It was actually a chemical tracing device which, when attached to an ordinary shortwave radio, could detect the whereabouts of any individual on Earth by homing in on that person's peculiar organic makeup. The opening bid of three hundred dollars came from somewhere near the front of the room.

Luthor pressed a small button in the palm of his right hand three times in quick succession, and on the right-hand side of the room, the actor who had convinced Seventy-Second Street that he was the fictional Lucius D. Tommytown rose and said, "Let's get this rolling. A thousand dollars."

Luthor pressed a similar button in his left palm, and to his left and in front of him the *eminence grise* who had driven up with his motorcycle escort said in overstated brogue, "A thousand and one."

"Some brotherly love," Tommytown said to his contrived adversary. "Fifteen hundred."

"Fifteen-nought-one," returned the great white buffalo.

"This man is annoying me," Tommytown said, pointing at Wainwright McAfee. "Isn't there a rule against what he's doing?"

"Look at the summons evader talking of rules," McAfee grumped.

"Every reputable auction hall has a minimum overbid rule. You can't bid just a dollar more than I bid. What kind of bulldink is this anyway?"

McAfee finally acquired the "Crystal Cave" for twenty-seven hundred fifty-one dollars when Tommytown finally threw up his hands in disgust. For all subsequent purchases, the auctioneer ruled, a bidder would have to bid at least fifty dollars more than the previous bidder. This had not been a rule before, simply because the Grangerford-Shepherdson Galleries had never before been witness to behavior as ungentlemanly as that between the put-on McAfee and Tommytown. Lucius D. Tommytown successfully bid for all the McAfee sculptures that followed the "Crystal Cave." Luthor, from his disguise in the back of the room, engineered the entire proceeding. Even the ersatz McAfee and Tommytown did not know it was Luthor for whom they were working. They were just a pair of off-Broadway actors looking to fill up a day with an extra gig, and Luthor paid better than scale.

By the time the jubilant Tommytown gallantly gave a depressed McAfee a ride to McAfee's hotel roof by helicopter and flew off to a hangar on the east side of town, everyone had had a fine time. The auctioneer had an unusual day. The process servers had at least been able to see Tommytown from across a row of people. The society and art reporters who attended the auction had a winning story. The art collectors had a good show. The Grangerford-Shepherdson Galleries had lots of publicity. Luthor had his sculptures back. And the pair of actors had their best payday of the year. Neither knew that the other was an actor. The man playing Tommytown had played him before, and was under the impression that although the real Tommytown liked the notoriety, a public appearance was simply too dangerous. The man playing McAfee had no idea why he was hired to do this, and cared less.

Lex Luthor now had sculptures that were actually an illusion caster, a weather controller, a sonic cannon, a chemical tracer, and a navigational compass for an interstellar vehicle which homes in on Earth's sun from halfway across the galaxy. Luthor had never been that far from home, but he did enjoy travel. The devices would all be shipped by the gallery to a warehouse upstate where they would sit until Luthor could be sure Superman did not know where they were. Then he would use them as he needed them. Meanwhile, still dressed in his rent-a-cop outfit, he would walk across town to his small apartment on Sixty-sixth Street. He could not go to the penthouse where his main headquarters were. He probably would not be able to go there at all this time out. He was not secure.

Superman had found out Luthor was Jeremy McAfee the artist. These things slip sometimes, Luthor realized. He could shed identities like disposable razors or used Band-Aids. He had no psychological dependence on Jeremy McAfee, so, for the benefit of the art world, he invented a story of the artist's strange and spectacular death by swinging into the steeple of an old Spanish church while dangling from a helicopter, and then falling two hundred feet to the ground, taking a large chunk of the church's roof with him. Not only would the story benefit the art world, but it would benefit Luthor. Stories like that, and displays like that of Tommytown and brother McAfee today would, for a time, cause the market price of a McAfee work of art to skyrocket. Whenever Luthor needed some spot cash now, he could simply throw together a few scraps, say it was done by Jeremy McAfee before his death—which would be true enough—and have somebody like Wainwright McAfee sell it to a museum or a collector somewhere for an outrageous sum.

It would probably have be a simple matter, had he chosen to do so, for Luthor to figure out what Superman's secret identity was. Luthor did not think the information would do him any good. He assumed that Superman had the same sort of setup as Luthor had with his made-to-order people, and that if he were exposed, Superman would simply create new aliases. Luthor had always assumed that Morgan Edge, the communications tycoon who had appeared out of nowhere sometime in the 1960s, was one of Superman's elaborate disguises. He was probably at least two or three other people Luthor had heard of. Maybe he had been Joe Namath. Possibly Bruce Wayne. In Smallville there was a kid named Pete Ross who always seemed to disappear when Superboy came around. Pete Ross was probably Superboy. Luthor had once considered that Superman could also be someone like Graig Nettles or Jim Rice, but a baseball player's schedule is much too demanding for someone who has to fly off unexpectedly at all hours of the day. He was probably Muhammad Ali. Or maybe even Edward Kennedy. None of that mattered.

What Luthor did not realize was that while his own aliases were tools and nothing else, Clark Kent was Superman's fetish and preoccupation. Kent was Superman's demon.

"We must have words, Lex Luthor," said the voice he heard from behind him.

Luthor was a block from the Grangerford-Shepherdson Galleries and he was about to slip a dime into the phone at the corner to call the penthouse. Still in his Pinkerton guard disguise, he decided to walk among the plow-piled snow to the next telephone and hope the owner of the voice would go away.

"That is not likely, Lex Luthor," the voice said, following him. "I will not be avoided."

Luthor walked a few more steps until a hand, the iciness of which he could feel through his coat, gripped one shoulder. Before Luthor could turn to face whoever it was, there arose in his pathway a shrouded human figure, far larger in its proportions than any dweller among men. And the hue of the skin of the figure was of the perfect whiteness of fresh snow.

It's Real

"I am called C. W. Saturn," the white figure said to Lex Luthor. "Do you know of me?"

"I have heard of C. W. Saturn," Luthor said, "and I have also heard of the Easter Bunny and the Tooth Fairy, but I don't generally see people dressed up as them making a scene on a public street. Aren't you afraid you're going to get arrested? I certainly am."

The demon, or apparition, or whatever it was, stood nearly on Luthor's toes, looking down into his face. Even its eyes were white. It had a big white widow's peak and hair that was swept back, a white goatee, and white flowing clothes over bleachy skin. Luthor scrunched up his eyes in order to make out the thing's features, but the face was so ghostly it seemed to glow.

"No one among the passersby sees me, Lex Luthor," the thing that called itself C. W. Saturn said in an eerie whisper, "only you. The only eccentric display they can witness is your own. You might

115

wish, therefore, to converse in a place hidden from the senses of the residents of this place."

It appeared to be true. People certainly were walking by as though there was nothing untoward happening in their icy way. Luthor thought of asking the woman making her way along the sidewalk if she saw a tall white-shrouded person with a widow's peak standing there, but he thought better of it. What if she saw nothing there? Worse, what if she recognized Luthor? It was fairly clear that the people on the street saw nothing. Then again, these people were Metropolitans.

"Please walk this way," Luthor suggested. Luthor led his demon to a small unused park a block away that was once a school yard. Now it was furnished only with broken bottles, pet droppings and structures suggesting the stationary parts of ancient playground equipment. Luthor and his spectre stood behind the ruins of a wooden dome-shaped jungle jim.

"So," Luthor said, "now prove it."

The big white thing pointed at the ground around Luthor, and as its white finger moved, a circle of flames surrounded the two where the finger pointed out the path of combustion.

"Oh!" Luthor started as though with surprise, lost his balance and fell onto the demon, who caught him.

"Very good, Lex Luthor," the apparition said. "Evidently you do know of me."

"Just a prudent safeguard," Luthor said, self-satisfied as all hell, as he untangled himself from the demon's grip.

"Prudent indeed," said the hollow voice, "so that I could have no claim to your immortal soul, having laid hands upon you before we transacted any agreement."

"I did a lot of reading on you before my last prison break, Saturn. I figured out that part of the Dracula legend traces back to you. As with the fictional vampire, a person must enter your power willingly, of his own accord, before you can claim his soul. You just put your hands on me before I made such an agreement, and now you forfeit any claim to me you may have had as a result of any agreement we make. Am I right?"

"Correct, although we still hold out hopes that you will join us when your time comes, Lex Luthor." There followed a horrible cavernous laugh that would have been more than worthy of Lamont Cranston. "May we talk business now, Lex Luthor? It is not yours, but the soul of another that I require."

Luthor wanted further proof of this entity's identity before the two could talk of business. Luthor was very prudent indeed, for there were things Luthor wanted that other men could not possibly have. He was as prudent as he was bold.

There was a time, years ago, when all young Lex Luthor wanted was to be President of the United States. This seemed an admirable enough route to immortality. For a little while in Smallville, everything Lex did—getting good grades in school, writing letters to the *Smallville Times-Reader* which were usually published, reading books by Arthur Schlesinger and Irving Wallace—was directed toward the end of someday being President. So the year of the Presidential primaries, when the senator from that state to the north came campaigning through Smallville, Lex decided to meet him.

The senator's idea, in this campaign, was to be identified with youth, and it seemed to the senator that there was nothing better for him to be seen with than a precocious teenager. The senator sent an advance man to Smallville to find him some precocious teenagers with whom to be seen.

"The commercial for the campaign will be filmed this coming Friday afternoon," the advance man told Miss Roberts's eighth-grade social studies class, "and your principal has been gracious enough to allow us to use this room after school. The senator will be coming right here, right where I'm standing."

The class suffered two or three seconds of undirected excitement before the advance man continued.

"So what I would like to do here today, with your teacher's permission, is pick four students from among you, and bring those four back here Friday at three-fifteen for a conversation on film with the senator."

"Oh, can I do it?" somebody said.

"Me, me, me," somebody else said.

"You want volunteers? I'll volunteer." There was no shortage of enthusiasm for the idea.

"What I'd like to do," the advance man continued, calming the group, "is find the four most informed students in the class and have them come. My idea is simply to have each of you take out a pen and a piece of paper"—Lex's desk was the first one to have the necessary equipment—"and write down the three questions you would most like to ask the senator. Put your name at the top of the page and list three questions. I'll look over the lot of them and I'll come back

117

tomorrow—tomorrow's Thursday, right?—I'll come back tomorrow and let you know which four of you will get to be on television with the next President. Fair enough?''

Lex thought up the three most pointed and relevant questions he could devise: Do you believe that we have a ''missile gap'' with the Russians? Do you think the owner of a restaurant should be required to serve a person he does not want to serve, if that person can afford to eat at the restaurant? Would you order American agents to try to overthrow the government of another country if the other country's government did not agree with us? If those three questions, well-rounded and issue-oriented, did not impress the advance man, Lex thought, then the guy didn't know his job.

The advance man happened to know his job very well, and he was very impressed with Lex's three questions. If Lex had been an adult the advance man might have asked him to lend his talents to the campaign. Nevertheless, the four students he chose to meet with the senator were Lana Lang, Pete Ross, Brad Herman and Clark Kent. Lex had no idea why.

''Hey, Clark!'' Lex called through the hallway during the four minutes between his social studies and physical education classes on Thursday. ''Clark, wait up.''

''What's up, Lex?''

''Lissen, Clark, lemme see your three questions, willya?''

''For the senator? Sure, Lex, they're in here somewhere.'' Clark held his pile of books in his left arm and riffled among the papers hanging out the ends with his right hand. Clark always seemed to carry more books than anyone else did. Lex ignored the fact that when Clark pulled the folded page with the questions out of his history book, he splattered his armload all over the hallway.

As Clark regrouped his books, Lex read the questions: What do you think of conservation? Do you think the Russians should get out of Cuba? Of all the laws you ever wrote, which one makes you the proudest?

Bland, Lex thought. Evidently Clark watched the news sometimes, maybe he even read a newspaper once in a while. But the questions were boring as cornflakes, just like Clark.

Lex simmered a bit as he walked with Clark to the gymnasium. He did not understand that all the senator wanted was to be seen with a bunch of wholesome-looking young people who would look at him admiringly while he gave them generalized answers to nonspecific questions. All Lex understood was that this was unfair, just as many things turned out to be unfair when you played by rules that other

118

people laid down for you. Of course the senator thought the Russians should get out of Cuba, Lex thought. Everybody except the Russians thought the Russians should get out of Cuba. What kind of a dumb question was that?

In the wrestling room, where the gym class went that day, Lex Luthor paired off with Clark Kent and played by the rules, even though he threw Clark around the room a little. Having demonstrated to Clark that even wholesome-looking and bland kids like Clark sometimes get knocked on when they play by the rules, Lex was able to ask his friend a civil question.

"You're an old farm boy," Lex said. "How much do you know about cows?"

"Cows? They give milk."

"Oh, that's where it comes from. I always thought it grew in those little wax cartons. I mean what they're like—the cows. Like, for example, how do you keep them from kicking you when you milk them?"

Evidently, Lex learned, the productivity of a cow depended on its sedentary nature. The less a cow moved or became excited, the more of its energy it was able to use in the production of milk. It was very easy to excite a cow.

His plan was simple. That afternoon after school, Lex would rig up a few little remote-control milking gadgets out of party balloons and wire mesh which he would control electronically by altering the wiring in his father's remote television controls. That was the easy part. Tomorrow, shortly before dawn, he would sneak into the Herman barn, which was the closest cow stall to the school, and pick out two hefty cows to play with. Lex would wear Indian war paint and dance around in the barn waving two flashlights. That should scare most of the milk out of them. Their innards would be all tensed up and they'd have constipation of the milk glands. When old Leon Herman came to milk them that morning, they'd be all stopped up and save most of their milk for that afternoon. Then in the afternoon, when they were all relaxed and bloated, Lex would gently walk them from their grazing field through the fence to the school. He could get them there without anyone seeing him if he did it as soon as the first classes let out for the day; all the spare teachers would be on the far side of the building making sure everyone in the first and second grades got into their buses all right. Lex would slip his little balloon devices onto the cows' udders and get the cows into Miss Roberts's classroom before the goody-goody kids got there with the senator.

Then, hiding in a supply closet, Lex would press his remote

control device, pointing it through the closet door at the cows just when the advance man was likely to be the most embarrassed in front of his boss. The signal to the balloons would squeeze the cows' nipples and spurt unpasteurized milk all over the classroom floor. If Lex was lucky and the camera technicians had set up their equipment before the senator or anyone else got there, Lex could work it so the senator's fiasco was on film.

That morning, just before dawn, a boy in Indian war paint, carrying a flashlight in either hand and a handful of wired party balloons in his pocket, stole into the Hermans' cow barn. He slipped through the barn door, picked out a corpulent pair of sleeping cows, and shone a flashlight into both of their faces.

Just then, from the vicinity of the barn entrance which Lex's back was now facing, came an awful crash of metal and rock and clanging and a human voice howling in pain. All the cows woke up and mooed for all they were worth. Through the gauzed-over window at the rear of the barn Lex saw a hallway light in the big Herman farmhouse flash on. He spun to face the barn door.

"I wasn't doing anything, I swear!" Lex edged closer to the figure near the door, scared witless.

"Lex?" the boy's voice said.

"No, it's not Lex. Lex who? It's just—who is that? Is that you?"

"Yeah. Sorry, Lex," Clark Kent said, scratching his feet on the ground like an embarrassed bull.

"You turd, Kent. What's with you?"

"I just saw you walking around. I got up early, see? And I figured you had something neat to do. You're always doing all this neat stuff. I had to walk Chief Parker's dog because the chief had to go to a convention, see? So when I brought the dog back and saw you in war paint, I followed you here because I thought maybe you were going to do some neat stuff. What kind of neat stuff you think you're going to do?"

"A rain dance, you dunce."

"Can I watch? You know about—"

"Oh!" Seeing the porch light come on and the door start to open, Lex shoved Clark aside and ran out of the barn.

"Hey," Clark called after him with as vacant a voice as he could find, "you dropped a balloon."

Mr. Herman appeared at the barn door, however, as quickly as Lex had disappeared through it, and he wanted an explanation for Clark's presence.

"I was just walking around," Clark said, "and I really like

120

Superman (Christopher Reeve) shares a tender moment with reporter Lois Lane (Margot Kidder).

Lex Luthor (Gene Hackman) and Eve Teschmacher (Valerie Perrine) make a startling discovery in the Fortress of Solitude.

Clark Kent (Christopher Reeve) attempts to rescue Lois Lane (Margot Kidder) at Niagara Falls.

The three villains from Krypton, Ursa (Sarah Douglas), Zod (Terence Stamp), and Non (Jack O'Halloran) prepare to enter the small town of Houston, Idaho.

The three phantom-zone villains, Non (Jack O'Halloran), Zod (Terence Stamp), and Ursa (Sarah Douglas) arrive at the offices of the *Daily Planet*.

Superman (Christopher Reeve) and Zod (Terence Stamp) square off in Metropolis.

The phantom-zone villains Non (Jack O'Halloran), Zod (Terence Stamp), and Ursa (Sarah Douglas) don't believe in doorknobs.

Reporter Lois Lane (Margot Kidder) comforts her editor Perry White (Jackie Cooper).

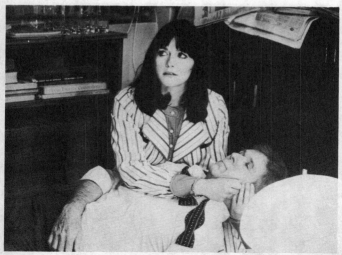

Otis (Ned Beatty) and Lex Luthor (Gene Hackman) reminisce about the good old days.

Ursa (Sarah Douglas) threatens Lois Lane (Margot Kidder) as Zod (Terence Stamp), Non (Jack O'Halloran), and Lex Luthor (Gene Hackman) negotiate with Superman (Christopher Reeve).

The three villains from Krypton, Zod (Terence Stamp), Ursa (Sarah Douglas), and Non (Jack O'Halloran) wreak havoc on the moon.

Eve Teschmacher (Valerie Perrine) helps Lex Luthor (Gene Hackman) escape from prison.

Ursa (Sarah Douglas) demonstrates that she has the same super powers as the Man of Steel (Christopher Reeve).

General Zod (Terence Stamp) forces the President (E.G. Marshall) to read a statement on television.

Lois Lane (Margot Kidder) goes for a spin in the sky with Superman (Christopher Reeve).

General Zod (Terence Stamp) in the Fortress of Solitude.

Jackie Cooper portrays Perry White, the editor of the *Daily Planet*.

barns. Dad doesn't have a barn anymore and I just came around because I like barns. Isn't that all right?''

It was not all right, as it happened, since none of the cows yielded up very much milk that morning. Meanwhile, Lex waited through his classes for most of that Friday for someone to drag him into the office of the principal or the police chief or the mayor or the senator—that would be nice—or someone in authority, so that Lex could be chewed out for his aborted plan. Lex did not see Clark until fifth period and Miss Roberts's social studies class The room was cluttered with film equipment.

Clark was downcast. Lex sniffed a hello and got a less articulate response from Clark. Then Miss Roberts said, simply, ''We are going to need another person for the group who is to meet with the senator this afternoon. Jacqui, will you be free after school today?''

''Boy, I sure will!'' the girl in the fourth row said. ''When? Where? How?''

Immediately, Lex caught on. Was Clark Kent a total moron, he wondered, or some self-sacrificing nincompoop? It did not matter He had not even mentioned that Lex was in the barn that night. He took the entire blame for scaring the cows milkless. He had probably even pocketed the wired balloon that Lex had left behind, so that suspicion would not fall on the young inveterate tinkerer Clark's inadequate explanation for his presence in the barn—in light of his stature as a model bland and wholesome-looking young midwesterner—had brought no more punishment than his exclusion from the great man's acquaintance. What a guy—the jerk!

On the way out of that class was where and when Lex said to Clark, ''I might've forgot to tell you this before, Kent, but don't trust me.''

''Wasn't planning on it,'' Clark said.

''Am I supposed to trust you?'' Lex Luthor asked the creature who claimed to be the arch-devil of cross-cultural fable.

''Certainly not,'' the apparition answered. ''Simply adhere to your half of any bargain we strike, if we can come to an agreement on terms.''

''Ah, yes. The bargain. I hope it doesn't involve my having to believe that you are who you say you are.''

''That is not necessary either. I am aware that you are a cautious enough man to feel comfortable simply adhering to the rules we set. First tell me—assuming I am who I say I am—what would you like from me?''

"That's simple. I want you to teach me enough about the physical laws of your realm—the Netherworld or whatever they're calling it these days—to construct a cheap, practical source of energy from the interface of the two worlds."

"You want to run turbines and generators by harnessing the clash between Earth and Hell, the same way a dam harnesses the clash between rivers or a windmill harnesses the clash between land and sky—"

"Or the way a nuclear reactor directs the energy from the conflict between Order and Chaos."

"That is simple enough. In return, I would like you to procure for me a lock of Superman's hair. Do we have a bargain?"

Overachieving

In the morning, while swimming through the twilight land between awake and asleep, one can sense what sort of a day it is going to be. From this interface between the two states of consciousness, one can gather, with a little effort, enough psychic energy to get a sense of the next several hours of one's life. It is really possible. Anyone can do it simply by being careful to catch one's self before one is quite shed of sleep. Superman did it all the time when he woke up in Clark Kent's apartment after his daily thirty or forty minutes of sleep.

This April morning, however, as Superman was lying in twilight, Clark Kent's telephone rang next to his head. Telephones and other such machines inflicted the life of Clark Kent just as they inflicted the lives of most people Superman knew.

Several blocks away, linked by an electronic arc to Clark Kent's machine, Morgan Edge had a similar machine of his own. Into his own machine and out of Clark's machine, Edge said, "Kent, did I wake you? Too bad."

"Fine, thank you," Superman said in a groggy version of Clark Kent's voice, "and yourself?"

"It's Edge, Kent, and I called to tell you this could be the most important day of your career."

I get one of those every week and a half or so, one of Superman's cerebral hemispheres said to the other. "Oh, sorry, Mr. Edge," Clark Kent fawned. "Did I wake you?"

"Think now, Kent. Do you remember dialing?"

"Oh, you called me. I'm sorry."

"Don't let it happen again. I want you to grab a pad and write this down, Kent. Do it before you fall back to sleep and forget about it. Got that?"

"Just a second. I'll see if I can find a pencil."

"No no, scratch that. Just get up and—"

Superman dropped the receiver of the telephone loudly between the night table and the mattress frame in such a way as to make it dangle on its cord and continue to make noises in Edge's ear while Superman walked to the far end of the room and called, "Just a second, Mr. Edge. . . . be right there . . . no problem . . . I've got the pad," and then Superman gently tossed a small chair into the night table.

Several blocks away Morgan Edge bit through his first cigarette holder of the morning and slam-dunked his third cigarette of the morning into his office wastebasket.

With telescopic and X ray vision Superman watched Edge throw out the cigarette. Satisfied that he had sufficiently gotten back at Edge for disturbing his rare chance at sleep and simultaneously extended the executive's life by about fifteen seconds, Superman put on his glasses.

"Sorry, Mr. Edge," Clark Kent said, "but I guess I'm not quite awake yet. I knocked over a chair."

"Sounded like you knocked over the Seventh Fleet. Listen, Kent, forget the stupid note pad. I want you to get dressed right away. Drink some coffee. Better—swallow a few spoonfuls of instant coffee out of the jar. It'll work faster. The copter is on the way to the roof of your building. There are four major stories in town this morning and you're going to cover them yourself. You'll anchor the news tonight from your remote location using the copter's equipment. Coyle and Lana will take up what slack you leave behind at the studio, if any."

"Hold it, Mr. Edge. Excuse me. Four major stories? What are the stories?"

"They all broke in the past hour. The pilot, what's his name,

124

has your working orders. You just follow him wherever he takes you and be lucid for the camera."

"I'd appreciate it if you told me what the stories were, sir."

"Oh, I don't know. Where is that sheet of—yes, hello, right here. Let's see," Edge said as he sat at his desk and read from the list he held. Superman could not see through Edge's chair to the desk. There was probably just enough lead derivative in the petrochemical stuffing of the chair to block the X rays. "Let's see now, a collapsed brownstone on the Upper West Side."

"Yes?" Clark found the building across town through his apartment window. There was no one in immediate mortal danger. "What else?"

"A fairly destructive minor earthquake along Fourteenth Street A subway derailment under Christopher Circle on the D-line"

There were no major injuries at either place. There were some due in a few minutes, though, if Superman did not do something soon.

"And there's a tramway car hanging by a fraying cable over the Outerborough Bridge."

"Oh, my Lord," Clark Kent said before he blew himself out the window.

"Hello? Hello?"

The cameraman in the helicopter that was approaching the roof of 344 Clinton Street considered himself very lucky. He had just finished loading and checking out the videotape cartridge in his videotape recorder when Superman slowed his flight enough for the cameraman to see him. The hero did not want to upset the air around the helicopter as he flew by, so the cameraman was able to whip the recorder into position and film the Man of Steel whizzing off toward the Fifty-ninth Street Tramway.

"Turn the chopper around," the cameraman ordered the pilot.

"That's Mr. Kent's building right in front of us. I know where I'm going," the pilot said.

"I know. I know. Clark's not even on the roof yet, and that was Superman who just flew by us."

"You seeing things?"

"No. I swear, I just saw him flying off toward the river Didn't you see him?"

"I was too busy flying this rig. You sure it was him?"

The helicopter was beginning to dip in the direction of the apartment building's roof. The main rotors shifted on their bearings and the bird that bore the decal WGBS FLYING NEWSROOM rose back toward the sky. Its smaller rear rotor revved faster and it spun around to the direction of the river. In less than a minute the WGBS news cameraman could see the figure of a flying man approach a pillar of smoke hanging over the bridge. The man in the helicopter turned on his videotape recorder and pointed it in the right direction and hoped Clark Kent would not have to wait on the roof too long early in this unseasonably cold morning in April.

Superman had sized up the situation seconds earlier from Clark Kent's apartment. There were seven people in the enclosed, heated tramway car. One of the two cables that held it as it made its trip over the river into the inner borough of the city had snapped. The car hung from the second cable, thirty meters above the bridge, and that cable was supposed to be strong enough to support the car in an emergency. It was not. The electric wires that carried the heat to the car from a generator in the outer borough were also fraying as a result of the first cable's snapping. The heating system was still working, but the fraying wire had ignited the paint on the outside of the steel cable car. If the paint fire reached the transformer on the roof of the car, it would explode. Meanwhile, the smoke from the fire outside the car was blocking the air filtration system into the car and of the seven people inside, only two were conscious. Superman knew exactly what he had to do.

From several hundred meters away Superman blew the pillar of poisonous smoke off the surface of the cable car and cleared the air filtration system. He shot a searing beam of heat from his eyes to the smoldering wire that had set off the hot smoky fire on the exterior of the car. The dangling wire fell, swirling and leaving a trail of light like a Fourth-of-July sparkler. The fire was gone, but at least for the instant, the heated air was still there. The air was still hot enough to push the transformer to critical heat.

With a burst of speed, Superman closed the remaining distance between himself and the tramway car. He ripped the transformer from its perch, stuffed it under his arm like a football, and shot upward into the sky. As he let go of the transformer and it continued to rise on its momentum, enough of the cable's frayed strands of wire snapped so that what was left of the single cable could no longer hold the dangling car. Superman arced downward as the hissing piece of machinery rose above him and, the remaining strands of cable having wrenched apart, the car with seven people aboard fell free.

Inside the car the air had cleared a bit and when the smoke dissipated and the two conscious passengers saw Superman—or a red-and-blue flash of light that must have been Superman—streak past the window, one of them had the presence of mind to shove out the emergency exit window and let the poisonous air inside clear. Seconds afterward, as the cable car wrenched downward, one of the five who had been overcome by the fumes opened her eyes. Neither the two women nor the one man who was awake when the cable snapped knew that they were in free fall. What they did know, as Superman held the cable in one hand and the car itself by five finger holes he had made in its steel roof and lowered it gently to the sidewalk at the corner of Fifty-Ninth Street and Polis Avenue, was that somewhere half a kilometer overhead, there was a burst that sounded like an extended rifle shot. As the sound of the explosion echoed off the walls of the nearest buildings, the muffled sound was joined by the splash of scores of tiny chunks of the shattered transformer hitting the river. While his hands and his flight softened the descent of the seven passengers, Superman's breath diverted the fall of the three charred chunks of transformer from appointments with the rush-hour jam on the bridge.

The passengers who were conscious hauled the others out onto the sidewalk, and two sat with their heads between their knees as policemen gave the four unconscious ones mouth-to-mouth resuscitation. Two ambulances were making their ways, with police motorcycle escorts, through the morning rush to the scene. Superman flew off to the northwest, followed by the WGBS Flying Newsroom that had hovered like a honeybee through the scene.

The WGBS helicopter landed on the roof of 344 Clinton Street where the pilot and cameraman found Clark Kent standing in the shelter of the roof stairway door, lost in a massive overcoat. He was hopping on one foot, then the other, and breathing condensed vapor the way a dragon breathes fire. The rotors of the copter continued to beat as the cameraman rushed out of the cab to find Clark and realized that it had not been this cold in weeks.

"Sorry we're late, Clark."

"What?" Clark yelled over the sound of the rotors.

"Sorry we're late."

"I can't hear you."

"Did you have a long wait?"

"Yes," Clark said, "I got out here late."

"Superman came by. We had to follow him. We got it all on tape for you."

"What?"

"Superman's on tape."

127

"Whose cape?"

"What?"

"Is it heated in the copter?"

"What?"

"Then let's get out of the cold."

The flying newsroom beat in the direction of Fourteenth Street where the earthquake had been. Clark knew that the extent of the damage included several broken plate glass windows, some roof ornaments shaken free to the ground and some broken dishes. Thirty or forty people had been shaken awake by the quake, but that was the extent of personal injury. There would be no aftershock and the damage would not be lost to the camera before this afternoon.

"Not that way, Jake," Clark told the pilot. "Christopher Circle and the subway derailment first."

"That's not what Mr. Edge said, Mr. Kent."

"It'll be my responsibility. Christopher Circle is a more immediate story."

"How do you know?"

"My nose for news," Clark Kent said and meant it.

At Christopher Circle there was a crowd surrounding a police line that kept them back from the subway entrance. The crowd got bigger as the WGBS helicopter lowered Clark Kent to the street from the height of a small building. The cameraman was supposed to set up his equipment while Clark milled through the crowd looking for someone to interview on camera. As Clark and his notebook waded toward the subway entrance, the crowd ignored him and followed the helicopter as it landed on the roof of the museum in the center of Christopher Circle so that the cameraman could get his equipment to the street. Clark had assiduously cultivated the capacity to be ignored, even while pursuing the most intriguing of enterprises. There was simply nothing interesting about the way he climbed to the ground from a hovering helicopter.

Slipping out the far end of the crowd, the journalist sprinted at an agonizingly slow thirty-five miles per hour into the lobby of the Paramount Building which looked down on Christopher Circle. In the lobby a crowd of people sardined their way into an elevator and as the door closed on them, an X-ray beam caused the latch to trip, opening a door whose elevator was two floors below in the sub-basement. Clark Kent dove upward through the shaft, and before the door was fully closed again below him, Superman burst out the trap door on the roof, fifty stories high.

"Look! Up in the sky!" somebody called from the ground.

If not for the beating rotors of the helicopter, Clark Kent's cameraman might have heard the call in time to record the hero's downward plunge into the subway entrance. He missed that, but he would catch the exit.

The *truck* of a subway car is the heavy bed on which the passenger-carrying container of the car sits. The truck is made up of the car's eight steel wheels, the axles of each wheel, and a rectangular carriage into which the main body of the car is bolted. On the D-train heading downtown through Christopher Circle this morning, the second-to-last of eleven cars derailed when its truck split up the middle for the length of the car. The car jumped up somewhere in the tunnel between Christopher Circle and Sixty-Sixth Street, disconnecting itself from the nine cars that it had been following. The eleventh car, the one behind it, bashed into its rear wall and molded its front end into the impossibly creased shape of the derailed car. The two cars were now locked together like two pieces of some three-dimensional jigsaw puzzle.

Thirty-one people in the derailed car and forty-two in the one behind had suffered varying degrees of terror for periods ranging from four seconds to several minutes. Miraculously, no one was hurt more than Edna Lerner, whose ankle was sprained, swelling to roughly twice its normal diameter, when the crash flung her against a retaining pole for passengers who had to stand. The only two persons in the two cars who were still terrified were Luis Izasa and Naomi Greensleeve who communicated with each other between the two cars by two-way radio. They were still terrified because they were the conductors and the only people among the seventy-three trapped here under Metropolis who knew the extent of their predicament.

Each subway car had two sets of walls, one inner wall and one outer wall. The inner wall, as were the aluminum windowpanes and doors, was completely insulated from the outside wall. The outside walls of both trains were charged with enough electricity to kill a person instantly. When the first car derailed, it skidded along the track until the hull of the car rested on a chunk of broken truck and the electrified third rail. The outer wall of the car behind was fused into the derailed car's outer wall and was thus electrified as well. Luis Izasa made a show of laryngitis for the passengers when he noticed this, and yelled through a small opening to the rear car for his colleague, Naomi Greensleeve, to communicate with him by radio so that the passengers could not hear.

Neither, it turned out, was able to contact anyone outside the subway cars by radio, and both concluded that it was impossible for anyone to leave either car without climbing or sliding over electrically charged metal. It was to their credit that they managed to convince their passengers to wait patiently until help arrived. They could not imagine what sort of help short of a drill through the roof and a powerful crane could be provided by the Transit Authority. Both conductors simply waited in private terror until (1) the passengers realized the nature of their problem; or (2) a miracle came to pass. This was Metropolis, after all.

"Please sit down and hold tightly to the nearest stationary object, ladies and gentlemen," the miracle called from in front of the derailed car.

Standing on the tracks was a large human form, glowing with electricity as white as fresh-blown snow. Everyone aboard knew who it was. As he hopped up over the roof of the derailed train, passengers saw Superman for a moment without the blinding glow. Then passengers in both cars heard the sound of metal prying free from metal. Seventy-three people wrapped white knuckles around chairs, armrests and standing bars while, gently, bit by bit, Superman worked the two subway cars apart without damaging the insulation that kept the interiors from burning the occupants of the cars to ash.

The hero pulled the cars free of each other, and the one whose truck was still intact rolled backward a few paces as they wrenched apart. Superman dropped from the ceiling of the tunnel to the track and pulled the misshapen front end off the rear car as though it were the top of a milk bottle. "Conductor?" he called, folding up the double wall of steel like a sheet of scrap paper.

"Yes?" Naomi Greensleeve said to her miracle.

As he folded and crushed the sheet of metal, it occasionally brushed against the electrified rail and Superman glowed for those instants with white-hot energy. Clark Kent would have liked to get that on camera if Clark Kent were here, but he wasn't.

"Miss—um, Greensleeve," he said, looking at her lapel tag, "this car is no longer electrified, so as soon as I clear the track in front of you it will be relatively safe for you to lead your passengers along the tunnel to the Christopher Circle station. It's less than a block down the tunnel, but be careful to tell them how to avoid the third rail."

"Uhh." Naomi Greensleeve nodded and turned around to face passengers who were nearly as awestruck as she. After a moment, she swallowed slowly and said, "He called me by name. Right? He said 'Miss Greensleeve.' You heard him, didn't you?"

"Maybe you should have your first name legally changed to 'Miss,' eh?" one jealous commuter suggested.

"Hold on tight now," Superman called into the electrified car in front.

He lifted the rear end up from the damaged truck as his body flashed and crackled with light. He had a deadly white halo over his whole form as he hopped between the truck and the elevated passenger container, lifted the body of the subway car over his head, and balanced it on his back, flying forward, until he deposited it, passengers and all, on the Christopher Circle platform almost a block away. He doubled back and leaned the steel pieces of the broken truck against the tunnel wall, and he was gone before Naomi Greensleeve began to help the passengers past the two halves of the truck toward the platform.

Clark Kent and his cameraman were on the platform waiting for her and her charges. "He said my name, I heard him. Tell the man he said my name," was all the heroine subway conductor could say to Clark's microphone.

"All right," Clark told the cameraman, after what Clark decided was the requisite number of expressions of relief/gratitude/indignation/wonder from the people who had been in and around the two subway cars during the crisis, "back up to the copter."

From the bubble front of the airborne helicopter, Clark got a better view of the collapsed building on the Upper West Side than he had gotten from his apartment window. As he had seen earlier, there were no casualties as a result of the collapse. There was, in fact, only one person caught inside the building when it fell; and in an evident fluke, the woman's second-floor studio was the only room in the building completely untouched by the disaster. As far as Clark could tell, while neighbors and fire trucks with their ladders swarmed over the sidewalk trying to make some sense out of the pile of rubble, the young girl sat comfortably on a couch reading a paperback edition of *Ragtime* by E. L. Doctorow. She could not leave her studio apartment, since the fire escape was gone, the hallway floor was piled up in crumbs under the floors from above, and the doorway was caked with ancient building materials. No one among the crowd gathered out front knew that there was anyone in the building, and nearly everyone there was horrified at the possibility that there might be. The young woman's window faced an alley and it was inaccessible to anyone who did not fly.

Clark was quite startled, now that traces of lead in building walls no longer blurred his view, to see that the woman sitting among the ruins reading pseudohistory was Kristin Wells.

The WGBS Flying Newsroom alit on the building across the street. This time the cameraman decided to set up on the roof facing

131

the shattered brownstone while Clark went down to ground level with his wireless microphone. Between eight and nine seconds after Clark and his microphone disappeared from his cameraman and pilot behind the rooftop door, Superman crashed through Kristin Wells's window.

She looked up from her book with a vacant stare. Unnaturally vacant. She looked at the glass around Superman's feet, closed and opened her eyes once and said, "Oh, that's all right. I've got a carpet sweeper." She stood and walked toward the door of her broom closet.

"Miss Wells?" Superman took her arm. "Are you all right? None of the falling debris hit you, did it?"

"Debris?"

He looked at her blank eyes and through them. If only he could decode the mess of circuits and connectives in the human brain, he thought. That would save a lot of questions.

But as he looked into her eyes they changed their expression. They widened. The tear ducts were sucked dry in an instant. They went from blue green to a chalky gray. Suddenly they were different eyes.

"You like my handiwork, Superman?" a voice hollower than Kristin's asked him.

"Your handiwork?"

"The earthquake, I thought, was a masterpiece of surgical destruction, though I admit the tramway was a touch sloppy. But the subway car was very inventive and I think this building's new configuration is the best of all of them. Do you not agree?"

"Who are you?" Superman still stared at the eyes.

"Who is Kristin Wells? Is that what you want to know?"

"No. Who are you?"

"Someone you are going to get to know better."

"I have no use for riddles." But as Superman said that, the eyes resumed their ocean color, more clearly awake than when he had come in.

"Superman?"

"Yes?"

"Have you been here long?"

"No, not long. Who are you? Are you all right?"

"Don't we know each other?"

"Do we?"

"I'm Kristin Wells, a metaphor in the mind of God, as are we all."

Superman took Kristin to a nearby hospital, from which she was released within an hour. She had arranged perfect health for the occasion.

132

Again, the Journal

At last, I have taken the identity of the girl
Kristin Wells. I will no longer have to relinquish
control of the mortal's mind, even for brief
periods, and I shall put her body through its
physical habits only once more. This will be the final
entry she makes in her precious journal.

She jogged her last half mile this morning.

She lay down in her bed for an hour today
for the last time, and even then she was not allowed
to sleep.

Tomorrow she will resign from both of her sec-
retarial jobs.

She has been weaned from her normal routine,
a routine that was fairly new to her when I began
the weaning process. Her body is adapting, for as long
as it will function, to a new routine—my routine.

Some weeks ago we—she and I—began by bringing to pass a number of emergency situations with which Superman was moved to deal. These included a ground tremor, two mechanical disasters and the collapse of the building in which my hostess body and I had taken up residence.

We currently reside in a small apartment in the building inhabited by Lois Lane, one of the women from whom Kristin Wells will soon terminate her employment. These past weeks we have extended our power over the face of this world. In all cases, as planned, Superman has moved to avert a near disaster.

In Shoreham, Long Island, Superman compensated for an excessive nuclear reaction that threatened to destroy that part of the Atlantic coast.

In the Marianas Trench I awoke a hibernating sea creature whose interrupted hundred-year sleep caused it to be hungry for the creatures—most of them human—on board an oil tanker which Superman saved before he put the creature back into its undersea cavern.

In Antarctica I caused a group of human hunters to discover the secret nesting ground of millions of endangered seals so that Superman had to build the animals a more secluded home.

In the sea south of Singapore I threatened a shipload of homeless refugees with a rising island of rock and Superman raised the boat over the menace.

I have caused twins in their mothers' wombs to cease separation and to be born joined at inconvenient parts of their bodies. I have coerced world leaders to greet crises while their mental and emotional perspectives were clouded. I have brought about malfunction in the controls of weapons of holocaust such as nuclear warheads and laboratories of cancer and plague research. I have compromised the world's natural balance, and the mechanisms men have raised to augment that balance.

In all these cases, as planned, Superman has thwarted the onset of chaos. He will continue to do so, but he is growing weary.

It will be after I destroy the creation he values beyond all else, beyond even his own realization, that I will tempt him beyond even his ability to resist. My prey has had several busy weeks. He will soon be busier.

C. W. Saturn/Kristin Wells
At the Onset of a Frigid May

Skvrsky's Plague

Along with the fires, earthquakes, mechanical malfunctions, oceanic upheavals, uncommon belligerance of national leaders, an ominous spate of unusual births and birth defects—all of which contributed to a worldwide sense of malaise and possibly impending doom—there was the Itching Sickness. No one seemed to know very much about the Itching Sickness except for Dr. David Skvrsky. Everyone knew about Dr. David Skvrsky.

Skvrsky was one of those rare men, a few of whom show up in a generation, who seem to the world to be a vestige of a bygone era. No one could agree with anyone else, however, as to precisely in which bygone era Skvrsky belonged. In fact, for all his individuality, inventiveness, intrigue, for all the swash in his buckle, the mustachioed Skvrsky belonged to no age but his own. Above all, David Skvrsky was a physician, a man of twentieth-century reason and values.

Skvrsky was considered, in circles both informed and otherwise, to be the greatest diagnostician in the world. There was the story of how Skvrsky had created a stir when he turned up unexpectedly at a party in Washington, D.C., where, after noticing the grip of a welcoming handshake, the doctor told the Vice President of the United States that he had a calcium deposit on his shoulder that would have to be removed. Another time, while looking out the window of a passenger plane, Skvrsky had supposedly determined from the rhythmic wobbles the plane was making as it passed through some clouds that the pilot had an infection in his inner ear and that the copilot should take over the controls before the pilot tried to land the plane. There was the incident not long go when Skvrsky predicted, on the basis of a photograph of the Soviet president in *Newsweek,* that an agreement on the SALT II treaty would be delayed so that the communist leader could recover from the stroke he would suffer sometime during the coming week.

As far as anyone could tell, Skvrsky spent most of his time out of the public eye's range of vision, being spotted occasionally at various locations around the world, honing his skills in medical research. This made him mysterious and thus more interesting when he periodically broke his anonymity with a public pronouncement. Often, other doctors were inclined to trust his judgment because they envied what they supposed to be his life-style.

A CARE volunteer swore he saw Skvrsky in Nicaragua after the devastating earthquake there, dressed like a seedy Roy Rogers, overseeing a neighborhood disaster clinic set up in a church in the ravaged city of Managua.

A group of West African villagers whose farmland had been reclaimed by the expanding desert told a French newsman that a man named David who fit Skvrsky's description had treated some of the village children for malnutrition and put the chief in touch with the national government's relocation administration.

More recently, a boatload of overcrowded but unanimously healthy Vietnamese refugees floated unannounced into San Francisco Bay with the story of how the miracle-working physician had dropped from a helicopter onto their deck somewhere in the south Pacific, examined ailing passengers and took blood samples. Then he synthesized, from a gel produced under the gills of sea bass, a serum to combat a virus that was sweeping the boat. Soon afterward, the health ministers of sixteen countries in Asia and North America received identical manila envelopes stuffed with formulas and explanations in their respective languages, detailing nearly a hundred cures, treatments and foods that could be made from this plentiful sea bass gel.

And so forth.

Skvrsky had been reported doing one thing or another this week in diverse parts of the world. Burma, Sri Lanka, Afghanistan, Togo,

Colombia, Senegal, the Dominican Republic, Byelorussia, Lichtenstein and other places turned up, in just about that order, in a wild itinerary of Skvrsky sightings. A free-lance foreign correspondent from London named George Laderbush noticed, according to the "People" section of *Time* magazine, that someone claimed to have seen Skvrsky in each of those countries immediately following a reasonably reliable report of the outbreak of the Itching Sickness in each place.

Four days earlier in Reykjavik where, the day before, Superman had caught a toddler falling from a hotel window, there were three reports of Itching Sickness. Laderbush went there immediately, and yesterday's *Daily News* carried a story by a European stringer named John Hughes to the effect that Hughes's sometime collaborator Laderbush had run into Skvrsky in a hospital lobby there. According to the Hughes report, the only quotable phrase Skvrsky uttered to Laderbush was, "Can't you see I'm busy?"

Meanwhile, through the courtesy of some force whose pattern only Superman was beginning to recognize, there had been plenty of short-lived phenomena of interest to scientists this week. The small staff of the Center for the Study of Short-Lived Phenomena, which occupied one floor of an old university building in uptown Metropolis, was busy enough this week. No one was prepared when Dr. David Skvrsky, in a Livingstonesque bush jacket and a three-day growth of whiskers, appeared at the head of the stairs and demanded the use of a telephone.

A young biologist trying to come up with some rational explanation for the strange red coloring that had lately appeared in the Nile River was summarily taken off a phone in favor of the eminent man. Within twenty minutes, Skvrsky was assured by the Under Secretary of Health and Human Services in Washington, that he would have all the federal money he needed to study and cure the Itching Sickness.

The illness had never been fatal so far, but the symptoms were nothing short of horrifying, and death was theoretically possible. It started, in each of its supposedly verified cases, with a severe form of eczema of the scalp. No matter what the patient's genetic background or natural hair condition, dandruff began to fall like snowflakes. The skin began to get scaly, and the condition spread quickly—in less than two hours in some cases—over the entire surface of the body. If the patient was not hospitalized, restrained and injected with massive doses of pain killer immediately, he or she was driven to scratch off two layers of skin. There were three cases, reported on three different continents, where those who had the disease scratched off their hair down to the follicles over the entire surfaces of their heads. Within

139

two days, whether or not he or she was restrained and hospitalized, the patient resembled a vampire left out in the sun too long.

After four days, the Itching Sickness simply went away, often leaving nightmarish scars behind. It did not seem to be communicable between humans; there was no known virus or natural abnormality that seemed to cause it; there was no apparent reason for it to disappear after four days. No one but Skvrsky had any idea why it popped up in the far-flung and diverse places it appeared. Skvrsky said that he had an idea of the disease's source, but that it was no more than an idea.

At the Center for the Study of Short-Lived Phenomena, Skvrsky was brisk and oppressively competent. In the main reception room there were a collection of cluttered and disheveled cabinets, a secretary-receptionist at a small desk, enough folding chairs to seat all eleven staff members who were generally in the building, and a blackboard with chalk. Within three minutes of the end of his telephone call to the Department of Health, Education and Welfare, Skvrsky assembled the entire staff and held their complete attention.

"I have prepared a list," Skvrsky began, "of the reported locations of the so-called Itching Sickness incidences during these past six weeks. I also have another longer list of cases which I have personally learned of through various contacts in parts of the world normally inaccessible to the American public. I have mimeographed the documentation for you. You will please hand these out to everyone, my dear. Thank you. As you can see from page six of my report . . . I said page six of my report, young man, and it might be appropriate for you to turn there in order to perpetuate the illusion that you are paying attention to me . . . as you can see, the two most serious cases of outbreak occurred this past week in the cities of Shanghai and Medina, two locations all but totally cut off from Western contact. Those of you who have seen fit to browse ahead of my fascinating narrative have doubtless encountered some consternation at finding a day-by-day account of Superman's known whereabouts during a period roughly thirty-six hours preceeding the disease's appearances. On page eleven . . . that is page eleven, young man. You'd better keep up because we're easing on into the exciting climax now . . . is a chronological correlation between Superman's presence and the outbreak of the disease. Apart from some predictable gaps in the data, you—even the gentleman over there in the flowered shirt, I suspect—can deduce from the information here that the disease's appearance consistently follows by approximately thirty-six hours the appearance by Superman in that area.

"You will see, for example, that in Shanghai seven days ago

Superman, according to an associate of mine in the Chinese Ministry of Health, saved the lives of several score people when the walls of the sixth floor of a nine-story hospital building mysteriously disintegrated. I of course have only speculation to lead me to an explanation of why the sixth floor wall disintegrated, but I can surmise with relative certainty that Superman is carrying the Itching Sickness, because five days ago thirty people in that Shanghai hospital, including two lab technicians and four doctors, came down with it. I have reason to believe that the Kryptonian is carrying the disease in his indestructible hair and, immune to it himself, is passing it on to people with whom he comes in contact. Considering the fact that our suspected carrier's daily itinerary may routinely include the entire globe and several neighboring planets and star systems, I do not suppose that we have any hope of finding out where he picked it up, but that is quite irrelevant. I propose to cure it.''

Skvrsky paused for several moments to allow his audience to murmur learnedly and sit in awe of him a little bit. He noticed that two women in the second row of seats, both certainly case-hardened scientists, were gazing at him quite intently. This pleased him, although he assiduously avoiding showing it.

"On the sixteenth and final page of my data," he went on, "I have included a graph detailing the spectragraphic analysis of Superman's hair. Those of you familiar with such things will note that it resembles hair much less than it resembles tiny strands of titanium. Titanium, however, is closer in resiliency to normal terrestrial hair than it is to Superman's hair. No matter.

"I propose that we do two things immediately. First, the Center will request Superman to submit a lock of his hair for testing. Second, we will use the federal money that you all saw me so skillfully wangle a few minutes ago to produce, in the laboratory, a super-strong organic strand that is physically and spectrographically identical to Superman's hair. Those of you who consider this second task impossible may be assured that you have a lot to learn from me. I trust that for this project I will have your complete cooperation and access to all resources of the Center for the Study of Short-Lived Phenomena. Any objections? Good.

"I will require a small office and a large laboratory equipped for conventional chemical and biological work. Later today I will choose two special assistants from among you. If you would be so kind, Mr. Golob, as to show me a suitable laboratory space now, I will order any additional equipment I need to be delivered tomorrow morning."

Richard Golob, the distinguished director of the Center for the

Study of Short-Lived Phenomena, quietly led Skvrsky to another room.

When they were gone somebody said, "Whew."

Almost nothing of what Skvrsky said was true. The only true information in the sixteen-page report was the accounts of Superman's appearances during the previous weeks and the spectroanalysis of Kryptonian hair.

There was no Itching Sickness.

There was, in fact, no Dr. David Skvrsky.

Skvrsky was one of Lex Luthor's elaborate creations, and the man who had breezed out of the room with Golob was Luthor himself in disguise. The reporters, George Laderbush and John Hughes, were also born of Luthor's brow. There would be no more need for fictional reporters to issue falsely documented accounts of the disease's outbreak. Once the news of Skvrsky's involvement got out, hysterical cases of Itching Sickness would actually begin to appear around the world wherever Superman went.

It was a charming little conundrum, Luthor decided.

The Special Report

The networks all preempted their regular programming that evening in early May for hour-long news specials. They often preempted their programming for reports on major events in the news: when kings and presidents took office or died; when war or peace was declared somewhere; when aliens from other worlds appeared unannounced in major population centers; that sort of thing. This time, however, there was not any particular event of the past week worthy of a special report. There were so many little unexpected events this week that were of almost major proportions that the networks decided to run specials on all of them together. The last time something like that happened was in 1964. One week back then, among other things, the Chinese exploded their first nuclear bomb and the Soviets deposed their premier to replace him with two younger men. That week, like this week, the Galaxy Broadcasting System titled their special report, "A World Turned Inside Out." This time, though no one knew it, the title would be more appropriate than it was in 1964.

Without any introduction other than the title of the report, the images on the millions of televisions across the country switched to a quick series of excerpts from news reports of the past week. John Keepe in Charleston reported on the pollution of most of South Carolina's city reservoir systems with tadpoles. There was Blake Thiebass in Duluth reporting on the inexplicable lowering of the melting point of steel in the mills there. From Tacoma, Kerry Tarsneaux gave an account of the disappearance of snow on mountaintops overlooking blizzard-bound towns. Donna Toothe in Belgrade talked about the outbreak of the previously unknown strain of eczema wherever Superman had appeared thirty-six hours earlier. Paul Grinn in Cairo gave an account of the migraine headaches that were afflicting virtually every head of state in the Middle East this week. In Paris, Marcel de Stonne reported on the swarm of locusts raging over the western European countryside. In the Metropolis studio, Clark Kent recounted the various major crimes and near disasters, natural and otherwise, that Superman was known to have defused around the world this week.

When these brief snippets of the week's regular newscasts ended, national anchorwoman Lana Lang appeared on the air and said, essentially, that there was a lot of weird stuff going on in the world these days. Most of the people watching had already surmised this, but Lana realized that restating the obvious in a clear manner seemed to be a large part of a newscaster's job.

A good many of the millions who were watching the report, possibly a majority of them, had some idea that their understanding of the past few dizzying weeks would be enhanced by this clear restating of the news. People hoped that the astute collection of Galaxy Communications employees who confronted them in such a fluent array tonight would be able to discern some pattern in the madness. During the first half hour of the report, those who hoped for such a synthesis saw no evidence that the journalists briefly in charge of their senses had any such thing to offer.

Uptown from Galaxy Communications, at the Center for the Study of Short-Lived Phenomena, was a group of people accustomed to discerning patterns in apparent madness. All but one of them expected no less of these reporters. Only the man who called himself Dr. David Skvrsky gave less than total attention to the television screen. Skvrsky was studying a notebook full of acetate-covered spectrographic photographs of Superman's hair. The others in the room were eagerly awaiting the appearance on the television screen of their colleague Tami Muriello, who was the chief public affairs officer of the center. Skvrsky had decided that it was technologically possible to duplicate to the smallest atomic detail the hair of Superman's head. It would take about a hundred thousand dollars to do it, Skvrsky decided, but it would be a simple matter for the Center for the Study of Short-Lived Phenomena, using Skvrsky's prestige, to get a five-hundred-thousand-dollar federal grant to do it. Skvrsky would spare the Center the moral dilemma that the grant suggested by keeping the entire four hundred thousand dollars that he would not spend. Luthor, meanwhile, would lay out the hundred thousand dollars needed to manufacture a lock of indestructible fake hair. If Luthor were a law-abiding citizen, he would somehow justify a 400 percent interest charge on his loan. Since he was a criminal, however, he, like the center, had no moral dilemma to overcome. He was simply stealing the money, and that was fine with Luthor.

Luthor, masquerading as a dashing, romantic international Angel of Mercy, sat scowling in a corner of the studied chaos of his uptown Metropolis laboratory, trying to ignore a boyhood friend who had just appeared on the television screen on the far side of the room. Clark Kent was sitting in on a panel discussion with the anchorwoman and a few other savants, including a few Galaxy newsmen from around the country and Muriello from the Center, trading theories on the spate of disasters around the world. Luthor was watching through an electron microscope as, at his prodding, thousands of macro-molecules fused together, crashing in and compressing one another, forming something that looked like strands of titanium but which was many times stronger. Luthor had to keep watching the strands form as his colleagues across the room listened to the words of Clark Kent from the television. Luthor ignored Kent as much as he possibly could. There was something about the man that spooked him.

It was years ago—the year Abraham Maslow, the pioneering humanistic psychologist, and Noam Chomsky, the linguist from MIT, both had visiting professorships at Metropolis University and were teaching a course together on psycholinguistics. In December a nineteen-year-old Lex Luthor vanished without a trace from the Pocantico Correctional Facility and in January a gawky, big-footed, potbellied and stunningly brilliant transfer student from Anchorage named Michael Hemmingway (with two m's, he was always careful to point out) showed up at Metropolis University and his late registration for the popular psycholinguistics course somehow slipped past the registrar into the file cabinet. In order not to arouse suspicion, Hemmingway also registered for four other courses that semester at Metropolis University. No suspicions arose at all, however, from the fact that the

145

transfer student never showed up at any of his other classes. This was not unusual. Certainly no one had any idea that Hemmingway was Lex Luthor, the young hellion who already held the record as the person who had been placed on and taken off the FBI Ten Most Wanted list more times than anyone else on record.

The two great men, Maslow and Chomsky, conducted a very impressive class two days a week. On Tuesdays, Chomsky would lecture, blinding the students' minds with a phantasmagoria of observations and suppositions about the ancestries of various English words and why they had evolved the way they had. He traced the derivation of the word *phantasmagoria* and its relative *fantasy* one Tuesday, and then extrapolated its possible link, in the future, with *fanatic* or *fan* from an altogether different root. He supposed that someday there would be a marriage between these two family trees and a *fan* would eventually refer only to a fantasy fanatic.

Then on Thursdays, Maslow would pick two or three students from among the class and ask them to have a ten-minute conversation among themselves in front of the rest of the class. When ten minutes were up, Maslow pointed out each phrase, each word, each sound, each gesture of body language that had struck his fancy (from the same Indo-European root as *phantasmagoria*) and picked it apart the way a beginning biology student might dissect a frog or an earthworm. Maslow and Chomsky taught their students at Metropolis University to study language and human interaction the way a doctor studies a strain of bacillus or a good repairman studies the works of a sick washing machine.

Michael Hemmingway with two m's was fascinated.

Hemmingway went to ask Maslow for permission to do a special research project. Before the young man even told him what the project would be, Maslow asked the student why he held one hand in a back pocket as he walked into the professor's office. Then Maslow asked why he said the name "Hemmingway with two m's" with such emphasis. Then he asked why the student stepped in so decisively instead of shuffling the way most students did. And so forth. Michael Hemmingway tried to laugh off Abraham Maslow's questions and Maslow asked why he laughed so defensively. In fact, Michael Hemmingway did laugh defensively; he had a lot about which to be defensive.

The student gave up his mission for that day and went to propose the idea to Chomsky two days later. What he wanted to do was get a dozen volunteers from among the student body at Metropolis, students from diverse sections of the country, and make a study of their various accents. Hemmingway would record their pronunciations of certain key words, and interview each student about his or her background. Then, five months later at the end of the semester, he would interview each volunteer again, paying close attention to the two or three most unusual things that had happened to the student in the course of the five months—the births or deaths of relatives, the falling in or out of love, the peak experiences and the lows. He would again record each student's pronunciation of key words, noting any changes during the five-month period, and seeing if he could discover any reason for changes in pronunciation from the student's experiences during the same period. Chomsky made a few procedural suggestions, pointed out that Hemmingway should have some sort of a control group, and said it was basically a fine idea.

Luthor was amused that one of the first of the Metropolis University students to answer Hemmingway's request for volunteers was a sophomore whom Luthor knew from his days in Smallville named Clark Kent.

Kent pronounced words as though he were from Nowhere, U.S.A. He had a perfect midwestern accent and Luthor remembered thinking at the time that instead of trying to be a newspaper reporter, Kent should be broadcasting the news on television. Luthor alias Hemmingway was relishing the interview with his boyhood friend. He liked hearing— from Kent's mayonnaisey viewpoint—about the little hick burg that was the last place Luthor had lived with his parents. Luthor was mildly surprised to learn, for example, that Kent had been an adopted child, and for a moment Luthor felt a burst of resentment at his own parents for not loving their natural son Lex as much as the Kents evidently loved their adopted son Clark. Luthor even felt a touch of regret on hearing that Jonathan and Martha Kent had both passed on since he had last been in Smallville.

Luthor sat behind the studied solemnity of his Michael Hemmingway face, laughing at Clark Kent until the end of the interview when, getting up to leave, Kent said, "By the way, Lex, who do you think you're fooling?"

"Excuse me?"

"I asked who you thought you were fooling. Isn't this project for Maslow's class?"

"What of it?"

"Well, I just don't think you're fooling a guy like Maslow any more than you fool me, is all."

"I haven't got the slightest idea of what you're talking about."

"Oh come off it, Lex."

"Lex? What's a Lex? Is that somebody's name? I'm Michael Hemmingway with two m's. I assume you're—um, what did it say there?—Clark Kent."

"You're no Michael Hemmingway any more than I'm Superboy."

"I think he calls himself Superman these days."

"Whatever it is. That nose is pretty good, though. Did you have surgery on that or—"

"Get your hand off my nose. What're you, weird?"

"Listen, I won't tell anyone. Honest, Lex. But why on Earth don't you cut this master criminal stuff out?"

"Master criminal stuff?"

"Yeah, that's what the papers call you now, the bad papers at least. The *Times* and the *Planet* still refer to you as just an escaped felon. I mean you've just stolen property so far, right? Never endangered anyone's life seriously, at least since you turned eighteen, and that's what counts, right?"

"Look—um, Kent—I don't think I'm going to be able to use your data here. You're too hostile."

"Hostile? You know as well as I do that I'm as hostile as your average terrier puppy."

"Maybe hostile isn't the word. I guess it's schizoid. That's it. And if you insist on staying here I'm going to have to let the psychological counseling office know about you—um, Kent."

Clark stood quietly for a moment, wrinkled his eyebrows and said, "Sorry, my mistake." Then he shuffled out of the room.

When Luthor went back to Michael Hemmingway's locked dormitory room that afternoon he found an envelope lying on the unmade bed. There was a typed note inside:

Dear Lex,

I'm really sorry if I got you upset today and ruined your game, and I know you always have good reasons for doing the things you do, but I've got an idea. It seems to me that anybody who could invent a new identity for himself the way you have done can probably wipe out his whole past and start over anywhere with a clean slate. You could be a scientist or a doctor or a psycholinguist if you feel like it or anything else. Well, it seems to me that the only thing keeping you from actually doing this is Superman. No matter where you went or how you changed yourself, Superman could probably find you sometime. And it seems to me that if somebody could somehow guarantee that if you decided never to commit a crime again, to go straight, if someone could then make it so Superman never came after you again, that would be just like a pardon. What I'm getting at is that I can do that. Honest. I can make it so Superman will forget about your past altogether if you want to start all over and use your intellect and your talents to benefit humanity instead of to destroy Superman. You'd be famous and acclaimed, I'm sure, no matter what career you chose. By now, after six or seven years in jails and reform schools, I'm sure you'll agree that it would be a better life. You know me well enough to know that I wouldn't lie to you. I know you well enough to know that even though it would not be a good idea to trust you blindly, you'll stick with any agreement you make outright. That's why I want you to meet me in the lobby of this building at eight o'clock tonight and I'll tell you my secret. I know you think I'm just a wimpy kid from the sticks somewhere, but I can make you believe me. If you're not down in the lobby by five after eight, I'll just assume you're not coming.

Your old friend,
Clark Kent

Luthor hated being confronted with decisions he never anticipated having to make. He sat down on the bed and decided. Clearly, he thought, Kent had something to tell him. And clearly, he thought, if he is the same kid he was six or seven years ago, it is something Kent considers pretty big. A lot of things can change, however, in six or seven years. Certainly Luthor had changed. Certainly, with the loss of his parents and the move from Smallville to Metropolis, Kent had changed as well. It was even possible that the kid had gone nuts. Then again, he was sane enough to have seen through the Michael Hemmingway disguise. Kent looked normal enough this afternoon, for an incurable wimp. But if he really was a wimp, how could he really believe he had a way to get Superman off Luthor's back unless he really did?

This was too much to sort out without more information. The thing to do, therefore, was to miss the appointment with Kent, but kidnap him on his way home. That way, Luthor would be able to get to the bottom of these questions and still not immediately endanger his disguise.

At five past eight Clark Kent sighed a sigh mixed with equal portions of regret and relief, stepped out the door of Michael

Hemmingway's dormitory building and walked south along MacDougall Street toward his own dorm. A block behind, Michael Hemmingway, in black turtleneck and black slacks and carrying a handkerchief doused in chloroform, followed Clark Kent. A few blocks downtown, Clark turned left into a short, dark alley that cut through to Jones Street. With Clark out of sight, Luthor/Hemmingway started running quietly on crepe soles toward the alley.

Three steps into his trot, Luthor felt the Hemmingway toupee he had glued to his head being ripped off, and then Luthor himself was lifted into the sky by his armpits. Luthor remembered struggling for a few moments. He remembered Superman's hand pressing the chloroformed handkerchief against his face. He remembered his last conscious thought before he woke up at Pocantico—that now he might never know Clark Kent's mysterious secret. And, again, he remembered rage.

Luthor, now masquerading as Skvrsky instead of Hemmingway with two m's, heard someone across the laboratory say something that sounded surprised. He looked up at the television screen across the room and did not look back down at his microscope again that day.

For the past minute or so, the panel of newspeople and experts discussing the varied reasons for this news special had seemed distracted. There was some noise somewhere off the set, maybe somewhere in the hallway outside the news studio. Then there was a voice from off-camera that everyone, including the television viewers, could hear. It was harsh, inhuman.

"The calamities have one cause, and that cause is me," the voice barked, and then Kristin Wells bounded before the camera and the startled panel.

"Excuse me, miss," Lana Lang said, standing up and taking Kristin's arm, "but maybe you don't realize this is a live news broad—"

Kristin whipped her elbow up into Lana's chin and, with her free hand, pointed two fingers at the Galaxy Broadcasting System's star anchorwoman and blasted her backward through the cardboard set that formed the backdrop with what appeared to be a burst of light from her fingertips.

Everyone on the set except for Clark Kent scattered. The camera remained on, fixed in position without a cameraman. Clark yelled, "Lana!" and went to see if the woman was all right.

"You can see from where you are that she is unharmed, Clark

Kent," the inhuman voice said from the throat of Kristin Wells, "and that is why you go to her so slowly, at human speed. The charade will no longer be necessary."

Clark paid no attention to what Kristin was saying, although maybe he should have done so. He knelt cradling the head of the unconscious Lana Lang in one hand and placed it down again as the woman began to wake up. He stood up to say something suitably indignant but still in character when Kristin threw a dark, hollow laugh at his face.

"Kristin," Clark said, "this is hardly appropriate behavior for a—"

"I am Saturn," the voice from Kristin Wells said. "I was born when the elements of Earth and Krypton were still cooling in the heart of a dying star. I will live on when your memory and time itself have no meaning. I have occupied your time, alien, these past weeks, and I will complicate your life until your precious Earth is a husk smoldering with the stench of rotted dreams and your Universe is tumbling faster than life into the pit."

No one had any idea what she was talking about, but she was clearly addressing Clark Kent, who insisted on remaining in character as he walked toward Kristin, who stood resolutely in the eye of the camera. Lana was looking up, Kristin was gesturing insanely toward Clark with both her hands. Clark was speaking in tones and words of reason. Between twenty-five and twenty-six million people across the country were watching.

Kristin Wells's hands shot out a burst of cold Hell-born energy at Clark Kent and minds froze as, in an instant, Clark Kent was gone, what was left of his clothes draped indecorously over the unmistakable frame of Superman.

Kristin laughed once more, and then she too was gone. A puff of black smoke and a dying squeal replaced her.

"That son of a rabid terrier!" Luthor wailed from behind the still intact disguise of David Skvrsky. "That was his secret, damn him! He was that wimp all along."

Nobody noticed what Skvrsky was saying and in a moment he would pull himself together enough to stop saying it. Life would go on, for the moment.

Song of the Earth

It was over. He was horribly embarrassed. He was mortified. A big part of him, the mortal part, was killed. He wove through the sky in a random pattern above Metropolis. Maybe he had broken a window or a wall on his way out. If he had, he would fix it sometime.

There were species on this Earth for whom heartbreak was a common cause of death. Swans and pigeons died soon after the deaths of their mates. Dogs sometimes pined to death when their masters died or moved away without them. Last year, twenty healthy sperm whales, distraught over the use of their spawning area as a dumping ground for nuclear waste material, beached themselves and gently died on a shore near Peugeot Sound. Now, Superman felt that he too was slowly beginning to die.

The news reached the entire United States and parts of Mexico and Canada before it fully hit Superman himself. Now, the last of Clark Kent's clothing ripping off in the breeze and flapping to the Earth below, Superman turned north and sliced the sky alone. Totally alone.

By the time Superman crossed the Canadian border, the telephone cables and the microwave satellite relays linking the North American continent with Europe and Asia were overloaded with calls to and from diplomats, business leaders, journalists, friends. News offices in America and then in Western Europe, Japan, the Soviet Union, Africa, China, India—ultimately all around the world—sat in undirected silence for a moment before somebody in each office ordered everyone else to go about telling the story.

When monitors at Strategic Air Command in Omaha picked up evidence of an erratic, high-flying object crossing the Distant Early Warning defense line in Canada and heading out over the Arctic Sea, there was momentary mobilization. It could have been an enemy aircraft blundering into unauthorized space, but that was not what it was. The news had reached this underground fortress, and when somebody muttered, "It's him," everyone else knew approximately where he was going.

"He's moving awful slow," a young technician said. "He never moves that slow. You sure it's him?"

"Leave him be," an officer said.

One hundred thirty miles south of the North Pole—from the North Pole every direction is south—there was a hollow, artificially built mountain. The mightiest hands on Earth had gathered and fused together a huge mass of granite blocks which now sat collecting snow and permafrost, hidden from anyone who might be imprudent enough to linger over this forsaken corner of the Earth. From the sky, one could see only a golden arrow the length of two Olympic pools which pointed north, presumably for the benefit of airline pilots. Only Superman could lift the sixty-ton object, slide it into a camouflaged lock set into the mountain face, and open the door bigger than most medieval cathedrals.

This Fortress of Solitude, this repository for collectibles—the junk and the treasure of the great man's life—was the final privacy he had.

By the time Superman laid his hands on the base of the golden key, the fact of his formerly secret identity had passed, in most of the world, from news, to common knowledge, to a source of idle speculation. When Superman lifted the key a hundred meters into the air, faltered a moment and then, despairing, dropped it back to the steel-hard frost that covered the earth below, the human population of the world was astir with excitement mixed with confusion. The President of the United States got the idea into his head to issue a postage stamp bearing the face of Clark Kent, when the key cracked and shattered against the cold.

By law, no living person may be pictured on a United States postage stamp.

Superman sat on top of the mountain that he had built, in a temporary high-backed chair that he dug out of the ice. He leaned back his head, closed his eyes and listened. He listened for everything. He turned on his full super-hearing, not simply the directed sense that he had trained himself to use in homing in on distant conversations or on the noise of a distant underground rumble before the Earth moved somewhere. He turned on the whole thing, and in a moment, he realized that he had never done this before.

From his perch at the top of the world Superman heard the clatter of trains making their ways among the towns of central Europe, the hissing of a cobra in the basket of a Pakistani fakir, the tuning sounds of the Boston Pops Orchestra and the orchestra of a high school in La Paz as respectively they rehearsed ''Maxwell's Silver Hammer'' and the second Brandenburg Concerto. A geyser bubbled below the surface of Colorado. A company of humpback whales howled an ecstatic, intricate symphony whose orchestration stretched for half the width of the Indian Ocean. Quintillions of snails dragged quintillions of jellied tails over the surfaces of quintillions of leaves.

The slap-slapping of a runner's feet against the outskirts of Kampala made a perfect syncopated rhythm with the singing of a thrush in Singapore. When the thrush stopped for a moment, the runner would stop for a gulp of water from his wineskin. When the runner stepped up his pace, the thrush soared into a new rhythm, as though the man in Africa and the bird in Asia were following signals from the same conductor.

The wind-songs ripping through the Andes made a counterpoint for the wagging tails of the dogs in the Bide-A-Wee Animal Shelter in Wantagh, Long Island.

An ant's breath, as it struggled to press a cake crumb up a centimeter-and-a-half-high hill in Bali, traced the precise pattern of the whirring of a machine mixing cavity-filling in the office of a dentist in Tel Aviv.

The hums of all the beehives and all the Xerox copiers in all the world together created an eerily beautiful collection of sound that clearly constituted a fugue.

An angry golfer in Palm Beach, when he smashed his putter

against a tree, compensated for the drummer in the Sussex disco band who missed a beat.

Then something even more remarkable happened. There was a flutter of flying fish in the Caribbean west of Bermuda whipping past the cruise ship *Raffaelo*. Together, in a pattern whose precision Superman could now begin to notice, they flashed out of the water and splashed back in, soared up, fluttered, tumbled back, broke the water again. And as they arced through the sky, two of the fish hit the hull of the *Raffaelo* and broke their part of the pattern. A line of people who applauded as they watched the fish performance from the liner's rail did not even notice the falling out of the two members of the school. And as Superman heard, from his icy throne, the sound of the pair of flying fish splashing clumsily into the sea, a few chunks of ice chipped off the rest under his heavy arm and scattered down the hill, making a noise comparable in quality to the noise of a flying fish duet fluttering on the wind and splashing into the Caribbean.

Superman was part of the song.

He had an instrument in the orchestra of this Earth.

He was not, in the overall scheme of things, an outsider.

He listened to the world, sitting in one of its most desolate spots, and he began to put together the pieces. He heard the howls of wolves, the roiling of cyclones, the bouncing of children's balls, the sounds of his own digestive system, the sounds of the mandibles of ticks attaching themselves to the skins of dogs' ears; everything, working together to create an ineffable symphony.

Maybe Superman, today, was the first one ever to hear the music that the Earth made in its totality. Maybe, on the other hand, every human who ever composed a concerto, wrote a song, whistled a tune, or listened intently to the heartbeat of a woman carrying a child had heard the song of the Earth in his or her own peculiar set of perceptions. Maybe Pythagoras, Mozart and McCartney had heard the song, and had spent their lives trying, in their primitive ways, to imitate it. Maybe every whippoorwill and meadowlark Superman heard today was imitating the Earth as well. Maybe that was what Superman had been doing—bouncing to the rhythm of this planet that teemed with life and melody, ever since the day he first arrived on Earth.

He listened, heard the sound of the Order of life and growth for which the planet had been created, and wondered what the sound of the Universe might be. He wondered what he would hear if, through some miracle, his super-hearing could pick up sounds across the vacuum of the continuum.

Somewhere to the south, a devil inhabiting the body of an innocent young woman had destroyed the one thing that had made him feel a part of this world. But now he heard, and began to realize, that by his very presence he had become of this world and a part of its encompassing Order.

Somewhere to the south, a demon had begun the process of disrupting that Order, ending the song, and spreading the word of Chaos from this point through all time and space. Not even the past and the future would be safe from a gathering wave of the Dark World's power.

Somewhere to the south, sounds of cacophany originated and found Superman's ears. The man from another world rose into the sky, through the aurora to the edge of space, and dove to meet the agent of Hell on Earth.

General Destruction

Determination does not necessarily make for an end to struggle. At best, it only helps. Superman was determined to put an end to the destruction that was promised by Kristin Wells. When he dove from the sky to find Kristin merrily prancing up Sixth Avenue, the following things had already gone wrong:

1. The Pan American Building was upside down, standing on its heliport above Grand Central Terminal.

2. The statue of Horace Greeley was running around Journal Square pinching tourists.

3. A geyser of crude oil was spurting out the top of the Exxon Building and tying up traffic on Sixth and Seventh Avenues.

4. All three hundred people inside Radio City Music Hall for a revival of *Singing in the Rain* had grown too big to fit out the doors and were caught in a downpour from the malfunctioning sprinkler system.

5. Fifty-Second Street from Eighth Avenue to Park Avenue had become a chasm at least forty feet deep.

6. The steering wheels of all the cars in midtown had suddenly vanished, whether the cars were moving or not.
7. Fifty-sixth Street and its restaurants were infested with frogs.
8. A supersonic wail permeating the air in the vicinity of Christopher Circle was driving a horde of dogs crazy.

The biggest problem was the Pan Am Building.

After Superman smashed through the pieces of the Horace Greeley statue, the pieces lay twitching on the ground for a few moments and stopped. After minor accidents, all the drivers in midtown, with expressions ranging from spooked horror to resigned annoyance, abandoned their vehicles where they were. Platforms full of garbage and landfill that Superman carried from various dumps around town were an adequate temporary solution to Fifty-Second Street. When Superman saw that the oil on the Exxon Building was apparently originating from nowhere but the base of the gusher itself, he quickly rigged up a well and a pipeline from the metal of junk cars, and the supply of crude oil ended after less than a barrelful drained into the fountain forty stories below.

When Superman sheared the corners and removed the walls from the Music Hall, three hundred people shrank back to their normal sizes. The three hundred, all soaking wet, wandered about their respective businesses. Superman was careful not to damage the walls of the national monument to pop culture. Superman had a soft spot for American pop culture.

When Superman couldn't find the source of the supersonic whistle—it had no source but the air itself—he airlifted fifty-four dogs from the area. The sound ended as suddenly as it had begun.

He pulled a water main from the ground under Fifty-Sixth Street and flushed most of the frogs off the street into the river, while citizens too stubborn to get out of the way—there were three of them, two restaurant owners and a chef—held on to a fire escape ladder and two light poles. The frogs would actually have been good for the river's damaged ecology, but they vanished soon afterward.

In the Pan American Building, only the inorganic things were upside down. People walked on the ceilings, sat on turned-off light fixtures, and looked up at their desks and chairs hanging from above. Superman had the superintendent of the building call all the floors and get the occupants ready for evacuation. The elevators did not work, since cables that depended partially on gravity had no weights to pull them, and the stairways were useless. Superman stretched a system of ramps and wooden staircases from the top of the Pan Am Building all the way up to the bottom. He spent most of the afternoon, after the building was emptied, lifting the building and slowly, gently, moving at super-speed to buttress scores of points on the surface of the building at what seemed to be the same time, flipping the Pan Am Building back onto its foundation and sealing it there the way it belonged.

What was she trying to do? Superman screamed in his mind as he finished his job. Kristin Wells was sitting on the stone wall that marked the southern border of Central Preserve, filing her fingernails. She was surrounded on all sides by a circle of flames a few centimeters high that flared up menacingly whenever anyone among the crowd watching her ventured too close. When a man tried to throw a rock at her it boomeranged back at his head; she said something about he who is without sin casting the first stone, but seemed unable to remember the source of that particular quotation.

The crowd threw stones of verbal abuse at her instead as she sat impassively. That was until the wall of fire rose again and Superman flew through it to land with his livid face an inch from hers. In a soft, painfully controlled voice he asked her, "What are you trying to do?"

She looked up blankly for a moment and went back to her filing. He grabbed the file from her and tossed it over his shoulder into Connecticut, but long before it landed another nail file appeared from nowhere. Resigned, he waited for her to look up again.

When she looked up she said, "I am C. W. Saturn, Superman, and I have come to make you unnecessary."

Then she laughed sweetly and disappeared in a puff of black smoke.

Superman visited Lena Thorul, but when he knocked on her door she pleaded with him to go away. He persisted, and when she finally opened the door she shrieked and fainted. She would have been a highly sensitive woman, even if she had never been psychic.

In his apartment in Los Angeles, Max Maven was practicing card tricks. Before Superman knocked on the door, he heard Max say, in a voice low enough so that only he and the cards could hear it, "Come on in, it's open."

"Hello, Max."

"Lena's going to be all right, or at least as well as could be expected. You look a little peaked, though. Sit down. Sorry about Kent. Here, pick a card."

"I'd rather not. I need some information."

"I don't know much."

"You don't know much?" the hero bellowed.

161

"Quiet," Max whispered and sat Superman down on the couch. "Half the neighbors are trying to meditate the evil spirits away. They're scared out of their minds. You'll disturb them."

"Meditate?"

"This is California," Max said, motioning in the direction of his head.

"What do you mean you don't know much? A few weeks ago you were a regular fountain of inside information. You were a guidebook to Hell, a half-baked cross between Virgil and Rona Barrett. What happened, smart guy?"

"Nothing happened. Saturn's got the girl, as you've doubtless figured out, and there was nothing you could do about that."

"Nothing?"

"Nothing."

"What about exorcism?"

"Exorcism? Out of the question. I'd laugh if it were funny. You can't exorcise C. W. Saturn. You're not dealing with one of Lucifer's handmaidens. This is the arch-demon, the agent of Hell on Earth. This is the entity that sits at the elbow of Samael. This is the Robespierre, the Rasputin, the H. R. Haldeman of the Underworld. This is the snake in the Garden of Eden out to make its biggest killing. You can't exorcise it. You've got to defeat it. And let me tell you, you aren't inspiring a whole lot of confidence in me right now."

"How do I defeat it?"

"How should I know? I'm no hero, I'm just a lousy stage performer trying to earn a living. I can't tell you the game plan, all I know is the gossip."

"You're saying it's up to me."

"I'm telling you it's impossible, but you're in the hero business. You're supposed to thrive on stuff like that."

"Then tell me this, Max. Exactly what's at stake? What happens if Saturn wins?"

"Okay. As far as I can tell, first of all, the laws of physics go out the window. Disorder is the rule of the day, at first in the vicinity of the Earth, and eventually throughout the physical Universe. Time no longer has any meaning. Ultimately, all four dimensions break down. The past disappears, and if through some miracle even a time traveler from the future were to come here, he would be caught in the mess too. Matter, space, time all become a mishmash and the Universe reverts to the state it was in before the Creation. I don't know what that looks like, but I don't suppose it's an environment that's very pleasant for living things."

"What you're talking about is a complete breakdown of the space-time continuum, am I right?"

"I'm no scientist, but I think it goes further than that. Here, pick a card."

But Superman was gone.

The next day the following things went wrong:

1. An American communications satellite fell on the White House lawn.
2. The President of Kenya, suffering a migraine headache for the first time in his life, was testy enough to order that his nation's air force attack Entebbe.
3. A school of sharks leaped out of the water onto the deck of a tourist boat off the coast of Virginia.
4. At the same instant, cables of elevators in six buildings in Metropolis snapped.
5. It snowed in Death Valley.
6. The water supply of the city of Silver Spring turned to formaldehyde.
7. The Panama Canal was filled with soil.
8. Anchormen of news programs all over the world laughed through their accounts of the day's news.

And so forth. This went on for weeks.

Around this time, Superman left a lock of his hair for David Skvrsky at the Center for the Study of Short-Lived Phenomena.

Getting Affairs in Order

It was another week before Superman could go back to Clark Kent's apartment at 344 Clinton Street. He hovered at the broken window for a few moments, watching Lois, who was inside gathering ripped and crumpled papers from the floor and flattening them out as well as she could before she stuffed them into a little Samsonite attaché case.

There was nothing left besides the papers. The tables, chairs, couch, snippets of rug had all been stripped away on that night a week ago when Clark Kent died. Somebody had taken the videotape recorder, the television and the collection of Clark's favorite television commercials, as well as all the books and records and cassettes that had recordings of extraterrestrial music. By the time Lois finally found the presence of mind that night to realize that Clark had no living relatives and that she had to take responsibility for his property, people had already stripped the small apartment of everything but scraps of paper. The telephones were ripped from the wall. In the building's elevator, the button for the third floor, Clark's floor, had been sawed or pried or bitten out of the elevator wall before the entire button console was ripped out and carried away. Most of the other tenants of the building had fled that night; perhaps some of them had even taken a souvenir of the consummate fiction that had been Clark Kent.

Now, with Superman preoccupied with the current world crisis and evidently uninterested in his former life, Lois had a court order appointing her Clark Kent's executor. She also convinced her old friend Inspector Henderson to pull some strings and cut some tape to get police guards around Clark's apartment. There was nothing anyone could see besides the papers all over the floors—financial records, bill stubs, discarded first drafts of news scripts, answers to Superman's fan mail—but she might find something else if she looked hard enough.

"Quite a mess, isn't it?" said the voice from the direction of the window.

She looked up from the bare floor against which she was straightening something that looked to be a manuscript and saw him standing on the ledge outside the window that had been shattered and whose shards had been carried off for souvenirs.

"What do you care?" Lois muttered and looked back down at the floor.

"My executor, I presume?"

"That's what the court says." Lois continued to work as he climbed in through the window.

"The reports of my death are highly exaggerated."

"Listen, hero, as long as you're here you might at least do something about those windows. It's cold as a—"

"Excuse me, miss, but do I know you?"

"Oh, don't play the lost little lamb with me, Superman, okay? Be a hero or a Romeo or a heel or some kind of sick, hormone-infested macho freak or anything you feel like being, but don't make believe you don't know what's going on in my head."

"You're upset that I never told you that Clark and I were the same person."

"Upset? No, amazed. You're a stranger. Do you realize that? In all the years I've known you, you've been a stranger. How do you think that makes me feel?"

"Alone?"

"That's a good word for it. Another good word for it is shitty "

"Lois, I'm sorry. I'm sorry you had to find out about it on television. If I'd known it was going to happen I would have told you first."

"Told me first? How about second? How about in the week or

two since the news broke? Where on God's Earth have you been all this time?"

"Maybe I've been busy making sure this remains God's Earth and not somebody else's."

"Oh, I get it. Now you're being the hero. The wide-eyed and innocent tactic didn't work. Well, I read the papers. I even write the papers. It's all very impressive the way you've been saving the world two, maybe three times a day. What would we do without you? And when you have the biggest personal crisis since you lost your parents, you have nothing to do about it but brood on the far side of the moon, for all I know. You certainly don't come and talk to your friends about it. You don't even drop a note to the person who's allegedly in love with you and tell her you're alive and well and you'll get back to her."

"I couldn't do anything else."

"Was I part of the disguise?"

"Excuse me?"

"The disguise. Clark Kent was the part of you that walked around looking and acting normal. A parody of normal. Was I just somebody to have tagging along on your arm in *Time* magazine so we puny mortals could think of you as a living, breathing Earthman who just happened to be an immigrant?"

"Lois, that's ridiculous. I don't think that's the real issue."

"Issue? I used to have a boyfriend before I met you named Barry Elkin, a psychologist. He was always talking about issues. He broke up with me because he said I still had too many issues to resolve. He said that out loud. I still don't know what he meant by that, other than the fact that he wanted to break up with me."

"It meant that he couldn't deal with a woman as strong-willed as you are."

"How do you know he wasn't even more strong-willed than I am? How do you know he wasn't the Lyndon Johnson of psychologists?"

"Because I once read a paper he wrote for a psychological journal on raising children. It was obvious from the paper that he was very strong-willed, although not as strong-willed as you are."

"Ah, the all-knowing, all-seeing Man of Steel strikes again. Is there anything you don't know?"

"I didn't know he was a friend of yours. Now I'll want to know more about him."

"Read some more psychological journals. I've got a mess to clean up."

"I'll clean up the mess. It was my apartment."

"I didn't mean the apartment. I meant my life."

Then she cried, which gave him an excuse to hold her in his arms, which made her stop crying and then made her angrier.

"Superman!" She pushed his arms away. "What is it you do to me? You know ants attract each other with smells?"

"Yes, they're called pheromones. They're a form of communication, like an insect language."

"Heartwarming. And did you know that now doctors are saying that attraction between humans is probably at least in part based on a smell we give off?"

"Yes, that's true. What are you getting at, Lois?"

"Well, how do I know that when you hold me like that you don't spray some weird pheromone up my nose at super-speed and make me fall madly in love with you?"

"Lois, that's completely incredible. You know I wouldn't do anything like that."

That's just the point. I don't know anything of the sort. I can't trust you anymore. For years you slouched and talked in a high voice and hid behind your glasses and for all I know you laughed at me that whole time."

This was a highly inauspicious moment for the two of them, Superman and Lois Lane. There are a lot of inauspicious moments in the course of such discussions between people who are momentarily insecure and in love. The purpose of such discussions is to slide headlong at these moments, bump around a bit, deal with them, and eventually resolve whatever it is at issue. There are always lots of issues coming up with the bumps.

What Superman wanted to tell Lois next was that he was unsure about his ability to have her without having Clark as well. He wanted to say that Clark was his means to be on a roughly equal footing with her, and with those among whom he had to live.

What Lois would then have said was that a woman arrogant enough to love a superman is uninterested in having a man who is on an equal footing with her. She would have said that she loved Superman, that she was born and raised to love Superman or someone like him just as surely as Prince Charles was born and raised to be King of England. She would have said that she firmly believed that if Superman had died as an infant with his parents on the planet Krypton, then there never would have been a Lois Lane, because there would have been no place in the world for her to fit in. She believed that everything fit into the Order of the world, and she would have impressed Superman by telling him this.

Before Lois met Superman, she would have said, she was both an overachiever and a lost soul, and without him she would have been a casualty of her own brute competence. She would still have been the first girl to edit the Hightstown High School newspaper, the first female valedictorian of her college class, and one of the first women to win a Pulitzer Traveling Fellowship from Columbia University. And with nothing better to do with her time, she would certainly have been a millionaire by the age of twenty-five, and a burned-out husk who had conquered all the worlds she had ever known by the age of thirty.

She would have said, in her characteristic colorful overstatement, that she used to go out with men who would have made Gloria Steinem and Lillian Hellman blush, and that, without exception, she was so unmoved by them she was in the habit of crying herself to sleep.

Lois would have said that before she met Superman she was a spoiled little girl who had never been said no to, who had never had her heart broken, and who would have died of loneliness by now if it were not for Superman. She would have asked him if he had any idea of what it was like to be totally alone, and he would have said that he did.

He would have confessed that now, without Clark behind whom to hide, he was afraid that he would soon die of loneliness himself. She would have cried again, he would have joined her, and they would have decided that they desperately needed each other.

Unfortunately, none of this was ever said. Unfortunately, at the inauspicious moment when Lois blithely accused Superman of using some sort of exotic hormone spray to get her to fall in love with him, the sky lit up with a new dire emergency.

This particular emergency was the result of C. W. Saturn, in the guise of Kristin Wells, whipping up all the pollution—all the nongaseous matter—in the sky between Metropolis and the edge of space, and weaving all that garbage together into a kind of flying carpet the size of the city itself. At the inauspicious moment when Superman streaked out the window, Kristin was riding the carpet from high in the sky down toward the surface of the city with the apparent intention of shrouding the city with it. Because it was so high, it reflected the rays of the sun off its surface like the moon, but as it came closer it would blot out the sun completely.

Superman would certainly be able to deal with this issue, just as he had been playing Kristin Wells to a stalemate ever since the devil took her soul. The conversation with Lois, however, would go unfinished.

The Alternatives

"There was the elfin character who claimed to be from the Fifth Dimension, whatever that was," the old man said. "I can never remember his name, but whenever we run a story on him I look it up and spell it out in big block letters and tack it up on the bulletin board in the city room. People have been comparing him to this girl, but I don't think the comparison goes very far."

"You're talking about Mr. Mxyzptlk?" Dan Reed the moderator asked.

"Probably, but I couldn't vouch for your pronunciation of it."

"The pronunciation's right, Mr. White," Jimmy said.

"Thank you, Olsen. I'll have to take your word for it. Mr. What's-his-name has certain powers of—oh, what shall we call it?"

"Magic?" Reed suggested.

"All right, for lack of a more precise description, magic it is. He comes to town whenever he breaks out of whatever zoo they keep him in back home, and he simply follows Superman around trying to get his goat. He has, as a matter of fact, done many things similar to what this girl Kristin Wells has done. He once made the statue in the Lincoln Memorial come alive, for example, and walk across the ellipse to the Capitol Building where poor Senator Stevenson found himself plucked up and sitting in a six-foot-diameter marble palm, holding a conversation with his fellow Illinoisian. He did all sorts of things like that.''

The man doing most of the talking was Perry White, the editor-in-chief of the *Daily Planet*, who once finished ahead of Walter Cronkite in an opinion poll to determine the man whose word the citizens of Metropolis trust most. White was a great gray mastodon of a man, three times a winner of the Pulitzer Prize, the person who had given Clark Kent his first job as a reporter. Barrel-chested and robust, White looked like the sort of man Bruce Jenner would be when he grew up. He was sitting between Lois Lane and Jimmy Olsen, talking on a special live interview with the new WGBS anchorman, Dan Reed, about Superman and Clark Kent, the man Reed had replaced. The biggest news of the day—still, and getting bigger by the hour—was the running war between Superman and Kristin Wells who, as everybody knew by now, was supposedly possessed by some sort of malicious demon. Perry White had some trouble swallowing that idea, but he had seen some strange things in the past sixty-six years, he admitted.

Jimmy Olsen, on the other hand, positively choked on the notion. Jimmy stayed as silent as he did only because the man sitting next to him was the person who had first taught him that personal feelings have no place in responsible journalism. White was, next to Superman, the person Jimmy respected most in the world. In fact, Jimmy was usually afraid of White and had never been afraid of Superman. Sitting next to the editor, Jimmy felt like a beer can, discarded by some witless tourist, lying on the ground beside the last of the redwoods. Jimmy's first impulse, when Reed asked him to be on the show, was to refuse. He had refused at first, but so had Lois, and Jimmy changed his mind only when he realized that if Lois did not have something to do today—something that had the illusion of usefulness around it— she might do something foolish to herself. She was so morbidly depressed that she might do something foolish to herself anyhow, but he convinced her to go on the show with him.

Meanwhile, Jimmy thought, if Perry White kept talking with such clinical detachment about Kris as though she were some kind of primeval monster, Jimmy might do something even more foolish. He might disagree with Perry White in public. Maybe it didn't matter, Jimmy thought, because it was probable that nobody was watching.

172

Most of the power was out in town and nobody wanted to hear the news these days anyhow.

"Whatever it is this little twerp's got," Perry continued on the subject of the mischievous otherworldly pixie, "Superman can't really handle it. Maybe it is magic. That was what we used to call it in the old days when Clark was with the *Daily Planet* and most newspapermen, except for Clark and a few others, hadn't yet discovered their responsibility to be precise in their writing. Whatever it is, Superman's vulnerable to it. And whatever it is, Miss Wells seems to have it or something like it in at least as great a measure as . . . umm—"

"Mxyzptlk," Jimmy said.

"Right."

"So what are you saying, Mr. White?"

"I'm saying, Dan, that whatever power this girl has is something from which Superman is really unable to protect us. I'm also saying that unlike—Olsen?—"

"Mxyzptlk."

"Unlike Mix-el-plix, whatever, this girl's intentions don't involve having fun. She has willfully waged a psychological battle against our friend Superman, taking away his clearest tie with the world around him. She has kept him occupied with trivia ranging in seriousness from zany inconveniences like upside-down buildings and vanishing walls to genuine crises like locust plagues and epidemics of maddening eczema. Superman knows as well as we do that she must be stopped. I assume he hasn't yet stopped her, but simply defused what she has done so far, because of two reasons. Firstly, he doesn't know what her intentions are and he would like to know. Secondly, he may not have devised a way of stopping her short of killing her."

"Oh, now you're going off the deep end. Really." It was Jimmy Olsen, and it was immediately clear that he was sorry he had said it.

"What deep end is that?" Dan Reed asked, doing his job.

"No, I was just—" Jimmy hesitated but saw it was not going to work. "Well, maybe I'm wrong, but she hasn't done anything but try to get Superman's goat, as you said. She's just more unfriendly about it. She hasn't killed anyone, right?"

"Except Clark." It was the first thing Lois had said since she said hello to Reed at the show's opening.

"Clark. Well, yeah, but there wasn't an actual murder involved. Hey, what's with everyone feeling like somebody really died? I mean, Clark was one of my best friends—maybe my best friend—and I'm kind of really happy for him that he turned out to be Superman. It couldn't've happened to a nicer guy. I mean, that's confusing, I guess, but I'd really like it if he'd come by sometime for lunch or coffee the way he used to. I don't know why he doesn't.''

"What would you call him?" Reed asked.

"Call him?"

"What would you call Clark Kent if he came by for a cup of coffee with you?"

"Oh, I get you. I'd say, 'Hi, Superman.' ''

"That's part of the point I was making," Perry White said, picking it up again. "If Superman masquerades as Clark secretly, he's living among us as a natural Earthman. If, on the other hand, he puts on those glasses and we all know it's really Superman, he becomes grotesque, a dangerously schizoid personality. Maybe one of the purposes of this Kristin Wells is to discredit Superman, to drive him past the brink of sanity. Who's to say?"

During the next few thoughtful moments Dan Reed decided to bring Lois into the conversation.

"Can you shed any light on this speculation, Miss Lane? Have you spoken to Superman recently at all?"

It was a mistake. Lois looked as though she were about to say something when, instead, she gulped hard and ran from the studio.

The remainder of the interview foundered in Dan Reed's unstudied ineptness, Jimmy Olsen's combative melancholy and Perry White's thinly veiled depression. The veteran editor, square-jawed and veiny-eyed, went on in an uncharacteristic rambling fashion until he reached the conclusion of his speculation and reminiscences. When he did reach the conclusion, however, it was quite a conclusion indeed.

"For the sake of argument, then,"—Perry was speaking in a quiet tone that suggested inevitability—"let's say that this girl is possessed by some kind of satanic entity. What then? Obviously, the demon needs her human form in order to work his—its—spells. One must assume that the girl is gone, as gone as somebody already dead, as one of the hapless victims bitten by Dracula in the old stories. Superman has no alternative but to destroy the essential tool of this creature, to kill the body of Kristin Wells."

Reed was silent. Jimmy Olsen's eyes were watering.

It was the Sunday before the third Monday in May and there was still frost on the windows of Metropolis and a cold front was moving south. Power was out through most of the city. Food supplies were getting low. Businesses were closed and stores were gutted. This was the last program that WGBS would broadcast until further notice.

174

Only seventy-eight televisions in the Metropolis area received the broadcast anyway, but Superman was watching one of them.

For a few minutes after the program Jimmy Olsen allowed himself to hate his mentor a little bit for advocating the murder of a young woman Jimmy liked. He hated the crusty self-assuredness; hated the argument that was so well constructed that logical disagreement was nearly impossible; hated the brutish experience of the man. But Jimmy was the only one among the stage crew and the hundred or so viewers and participants in the discussion from whom Perry's sorrow at his own words was effectively veiled. Jimmy Olsen hated Perry White until after the broadcast, when the young reporter walked into the men's room on the twentieth floor of the Galaxy Building and realized that the sounds of gentle and private disgust in the stall against the wall were those of that great gray mastodon of a newsman surrendering his latest meal.

The Standard Nightmare

A generation, still alive and still young, grew up in the United States, Europe and the Soviet Union, continually reminded of the apocalyptic circumstance that rode shotgun with civilization. The more intricate and refined life became in the twentieth century, the closer rode violence and the spectre of mass death. The nightmare of unbridled power came to pass on the morning of the third Monday in May. As everyone who grew up in the days of ice-cold war and white-hot visions in the dark had always known it would, it happened not by the hand of any human, but by that of a devil!

Superman slept in flight these days, with only one hemisphere of his brain at a time. He careened in a twilight of consciousness around the world from day to night to day to night and around again, keeping his mind healthy with what dreams he could gather from his few minutes per day of rest. He had a dream today of Jonathan and Martha Kent coming to dinner in the home of his parents on Krypton. Infant Kal-El seemed to recognize the farm couple when they walked in and wanted to introduce them to Jor-El and Lara, who did not speak

English. No matter, he realized. Jonathan Kent had learned Kryptonese for the occasion and brought the Kryptonians a Sara Lee cheesecake and a fresh cabbage from Mrs. Kent's garden. Cabbage went very well, as it turned out, with braised gryzmish, which was what was waiting in the dining room of Jor-El's house. Lara flushed the head of cabbage through the thresher and it came out cole slaw. Jor-El lent Jonathan a headband so that he could say grace, and Jonathan translated for Martha. Martha was under the impression that Kal-El had somehow helped prepare the meal and praised him copiously. The baby swatted his food around the surface of his separate table and energy fields and caught it in midair before it soiled the grasslike carpet of the dining room. Jonathan joked that he could have used energy fields like that back when he used to keep pigs, and Jor-El and Lara laughed. Martha Kent slipped and called the baby Clark and Kristin Wells woke Superman up.

"I have turned loose the holocaust, Superman," said the inhuman voice that came from the beautiful young woman with the freckle on the tip of her nose. Superman opened his eyes and saw the unholy leer that profaned Kristin's face as she sat cross-legged before him, her back shielding the wind in their course over the roof of the world.

Superman had no use for recriminations. He supposed that what scant effect even the most economical of oaths might have would certainly slip past the demon Saturn and slap the poor enslaved consciousness of Kristin Wells—whatever was left of her—squarely across the corpus callosum. Below, the world was going up in flames, and if it did, Superman would go with it.

The hysterical obscene cackle, ancient beyond words, that came from Kristin Wells's distorted throat, followed Superman wherever he went on this mission of undignified necessity. This was the worst one yet. Silos, bunkers and torpedo tubes all over the world had come alive and, with one will, had shot off every armed nuclear warhead in the world at its target. Saturn did not want to destroy the Earth, although if that happened in the process that would be fine with the demon. What the Hellspawn wanted was for Superman to allow the world to end. It was as simple for C. W. Saturn to explode every atomic nucleus on the planet as it was to unleash the weapons built by men. It was simply more dramatic this way. Saturn was living not on death itself, but on rancor, fear, and the promise of death.

The first problem would be the bombs for which nobody but their builders had any record. They were the ones most likely all along to bring about the end of the world, whatever that was. Secure in the knowledge that only he, of all the life on this planet, knew what the end of a world looked, felt and tasted like, he dove in the direction of Pakistan.

The small nation was a mass of humanity surrounding the opulence of a building that went by as many names as there had been despots to occupy it. With each despot came a new wave of inhumanity and a new caretaker for the obscenity in the basement. The mass of garbage and wires as big as a two-car garage with a globule of plutonium at its core was one of Dr. Robert Oppenheimer's more specific recurring nightmares. The bomb was aimed at nowhere; no one among the generations of bureaucrats and toadies and potentates who passed this way in the course of a year could remember how to explode or disarm the thing. No one but Superman knew that the chain reaction had begun, and when the outer roof of what was currently called the Presidential Palace spewed apart, the bomb was what everyone in the building first thought of.

Superman crashed through the roof, through a succession of floors of marble, granite, steel and wood to the wall that contained Pakistan's nuclear device, which was already beginning to glow red.

With the infrared rays of his eyes, he fused the hairline cracks in the corners of the steel container so that it was one solid piece. He burrowed underneath it and lifted it onto his back, and plowed back up in the direction he had come, widening the holes in the floors and the ceilings on his way back up. He prayed that not too much radiation would spew out in his wake.

Superman had reached forty kilometers over the surface of the Earth when his burden caught fire. The atmosphere below shielded the cradled world as it was supposed to, and most of the impact bounced off into space. New Haven, Connecticut, and then nearby Cambridge, Massachusetts, were next.

The physics faculty at Yale University had spent three years petitioning the New Haven municipal authorities for permission to build a basement nuclear reactor. They pointed to Columbia University which had operated a reactor for educational purposes for years in one of the densest population centers on Earth. When the department got the permission they had fought for, they cleverly rubbed their hands together and built a bomb instead. It would be much more educational than a mere reactor, and no one, not even the University administration, needed to know what it really was.

Fortunately, Superman knew. It was smaller, and not as crude as the Pakistani device. It had fewer wires hanging out where wires did not belong. It would go off sooner, however.

Superman plummeted from the sky into the institution that had seen fit, over the years, to give a voice to the likes of Eli Yale and William Sloane Coffin. Through the greensward of the Yale campus the man who had ridden a falling star to Earth bored, kicking up a storm of moss and loam behind him. His trajectory took him through a basement compartment under a physics building, and he followed a trail of burning nitrogen to his destination.

He scooped up the football-shaped object and continued on course, through the floor, through the crust of the planet, through the mass of molten soup on which the east coast of the United States rides, into a vast cavern miles below what humans think of as the world, from which an explosion sent tremors along the coast from Narragansett to Red Bank.

By the time anyone realized the sky was falling, Superman was in Cambridge where, overlooking the Charles River where a flurry of white sails refused to recognize the fact that winter had decided to stay around for a while, a man at the Massachusetts Institute of Technology who had the makings of a Nobel Prize winner had constructed something that was excessively stupid. It was a nuclear device whose trigger mechanism was operated by the stimulation of reproduction of cells of recombinant DNA.

The physicist who had designed it had figured out the idea in a dream. He supposed that although nuclear radiation was capable of wiping out virtually all forms of life now on the planet, he could stimulate the development of altogether new forms of life by placing their seeds at ground zero of a nuclear explosion. He had a lot of grant money left over the year before and, in a fit of irresponsible silliness, he actually built the thing.

The life-defining chemical at the trigger of the MIT bomb was already forming into something that was neither plant nor animal, and may not have been alive by any rational definition of the term. The bomb, however, was quite alive by the time Superman snapped it up in his cape, knotted it shut and flung it like a bolo in the direction of Polaris.

The package rose only a few kilometers before the bomb burst, but the cape of Kryptonian fabric stretched out of all proportion and contained it, continuing to rise until, on the edge of space, the knot finally flew out of its corners and the heat that was the only thing left inside the red sack poured into infinity. Superman would pick up the cape from its orbit later.

There were thousands more, but they were all the "responsible" bombs, aimed by the governments of the United States, the Soviet

Union, France, China, and India at one another's strategic locations and population centers.

They were all on course and, one by one, in order of their closeness to their targets, Superman disarmed them with the ringing cackle of the demon C. W. Saturn haunting his consciousness

He threw missiles into space.

He tossed warheads at each other.

He drove the heat-seeking devices driving multiple warheads crazy by heating up the tail of the missile carrying the warheads with his heat vision so that the steering devices wore out before the bombs let go of them.

He took direct hits on his chest.

He gulped down several ounces of hot plutonium and let his own underworked antibodies deal with the heat.

He caught giant armloads of deadly weaponry as if they were pickup sticks and threw them like darts into the sun.

It took an hour and forty-two minutes to rid the world of its various nuclear arsenals, and still he heard the ringing of primeval laughter from the throat of Kristin Wells. Emotionally spent and knowing he would have to gather his moral strength as quickly as he had gathered the mega-death that he had banished from the world, Superman turned his torso to his left and pointed his extended fists in the direction of the city of Metropolis below him.

Kristin Wells stood at a place Superman had once considered to be something like his home, on the roof of the Galaxy Building in the city of Metropolis. Around midday on the third Monday in May, he went there to meet her.

181

The Decision

So far, since C. W. Saturn had taken active control of Kristin Wells's life, the young woman had been moved to commit, among others, the following acts of destruction:

The disintegration of the steering wheels of the cars in midtown.

The attacking of pedestrians by the twenty-one statues in Central Preserve.

The growth of roaches until they were so large they scared rats.

The rising of killing winds across the countryside.

The division of families and friends by causing them to speak different languages.

The forgetting by people of the faces of their own children.

The disarray of the mass media by turning all the rubber insulation in the television and radio network buildings into highly conductive silver.

The emptying of the digestive systems of a horde of citizens so that they became hungry enough to steal food from the city's grocery stores and supermarkets.

The explosion of a fuel tank of every airplane to leave Metropolis International Airport during a certain two-hour period on the tenth of May.

The incitement of the planet's most powerful governments to the edge of nuclear war.

And she had stolen Clark Kent.

Max Maven the expert and Lena Thorul of intuitive near-infallibility agreed that Kristin Wells could not be exorcised of the arch-demon by physical or mystical means. The spiritual power of Superman and the entire human community could not rip C. W. Saturn out of Kristin Wells against Saturn's will without leaving Kristin a tattered mess of lifeless flesh.

There were those who claimed that the death of this pawn, this innocent child without family or past, was the only way to save the world. All she had to do was succeed in one act of destruction, according to that powerful argument, while Superman had to succeed in defusing her every try. Her demise was certainly one solution, Superman knew.

Now, he asked himself, what were the other alternatives?

Were there any?

The world cried out for the death of Kristin Wells before she succeeded once. This man who stood in space facing the roof of the Galaxy building where this possessed girl stood, soft and human and as vulnerable as any creature wrought by the hand of God, this man was the only power capable of carrying out that final solution.

But for one fact, he would have done it. The fact was that although it made perfect sense to the entire sentient population of the world with the exception of Superman, the logic of killing Kristin Wells honestly eluded him.

Other than the murder of the exquisite fiction of Clark Kent, she had done nothing and was likely, as far as Superman could tell, to do nothing that Superman could not reverse. Certainly the arch-demon C. W. Saturn could kill or disparage, could scar living sensibilities, but that was not what Saturn had used Kristin's body to do. Superman suspected that it would not serve Saturn's purposes, whatever they were, to destroy anything of this world outright, any more than taking Kristin's body was his final purpose.

What Saturn was interested in doing was not destroying life and liberty, but destroying innocence. If Saturn, through Kristin, tore down a building, then only the building and presumably its occupants were destroyed. If, on the other hand, Kristin were to prompt one of

184

the building's inhabitants to destroy the building, then Saturn would win the soul of the destroyer.

And if Superman killed Kristin Wells in order to stop her reign of terror, then it was Superman, along with all he stood for, that was destroyed.

"What will you do now?" the shrill, horrible voice of the possessed woman called to Superman from the roof of the Galaxy Building.

"Who wants to know?" the big man responded.

"Will you stand by and allow me to do as I would? You cannot confine me effectively, or stop me from committing whatever caprices I care to. Or will you kill me, good Superman?"

"You're talking nonsense."

"Nonsense?" She held up an open palm to the big Radio Corporation building across the plaza and a bolt of heat energy burst through the air in the building's direction. Superman met the bolt halfway with his chest and the force dissipated into the air. "Is this destructive power nonsense?"

"No," Superman said, "your power is not nonsense. The idea that I would kill you simply because you misdirect it, however, is ridiculous."

"You prattling, idealistic fool. Do you expect me to stop of my own accord?"

"No, I don't. Unfortunately, I don't expect that at all."

"Then what do you expect to do about me?"

"What I ever do with criminals and destructive forces like you. I'll follow you," Superman said, casually unshakable in his conviction that there was a good and an evil in the Universe, and determined to be a force for the good.

"You would follow me to the bowels of the Earth?"

"Certainly. Wherever you choose to vent your spleen I'll be there to stop you. It's as simple as that."

"To the rim of the Universe?"

"I think you're being melodramatic. I'll follow you to the ends of Creation. I look forward to seeing places where I've never been, and I don't suppose there could be a nobler mission for a superman."

The clouds rolled over the city. Thunder roared without a crack of lightning. The air shook. The eyes of Kristin Wells widened and, for the moment before they snapped shut, they glowed red.

Superman looked on, his own eyes widening against his will as he realized what was going on. The body of Kristin Wells dropped on the asphalt and a great black pillar of energy swirled upward from her head and toward the sky. A grotesquely obscene scream of pain and a great voice, equally unearthly, cut through the chaos of the third Monday in May.

"*Stop, damn you. Now you'll answer to me.*"

The voice was monstrous, harsh, inhuman.

The Raped Lock

On the Saturday that was two days before the third Monday in May, there was no broadcasting coming out of Metropolis, and very little news by other means. The food supply was dwindling because truckers refused to come into town. The cost of fuel in the coming summer, if the unseasonable cold did not break soon, promised to set new records. Private motor vehicles were banned from the streets. For fear of vulnerability to the arch-demon, gasoline was drained from the tanks under all the city's stations and was totally unavailable. Mass transit, even subways, had ceased to function. People were staying home from work. Strangely, the hotels were doing phenomenally good business. Dr. David Skvrsky walked down the steps to the empty subway platform under the corner of Fifth Avenue and Fifty-Second Street.

Skvrsky walked to the far end of the platform, then hopped down onto the track and walked on beyond the station. He pulled off the mustache and the shock of iron gray hair and became Lex Luthor again. He stuffed the hair into the right inside pocket of his coat, and before he entered total darkness he checked once more for the hair in the left inside pocket.

To his left in the darkness there was a small red light marking the entrance to a tunnel that had not been used for anything by the Transit Authority since 1942 when President Roosevelt came to town and it was secretly converted to a combination bomb shelter–command station to be used if the Nazi Air Force attacked the city while the President was in town. Luthor had not known about the bunker in the tunnel until he was told that it was to be his meeting place.

In the abandoned tunnel he found a wallpapered room whose eerie light seemed to have no source. There were three comfortable-looking chairs and a large empty desk behind which sat the large white figure who had ordered a lock of Superman's hair.

"I trust you have the item we discussed, Lex Luthor." The apparition's voice seemed even more cavernous than it had been at their first meeting.

"I have it right here." Luthor pulled a small envelope from his coat pocket and held it away as the white figure leaned across the desk for it. "You ought to know these things. You claim to be a supernatural being."

"I hardly need to claim it. Certainly you used to read the city's newspapers before I disrupted their production," and the thing laughed a horrible laugh. The Shadow used to laugh that way.

"Actually, I rather think you are who you say you are, or rather what you say you are. I am satisfied that you are bound by any contract you make. I wonder, however, if you could tell me what your game is. You've evidently managed to possess this girl Kristin Wells, is that right?"

"She is acting under the dominion of C. W. Saturn, that is correct."

"Then what keeps you from simply destroying the city, or taking over, or whatever you came to do?"

The white figure laughed again. Luthor hated that laugh. "In your world, Lex Luthor, you are a very powerful being, is that not so?"

"I believe it is."

"As I am in the Netherworld. But do you remember anything of the land you passed through in order to escape from prison?"

"Almost nothing. I saw some shadows, and I knew how many steps I had to take in each direction, but mostly I remember being in pain."

"As I was in pain when I entered your world at the time you

made your escape. As you would have grown in power had you remained, so do I become stronger here in good time. It is not my intention to destroy your world, Lex Luthor. But my power here is still limited. For example, I do not even know where your gateway to the Netherworld is located.''

Now Luthor laughed, not as menacingly. "Why would a phony demon admit to a foul-up like that? Here's your hair from Supie. You owe me now.''

"Indeed I do,'' and the ghostly figure gestured in the direction of the surface of the desk, where the standard puff of black smoke heralded the appearance of a single clothbound volume. "All the technical information on the physics of alternate dimensional universes that you will ever require,'' the creature said and handed Luthor the book in return for the envelope with the lock of hair.

Luthor coughed from the smoke. "What is that stuff, burnt rubber?''

"Pardon the histrionics. It is brimstone, actually. Traditional, you understand.''

"Of course. What are you going to do with that hair anyway, make some kind of Superman voodoo doll?''

The laugh again. "You seemed rather unimpressed that I did not know the location of your 'demonpass,' Lex Luthor. The information would be rather useful to me. I propose a trade. You answer my question and I shall answer yours.''

"Oh, I think I can get more out of you than that. Your information would do me no good at all, I'm simply curious.''

"Very curious. You are a scientist, Lex Luthor, among the most curious creatures in all Creation. You want to know the answer to your question quite a bit more than I want the answer to mine.''

"All right. I never was very good at bargaining. Demonpass empties out in the area of the New England Pontoon Reactor. The vicinity of a nuclear reactor was the easiest place to put it because the plant itself softens space in proximity to it. When Earth scientists realize that, they may stop building them. I came out under the reactor floor, on top of the easternmost pontoon. Now it's your turn, Saturn. What do you want Superman's hair for?''

"Oh, I don't know.'' The voice became clearly softer, more Earthly as he spoke. "Maybe I'll see if I can glue it back or something.''

And the lights went out.

Luthor began his howl of frustration under the city, and by the time he finished it, he was wrapped in Superman's cape, flying north toward Pocantico Correctional Facility. Superman had used his visual and flying powers so creatively that Luthor thought the demon was using powers that Superman did not have. Superman had reflected his X-ray vision through a collection of hidden mirrors to make the eerie light of the underground room; he had appeared and disappeared by flying in and out of sight at super-speed. The book was actually a freshly bound copy of *Catch-22*.

It was all in order to find the location of the demonpass, and now Superman would be able to plug it up against the entry of any more of Saturn's minions.

"You did very well," Superman told Luthor before turning him over to the new warden of the Pocantico Correctional Facility. "You might have put it over on me if it hadn't all been my idea."

Heroes, above all, are people who succeed. They sometimes fail in their immediate goals—staying alive, for example—in order to succeed in their ultimate goals—saving the Union, making the world safe for democracy, obtaining civil rights for their people. Ultimately they succeed, and generally this is because they set out on purpose to succeed. They keep control. The key, then, to success, and therefore to being a hero, is to be in control of surroundings, always to know what happens next.

The encounter between Lex Luthor and Superman disguised as C. W. Saturn ended the Saturday before the third Monday in May. All of this is by way of explanation for what happened next on the third Monday in May.

The Reckoning

"Stay, damn you! Now you'll answer to me!"
The voice was monstrous, harsh, inhuman. It was a voice that
Superman had never before realized that he owned. He used that
voice, rippling with righteous power, to order the demon escaping
from the girl's body to a halt.

"I've won, you Hellspawn. You owe me. Stop where you are."
The Man of Steel hurtled up into the sky beside the rising pillar of
luminous blackness, and at these words the pillar stopped rising.

Below, the city ceased its motion and the elements no longer
roiled. Above, the sun no longer burned, saving its energy until this
moment was over. The sky lost all light. Photons hung still in space.
The very heat of the Universe stopped its flight toward entropy.
Everything seemed to freeze in place, but nothing actually stopped
except for time.

Superman stood motionless in space and time, shortly before
four in the afternoon of the third Monday in May, one hundred fifty
meters above midtown Metropolis, facing the agent of Hell on Earth.

191

It was an instant suspended between the eternities of the past and the future where the pillar of obscene energy was the only thing that moved, in answer to the command of the last son of Krypton, who had made himself its master. The pillar spun and swirled into the solid form, four meters long from horns to hooves, of the dark fallen angel of fable. C. W. Saturn took the form he had devised an age ago to strike terror into the hearts of humans. It was the leathery-winged, goat-like devil, spurs at its joints, beard reaching from its pointed chin, nostrils distending in hypnotic rhythm. The creature was visibly—to the eyes of Superman, who needed no light—quaking under the Kryptonian's command and hating him nonetheless. No one who had made himself this creature's master would have needed light to see now.

"I was supposed to kill her, wasn't I?"

The demon only glared and sucked its nostrils.

"That was the plan, wasn't it? That was how you proposed to defeat me, by getting me to think I was freeing her from you by killing her, wasn't it?"

Saturn stared some more.

"You thought you'd use my pity for an innocent victim to make me abandon the principle I hold the most sacred, didn't you? Answer me."

"Yes. That was it. I could not find an adequate weakness with which to tempt you, so I tried to distort a virtue."

"Shrink yourself down to three feet. I don't care what you choose to look like, but I won't have you hovering over me."

The creature became smaller in an instant, but still it glared and hated.

"I know the rules," Superman said. "I'm in charge now. Am I right? Tell me."

"Yes, you are."

"And the girl. Tell me what happens to her."

"When time again resumes, when our conversation is ended, she will soon die."

"Why?" howled the indignant hero. "She was innocent. Completely innocent. I don't even think she belonged in this city full of fallible humans. She was too good even to be here. Why is she to die? Answer that."

"Her mortal form has been overextended by my possession of it. Her shell will collapse, her power to live used up."

"Fiend!" Superman swatted the back of his hand with all his power across the leathery face of C. W. Saturn. The hero was surprised

192

that the part of the demon's face that Superman's fingers had touched was now striped with fiery red welts. Saturn could not bear the touch of his vanquisher.

"No," Superman said, sorry now for his burst of temper. "That won't do. I won't waste my power on anger. You're going to undo your damage and we will figure out the best way to do that. First, tell me why, of all the people on Earth, you chose Kristin Wells."

"She was an alien element in the city. She was the most susceptible to my influence because she did not really belong here."

Superman was startled to hear this, not because it was of itself surprising, but because Superman had just said it out loud and it had been no more than an idle thought he had tossed out in a rage. What Superman did not realize—it did not matter whether he realized this or not—was that in this extended instant he could do or say no wrong. There was a right and a wrong in the Universe, and Superman was no more capable of erring here and now than C. W. Saturn was capable of defying him. He did not need Saturn to tell him what he instinctively knew about Kristin Wells. There was something else he wanted.

"Kristin Wells's life," he barked at the demon. "Tell me how I can save it. I will not have her indebted to you for that."

"You will find in the private notebook of Dr. David Skvrsky the formula for a life-preserving elixir which can save her."

"The notebook. Tell me where it is."

"It is in a drawer in Dr. Skvrsky's temporary office at the Center for the Study of Short-Lived Phenomena."

"How will I recognize the formula? Tell me which page it's on."

"The pages are numbered. It is written on page number thirty-one."

"Swear you're telling the truth."

"I must tell the truth," and C. W. Saturn swore in the name of his master.

Superman was disgusted by this, and spat on Saturn's hooves, which burned at the touch.

"You took Clark Kent away from me," Superman accused Saturn. "I want you to give him back. Tell me if there's any reason I shouldn't make you do that."

"It would upset the balance of nature that you hold so dearly," Saturn mocked his captor, "if I were to recreate a person the memory of whom has been destroyed through natural means such as this one."

Superman thought for a moment. "You can substitute Clark Kent for Kristin Wells. You can, can't you? Tell me."

"Yes, I can. I can remove the memory of Kristin Wells from everyone with whom she came in contact here, and balance that by replacing it with the person of Clark Kent so that you may resume your elaborate charade."

"Tell me if that would in any way disrupt the natural balance."

"That would not upset your Universe as it is."

"Then do it. Take away the memory of Kristin Wells from the human consciousness and replace her with Clark Kent. Give me back Clark Kent."

"It is done," Saturn said.

"And what do I owe you and your master for performing these services for me and for this world?"

"Nothing," the creature said with disappointment.

"Then I want nothing more to do with you. Get out of this world, out of the realm of humanity for all time. Do you understand that? Go see how your cursed master deals with you now."

Photons of sunlight streamed once again to Earth, the city resumed its motion from the moment it had left off. Life continued. The rolling waves of this Universe continued. Shortly before four in the afternoon on the third Monday in the month of May in the city of Metropolis, after an immeasurably long, short, or middling pause, the Universe resumed its course through time into the future.

The unholy shriek, the sound of the force of C. W. Saturn leaving the body of Kristin Wells, continued, then died on the air.

The Miracle

Shortly before four in the afternoon on the third Monday in the month of May, the people of the city of Metropolis learned the meaning of joy. They had no explanation for this feeling, and there were gaps in their knowledge of what had gone on in their lives so far that day. It was as though they were all waking up, or at least opening their eyes, for the first time in an awfully long time. The first thing many of them saw was the red-and-blue figure of Superman drawing a line across their sky, and he became the symbol of their joy. It felt like a miracle, though none could say why.

In the apartment building where Kristin Wells lived, the superintendent, Cezar O'Higgins, was inspecting an empty studio apartment. It was clean, free of vermin except for one roach who poked his head out a crack under the bathroom basin, and it was completely empty. The refrigerator door as well as the freezer compartment hung open, the machine turned off and dry. It looked to Cezar as though it had not been used for nearly a year, which was what his boss told him was evidently the case.

No one understood how the apartment could go empty for so many months without anyone calling the fact to the attention of Cezar or the owner of the building. The owner had been quite confused, as a matter of fact, when he called Cezar about it a few minutes ago.

No matter, Cezar thought, he could worry about finding a new tenant tomorrow. Or the next day. Right now he felt like calling his friends and having a party. He did not stop to wonder why he felt this way.

"Kent!" Morgan Edge yelled with the characteristic disdain for dignity befitting his position. "Kent, where are you?"

Edge had commandeered an elevator down from his office in the ivory tower of the thirty-third floor of the Galaxy Building, to the WGBS News offices on the twentieth floor. As far as Edge could tell, he had been speaking with Clark Kent on the interoffice picture-phone and the anchorman had shut him off.

Edge's natural reaction was to barrel into his employee's office and chew him out in person so that he could not be turned off. This is what he was doing now, but only on general principles, because his anger was now running on principles and nothing else. Edge felt odd, though, quite disinclined to snap like the cobra that his legend said he was. Edge regretted that he could only describe his mood as *mellow*. He disliked the word, much as he disliked the words *concept*, *transactional* and *outrageous*. Words like that and the attitudes they brought with them were a large part of the reason he moved his office here from Los Angeles a few years ago. Unfortunately, undeniably, the man putting on a show of careening down the twentieth floor hallway, biting the end of his cigarette holder and screaming for the blood of one of his pet newsmen, was mellow. Worse, he was *centered*.

Morgan Edge blew open the door of the office like the Big Bad Wolf and found Dan Reed sitting at Clark Kent's desk. Reed looked more surprised to be there than Edge was to see him. Edge looked at the sign on the door which said "Mr. Kent," and at the plaque on the desk which said CLARK KENT. The certificates and testimonials that customarily paper the walls of a television newsman's office—a Peabody Award, an Emmy or two, "Best wishes" from Hugh Carey and Eric Sevareid and so forth—were all in place and inscribed to Kent.

"What're you doing here?" Edge asked Dan Reed. He supposed the question was appropriate.

196

Reed looked around. "I don't know, Mr. Edge," he said. "Working, I guess."

"What's that noise?" Edge wanted to know, and both men went to the window and looked down at the street. Clark was the only newsman at WGBS who had insisted on having a window in his office.

It was the first really hot day of the year in Metropolis, an assurance from the heavens that there would indeed be a summer this year. Outside, people had left cars unattended in the streets. People were cheering at something, running through the plaza waving jackets and sweaters as if they were banners at the ends of sticks and umbrellas. People were reaching into deserted cars to honk horns, and then running on to other cars to do it some more. Mounted police were rearing ecstatic horses up on their hind legs.

"Looks like they're happy about something," Edge said absently.

"Yes, sir," Reed said. "Me too."

"Happy? About anything in particular?"

"No, sir. I mean, no, I don't think so, sir. Just happy. Kind of mellow."

"Hmm. Aren't you guys supposed to put today's news on the air in two hours?" Edge asked, also because it seemed appropriate.

"Yes, Mr. Edge."

"Right." They both looked out the window again. "Come on, Reed, I'll buy you a martini. You can wing the news tonight. It'll be good practice. Doesn't look like anyone's doing much of anything newsworthy today anyhow."

Throngs cheered through the streets as Superman passed overhead, and the feeling spread to the streets where people could not see him. The feeling spread into buildings, through subway catacombs, across rivers, over oceans, through the air. There was a collective consciousness about the people of this world, a mass mind personified by Clark Kent and other newsmen like him who told the entire planet Earth, almost all at once, as if communicating with one pair of eyes and ears, what had happened on this world today. This day, though, the souls who had subjugated the surfaces of the small planet needed no artificial aids like newspapers, radios, televisions, even word of mouth, to know it was a good day.

The next time Clark Kent would identify himself over the airwaves to a million Metropolitans, it would be Tuesday. For the next twenty-four hours or so, acting en masse and without any cue other than the conviction that such a thing was peculiarly appropriate, the human population of the entire city would take the day off.

A great miracle had happened here.

197

Across the top of the city Superman sped, warding off the feeling until his job was done. He landed uptown on the roof of the university building that housed the Center for the Study of Short-Lived Phenomena. The office for which he was looking was locked and unoccupied. He hovered at the outside window, hearing cheers from the street below. He scanned the shelves and cabinets in the room until he found the notebook in the drawer of a rolltop desk. He flipped through the pages long-distance by minusculely intensifying the radiation from his eyes. Page thirty-one was facedown and he read it mirror-fashion through the back of the page.

Immediately, Superman whizzed off to a laboratory at the medical school where he left an I.O.U. for the chemicals he lifted. He swiped the garlic and a paper bag from a grocery store on Columbus Avenue on the ledge of whose cash register, at eye-blinding speed, he left three quarters from Clark Kent's pocket which was in the pouch of his cape. He filled the paper bag with hawthorne berries that he found growing in Evenside Park. In the next three seconds he streaked the three and a half miles from Evenside Heights downtown to the Galaxy Building, tincturing and heat-bonding the substances as it had said to do in Skvrsky's notebook, and then cooling the serum with the air for the last four blocks. On the roof of the Galaxy Building, fallen and gasping at the air, was the girl nobody remembered.

"Kristin," he said after a while. "Kristin, can you talk now?"

He had no idea what the serum was that he had just made, no idea that it was the medicine with which Luthor had cured himself of heart disease years ago. He did watch what it did to Kristin Wells and he was impressed. The liquid seeped right through the walls of Kristin's esophagus before it reached her stomach, and lodged in the muscles of the upper chest, including the heart and the lungs. Rather than an added burden, it acted as a stimulant at first, then prompting the gradual growth of new and stronger tissue. From the looks of it, Superman thought, kids should start to take this stuff as soon as they were off mother's milk. Tomorrow morning he would submit a sample of the serum to the Food and Drug Administration. The agency would test it for several suspected impurities, and six years later they would rule it unacceptable because it evidently caused mumps in rhesus monkeys.

"Kristin?"

"Yes?"

"Are you all right?"

"Wonderful," she said as she opened her eyes and feeling reached her. "Superman?"

"Yes."

"Superman? Really?"

"Really. Kris, are you all right?"

"I think so."

"Then tell me something."

"Anything."

"Who are you?"

"Kristin Wells," she said. "Brandeis Class of '53, Columbia history Class of '55."

"Care to fill in a century?"

She looked up and squinted her eyes. She sat up and couldn't believe it. "Superman," she said, "it really is you. Columbia history, masters Class of 2855, doctorate, maybe 2859."

"That explains it."

"Doesn't it, though? Happy Miracle Monday, Superman."

"Excuse me?"

"Miracle Monday. It's the first Miracle Monday. It's a holiday. People will celebrate today for hundreds, maybe thousands of years. And only you and I out of all the people in the world know what they'll be celebrating. I'm a historian. Actually a history graduate student, but I came here to find out what no one's been able to find out in nearly nine hundred years. Now I can go home and tell the story of Miracle Monday."

"That's fantastic."

"So're you." She grabbed his face and went up on her knees to kiss him.

"What do you remember?"

"Everything. Saturn, the plagues, the fight, everything, all firsthand. I'm my own primary source."

"It couldn't be a very pleasant story for you to tell."

"Neither is the Civil War or the Nazi Holocaust, but I know about them. At least this one has a happy ending. Did you know that the hotels in town have been filled to capacity for at least a week?"

"Hotels?"

"Full of historians. Every few years every big University in the Solar System budgets a fellowship to send somebody from the history department back to the first Miracle Monday in Metropolis. Some professors have it written into their contracts that they get to go. There are more future Pulitzer Prize winners in this town today than there are in Cambridge, New Haven and Princeton put together. There were a lot of them hiding out in the woods and the wheat fields around the place where the Kents found you as a baby, but not as many as there are here. They're all going home empty-handed and empty-headed except for me, and now I know why."

"Wait a second. Saturn told me he picked you out to use because you were different. You weren't so different if there are hundreds more like you from the future scattered around the city."

"They weren't here yet when C. W. Saturn first entered the Earth. That was my idea, coming a year early, for my dissertation. That way, I figured, I could at least have some good stories to write about even if I didn't learn any more about Miracle Monday than any of the others had. Also it was cheaper. I didn't have to get Columbia University to cover my hotel bill."

At this Superman smiled, then chuckled, then he laughed, and soon he was roaring with laughter as was Kristin. The feeling Superman himself had authored finally caught up with him.

For a while Superman and Kristin sat side by side, dangling their feet over the edge of the Galaxy Building. He gave her a whimsical, giggly account of his conversation with C. W. Saturn. She teased him about the future and the futures of his friends.

"Jimmy's going to miss you," he told her.

"He won't even remember me," she said, "and besides, he'll do fine. Even his kids will go down in history, but not the way he will."

"His kids?"

"Well, there's got to be a James Bartholomew Olsen the Third, if for no other reason than the fact that James Bartholomew Olsen the Fourth has to marry my great-great-however-many-great-grandmother."

"You're kidding."

"No joke. That's why I wouldn't go out with him. It would have been indecent."

"What about Lois?"

"What about her?" Kristin grinned.

"Umm. Does she do anything historic?"

"Of course she does."

"She's probably the first woman President or something."

"Well, nothing quite that mundane, Superman. But you know that already, don't you?"

"I have no idea what you're talking about, Miss Wells."

"No, I suppose not. They're always the last to know."

He thought awhile, looked out over the city and found Lois skipping down the street like a schoolgirl toward her apartment downtown. He would be waiting there, hunkered down in a corner of the elevator, when she arrived.

He told Kristin how he had masqueraded as C. W. Saturn in order to trick Luthor into telling him where he had ripped a hole between Saturn's world and Earth in order to escape from prison. Then he reached into his cape pouch and gave her a lock of hair from the pouch, held together with a rubber band.

"Hair?"

"Mine," he said. "It was what I traded with Luthor to get the information. He gave it to me when he thought Saturn wanted it."

"How can you beat that? A lock of Superman's hair. That's better than Elvis Presley's scarf."

"Tell me one thing seriously, Kris."

"Can't promise. It's against the rules, even for you."

"Just one thing. Do I ever make friends with Luthor again?"

She thought about how to tell him and how much to tell him. He was Superman, after all, she had to tell him something. Finally, she just whispered, "Someday."

That made him happy. "Will you be all right here on the roof?"

"I'm fine. I don't need any saving or heroing anymore. I'll be going home soon."

He was about to soar off when she asked him to wait a second.

"Yes, Kris? What is it?"

"I just wanted to thank you for a wonderful time."

"No regrets?" He smiled his special smile.

"Nope. Well, maybe one."

"What's that?"

"I never got to meet John Chancellor."

He laughed again. "I'll give him your regards," Superman said, and he was gone.

Soon, Kristin was gone as well.

Final Entry

The lock of hair belongs to the University, of course, and before it was placed on display at the Superman Museum, a number of tests were done on it in the School of the Sciences laboratories. Evidently it is not human hair, indestructible or otherwise. It is, in fact, quite indestructible, as Superman's hair ought to be, though it can be cut with ordinary scissors when the peculiar radiations of a yellow star, such as Earth's star-sun, are excluded from it. It even has the genetic cell structure that was purportedly had by Superman. Through some highly sophisticated means, however, which is not understood by me, it was found that it is not hair but some genetic duplicate, probably produced in a laboratory of some sort. Certainly the authorities do not doubt my word that I got the lock from

Superman himself, and I do not doubt that Superman believed it to be his own hair. It simply is not, and that is a new mystery. No one possessed the technology in the twentieth century to produce a spectrographically and genetically perfect duplicate such as this. No one with the possible exception of Luthor, and that is the theory that the people at the University School of the Sciences are toying with now.

The question is, why would Luthor do such a thing. I have my own theory, and I will make it public with the publication of this journal a year from now, on Miracle Monday, 2859, once I am well beyond my period of time reorientation.

Primarily, I am undergoing an intensive language course, designed to refashion my speaking patterns in a manner more suitable to the twenty-ninth century. The disco slang must be eliminated, the subjects of my sentences must be removed from the beginnings to the ends of my clauses, and so forth, or I could develop a terrible stuttering problem, I am told. I met a number of actors and scholars in twentieth-century Metropolis, though, who spoke what amounted to Shakespearean English and they seemed to fare well enough. People seemed to like the way they spoke. No one likes the way I speak except me. This may be the last thing I ever write that could be understood by a resident of the outrageous Nineteen Eighties. Alas and alack.

I am typing this last entry, as I typed all the others, but this time I'm doing it on my very own antique Olympia portable typewriter. I bought it with the money I got with my postdoctoral fellowship that I won as a result of my mission in the past. There are no more discos around, so I have decided to take up typing as a hobby. Lord knows where I'll get any more carbon ribbons when this one it came with runs out. I understand these ribbons were once thought to have caused cancer in secretaires.

Here is my secret, and it will not be told until this report is tachyographed through the Galaxy next Miracle Monday. I think Luthor did switch his fake for the real lock of indestructible hair, and he did it precisely because he thought the devil wanted an artifact of Superman's body through which he could come to possess the hero's soul. Why, the reader will ask, did Luthor not want this to come about? Remember Hamlet.

In Hamlet, the hero hates his uncle King Claudius so much that he avoids killing him while Claudius is praying in church, because Hamlet believes that anyone, no matter how sinful, who dies while he is praying, will go to his reward in Heaven rather than Hell. He hates Claudius enough to let him live, rather than assure him of entry to Heaven, no matter how painful that entry may be.

So listen to how simple this is: Luthor did not hate Superman enough to send him to Hell. Luthor discovered the fact that there was an afterlife, that there may well be a Hell, and that if he gave C. W. Saturn the real lock of hair, Saturn might have brought Superman to Hell as a sort of trophy of profanity.

I believe I have discovered something about Luthor, and by extension, the human spirit, that neither Luthor nor Superman ever learned in their lifetimes. It is that even in the criminal's hatred, there was charity. Superman, then, was correct in assuming that even where he could not see it, there was good in all life, a good that made it important to treasure that life. Pretty nifty, isn't it?

Not a bad bunch of souls, these Earth humans.

Kristin Wells
June 1, 2858

LOTS MORE SUPERMAN BOOKS AND GAMES...

SUPERMAN: LAST SON OF KRYPTON
by Elliot S. Maggin (U82-319, $2.25)
A tiny space ship leaves the dying planet Krypton, carrying the infant who will become Earth's Superman. Here's the enthralling tale of his childhood in Smallville, his emergence as newsman Clark Kent, his battles with archenemy Luthor. It's the one and only original story.

SUPERMAN BLUEPRINTS
(U87-819, $6.95)
A complete set of 15 authentic blueprints of rockets, the star ship, Luthor's lair, the Fortress of Solitude, Jor-El's laboratory, Hoover Dam, the trial arena, Krypton City. Every scene is laid out to scale in exact size. Each drawing is 13⅛x19 inches. Includes a beautifully-designed plastic carrying case.

SUPERMAN CUT-OUTS
by John Harrington & Aldo Cappelli (U97-068, $7.95)
The diorama you make yourself. Just cut, color, paste and assemble using ordinary household glue, scissors and coloring materials. Features three action sets from the movie, including scenes from Krypton, Kansas and Metropolis. Over eighty pieces in all and hours of fun.

LOTS MORE SUPERMAN BOOKS AND GAMES...

GREAT TRIVIA BOOKS
FROM WARNER BOOKS

THE COMPLETE UNABRIDGED SUPER TRIVIA ENCYCLOPEDIA
by Fred L. Worth   (V96-905, $3.50)

Xavier Cugat's theme song? The bestseller of 1929? Miss Hungary of 1936? Here's more than 800 pages of pure entertainment for collectors, gamblers, crossword puzzle addicts and those who want to stroll down memory lane. It asks every question, answers it correctly, solves every argument.

HOLLYWOOD TRIVIA
by David P. Strauss & Fred L. Worth   (V95-492, $2.75)

Spotlighting the characters that made Hollywood happen, here are thousands of film facts that will delight and surprise you. Who was buried wearing vampire gear? Who stood on a box to appear taller than his leading lady? Why couldn't Clark Gable secure the leading role in *Little Caesar*? Almost 400 pages of fact and history.

CELEBRITY TRIVIA
by Edward Lucaire   (V95-479, $2.75)

Crammed with gossip galore, this book was written with the name-dropper in all of us in mind. It's loaded with public and private memorabilia on actors, writers, rock stars, tyrants—and the scandalous facts they probably wouldn't want you to know. From Napoleon to Alice Cooper, anyone who has caught the public eye is fair game.

THIRTY YEARS OF ROCK 'N' ROLL TRIVIA
by Fred L. Worth   (V91-494, $2.50)

Who thought up the name Chubby Checker? Who was paid $10,000 *not* to appear on the Ed Sullivan Show? Who made his television debut with his fly open? A fascinating and colorful compendium of pop memorabilia for both the casual fan and serious afficianado.
